The Five
A Mary MacIntosh Novel

Maureen Anne Meehan

Table of Contents

Chapter 1 1
Chapter 2 10
Chapter 3 14
Chapter 4 24
Chapter 5 31
Chapter 6 35
Chapter 7 43
Chapter 8 47
Chapter 9 50
Chapter 10 54
Chapter 11 61
Chapter 12 67
Chapter 13 70
Chapter 14 74
Chapter 15 78
Chapter 16 83
Chapter 17 87
Chapter 18 94
Chapter 19 101
Chapter 20 107
Chapter 21 111
Chapter 22 116
Chapter 23 121
Chapter 24 127
Chapter 25 136
Chapter 26 141
Chapter 27 146
Chapter 28 153
Chapter 29 159

Chapter 30 168
Chapter 31 174
Chapter 32 182
Chapter 33 190
Chapter 34 196
Chapter 35 204
Chapter 36 208
Chapter 37 213
Chapter 38 218
Chapter 39 226
Chapter 40 230
Chapter 41 237
Chapter 42 243
Chapter 43 248
Chapter 44 253
Chapter 45 258
Chapter 46 263
Chapter 47 273
Books by Maureen Anne Meehan 278
About The Author 279

Chapter 1

It would end up being the most heinous crime the citizens of Douglas, Wyoming would bear witness to for centuries to come, and certainly was the most gruesome that anyone could ever remember. On October 1st, Carolyn Patterson had driven the simple five minute trek across the small town of five thousand to check on her daughter Wanda Sue, and her two grandsons, Chance and Bridger, at their townhouse on Fairway Drive. Carolyn was not the worrying type, but on this particular occasion she was concerned because she hadn't heard from Wanda Sue for twenty-four hours. Normally, not hearing from an adult daughter for a mere day wouldn't be enough to sound anyone's alarm bells, but Wanda Sue was a single mom of two boys under the age of six, and she tended to call her mother three to four times a day for meaningless chit-chat or for childcare favors. Carolyn didn't mind the calls, as she was a widow and the time with the boys filled her life with noise and laughter and discovery. Wanda Sue normally carried her cell phone in hand—as if it was her lifeline—so when Carloyn couldn't get an answer or a returned call for twenty-four hours, she decided to put her mind at ease and drive to her daughter's house. She put her car in gear and began the drive down Fourth Street, proceeding under Interstate 25, and then took the left turn onto Fairway Drive, which was adjacent to the town's only golf course.

As she was driving, Carolyn couldn't help but appreciate the sunny day, and welcomed how the water on the North Platte River shimmered from the gusty winds which were customary for this rural area of central Wyoming. As she neared her daughter's townhouse, however, Carolyn noticed the first instance of dark clouds forming to the west, and realized that this was probably a telltale sign that the first winter storm was on its way. She rolled down her window as she pulled into Wanda Sue's driveway, inhaling as much moisture as she could from the otherwise dry air.

As she stepped out of her car and began the walk towards the front porch, Carolyn was relieved to not only note that Wanda Sue's Ford Fiesta was in the driveway, but that her front door was wide open; certainly that meant the kids must be out riding their bikes. Carolyn expected an immediate answer after she rang the bell since Wanda Sue was usually on red-alert when her kids were out playing in the front yard, so she didn't pause long before opening the screen door after her call went unheeded. As Carolyn was getting ready to shout out Wanda Sue's name, she barely missed stepping on Bridger's body, which was lying in the middle of the floor, twisted and bloodied and mangled, with his arms outstretched toward the front door as if his five-year-old body was trying to escape the horror which took place inside. Bridger had been brutally stabbed, the blade of the kitchen knife still protruding from his back.

Time suddenly stopped in Carolyn's world, and she stood there trapped in a moment that she wished she'd never come upon. She didn't process what happened following her discovery, and most certainly didn't hear her deathly scream echoing out the front door and along the neighborhood. She was still standing there, alternating between frozen gasps for breath and hoarse, tired screams when detectives arrived at the scene in response to a suspicious noise complaint called in by a neighbor. It took several officers to physically remove her from the scene and it would ultimately take many Xanax before Carolyn would ever be able to calm down.

As detectives combed through the Patterson crime scene, they reacted both physically and emotionally. Even the most hardened of detectives would go home that night feeling a bit more likely to wake up their children from a deep sleep to kiss them on the forehead and tell them how much they loved them. Newer detectives reacted with revulsion and disgust. No officer, regardless of their tenure, had ever seen such a vicious—and obviously prolonged—attack. As if the forty-two stab wounds to her head and chest weren't enough, Wanda Sue had also been bludgeoned and strangled. Whoever had done this to her had obviously disregarded her attempt to protect her eldest son, Chance, because his severed right hand was still clamped tightly in Wanda Sue's. And if severing the little boy's hand did not prove sufficiently depraved, the child's remains also showed that his head was nearly decapitated in the struggle.

News of the triple homicide spread quickly throughout the small town, and sent shock waves through this normally tight-knit and quaint western community. Many residents felt unsafe for the first time in their otherwise uneventful lives, and made it clear to law enforcement that the killer needed to be caught immediately. Rumors quickly spread that the crime must have been committed by one of the meth-using oil riggers, whose influx since the re-emerging energy boom had set off a wave of crime in the entire state. Many were quick to agree with this theory, as it not only made sense, but provided a door for many people to close on this stressful and tense situation. Detective Frank Brown was not one of them.

He'd been assigned the Robinson case a year prior–the only other unsolved murder in Douglas during the preceding fifteen years. Patricia Robinson lived less than a mile from Wanda Sue, and she had also been stabbed with a kitchen knife. Until this triple murder, Detective Brown had suspected that Patricia Robinson's estranged husband was responsible for the deed; his quick departure and currently unknown whereabouts only furthered the suspicions in Detective Brown's mind. The only problem with this theory was the fact that their daughter was not abducted, despite the fact that the little girl was at home when the crime was committed. In fact, she was still hiding in her closet when the police found Mrs. Robinson's fatally-wounded body.

The similarities in the two crime scenes were too great for the detective to overlook, and so he pulled out his old notes accompanying the Robinson file and began to compare evidence. Detective Brown sipped from his cup of coffee as he began to note the similarities in the two cases, many of which were not immediately apparent on their face. After quickly reviewing his handwritten notes and refreshing himself on some of the details in the Robinson case, the detective found himself surprised at just how parallel the cases actually were.

In both the Patterson and Robinson cases, the killer used a weapon that was already in the house. This suggested the killer entered the house for another purpose such as burglary or rape. Detective Brown knew from his thirty-some years of experience that robbers more often burglarized houses they are familiar with and often chose houses close to where they live. Since the two adult victims lived within a half mile of one another, the detective figured that the murderer might live in one of the homes or townhouses that lined the golf course. The golf course community was separated from the rest of the town by Interstate 25, so the perpetrator would have to cross under the freeway if he didn't live in the golf community.

In addition, each case documented a frenetic display of overkill towards each victim, which also suggested that the perpetrator was the same person. Few killers stab a victim with such force and frequency. And in the Patterson killings, the detective realized that the killer left behind blood, suggesting that he or she had been injured in the process of the crime. The detective took special note of this, because he realized that the perpetrator could potentially be seeking medical attention in the days to come. With that in mind, he notified all area hospitals and physicians to be on the lookout for a person who required emergency medical care.

When Detective Brown returned his attention towards his two case files, he couldn't entirely concentrate on the material within. His mind was still focused on the more recent crime, and the likely injury that was sustained by the unknown perpetrator. While trying to shake the thought from his head, the dark cloud forming in the back of his mind started to take shape, and he suddenly recalled the specific incident which his mind was trying to bring back to his attention. The incident in question was one which he'd initially written off as peculiar, but nothing more, although he now appreciated it a bit more for its unusual timing. Two days following the Patterson crime, Detective Brown spotted a familiar face. He stopped his patrol car in Riverside Park, which was located adjacent to the North Platte River, to speak with Chandler Craig, a dark-haired twelve-year-old kid whom he had once coached in a local soccer program. Detective Brown knew that Chandler had been caught a few times for petty theft and graffiti, and was disappointed that his son's old friend was turning into a defiant pre-teen. Detective Brown remembered being surprised at seeing the kid out so late, not only for his age, but also for the season. October 3rd in Douglas was generally brisk, but this late at night was outright cold—and dark. He'd approached the boy, asking him whether he was aware of how unsafe it was to be out alone that time of night, and whether he was aware of the recent crime over at the Patterson house.

Chandler was noticeably tense, but admitted that he was not only aware of what had happened, but actually seen the bodies coming out of the townhouse given that he lived just a few doors down the street from the Patterson residence.

During the conversation, Detective Brown noticed that Chandler had a dark colored sock wrapped around his right hand. When he'd asked Chandler about the curious wrap on his hand, the boy had responded roughly that his "son-of-a-bitch" step-dad had pissed him off, and he'd punched a golf cart windshield down at the club as a result. When the detective suggested that the kid get medical attention, Chandler shrugged, adding almost as an aside that he'd been soaking his hand in the river and that it was feeling better. The detective left, but was a bit bothered by the fact that a kid would admit to vandalism to a police officer, and even more bothered by the fact that he appeared to be avoiding medical attention for the obviously infected injuries to his hand. The kid's mom was a nurse, so she surely would have recognized the severity of the injury had she seen it. Why would an injury to this twelve-year-old kid's hand be something he'd want to hide from his own mom?

The disturbing connection between Chandler Craig and the Patterson perpetrator didn't register with the detective immediately, partly due to the fact that Chandler was a good-natured kid overall, and the petty crimes he'd committed were not atypical of a soon-to-be teenager. As the detective drove around Douglas, however, he couldn't help but think about the cut on the boy's hand and the fact that the youth lived on the same street as both victims' residences.

Detective Brown decided to stop by the country club Chandler said he'd vandalized to check on the condition of their golf carts. Despite some serious praying and a whole lot of second guessing throughout the drive to the club, the detective wasn't entirely surprised when management informed him that no golf carts had been reported damaged within the past six months. The supervisor in charge was very amenable to the detective's inquiry, and accompanied him towards the storage garage to complete a close inspection of every cart on hand. There simply were no carts anywhere on the country club premises with even a scratch to the windshield, let alone sufficient damage anywhere on it to cause the type of injury that the detective had observed to Chandler's hand. As the detective began the slow walk back to his car located in the upper club parking lot, he received a call from the crime scene investigator who was still processing some of the evidence picked up at the Patterson home. The detective was informed of several recent findings, but stood ramrod straight when he heard that the perpetrator left a bloody sock imprint at the scene, along with his foot measurement of size fourteen.

Detective Brown called his partner to see if he would accompany him on the drop-by that he realized he would have to make that evening at the Craig residence. When the two officers arrived at Chandler's home, they immediately asked for Chandler and his mom to come with them to the police station. Detective Brown was secretly hoping that the questioning would be routine and uneventful, doing nothing more than eliminating the lad from the radar screen of suspicions. Deep down in his gut, however, the detective realized that what lay before them would prove anything but uneventful. What Chandler ended up sharing with them proved to be vile and disgusting, and truly disturbing to say the least. He quickly learned that Chandler maintained several social networking sites, but most frequently updated his Twitter page with disturbing mental imagery. Past tweets to that account boasted about the sound of a knife slicing through human flesh and bone and were filled with gory details about torture and cruelty towards animals. He recounted the gleam and pleasure he had experienced watching a toad die after pitching it with a fork when he was five, and later incidents of killing snakes, mice, kittens, and a neighbor's dog. Chandler's mother appeared truly surprised to learn that her son had a webpage, let alone what the webpage itself contained, and admitted that she should be more diligent in supervising his computer use.

The detectives also learned that he had unusually large feet for his age—size fourteen.

This was enough for Detective Brown to get a search warrant to Chandler's home and on October 6th, in the early hours of the morning, the detective and his team of officers rang the Craig's doorbell. Chandler's step- father answered and reluctantly allowed the officers to enter. While searching his room, detectives noted that Chandler idolized rap artists whose primary genre promulgated violence and drug use. He was apparently allowed to listen to Eminem and progeny. His computer history denoted a preoccupation with death. The most frequent website hits included a YouTube video showing two kids pinning birds to the road and then filming them as cars drove by and crushed them. The detectives confiscated the computer for further criminal analysis before continuing their search of the house. Other than the items found in Chandler's bedroom, the rest of the Craig's house was neat and tidy and nothing appeared to link Chandler to the crime scene.

But the detective was truly shocked when he discovered what was located inside the Craig's garage–a trash bag full of bloodied clothing, gloves, household items, and a knife. Surely, enough time had gone by for these items to be better disposed of–someplace further away and less connected to the family home. Still, there it was, less than a few hundred feet from Chandler's bedroom, evidence connecting him to the hideous crimes that would forever haunt Douglas, Wyoming.

Chandler Craig, age twelve, was arrested for the murders of Wanda Sue, Bridger and Chance Patterson.

Upon booking, Chandler stunned the detectives with his flat demeanor and his willingness to provide details of the murders. He described in detail the events of the day, which had apparently started with the simple intent to burglarize. No one was home at the time and the front door was left standing wide open. Just as he began to disconnect the family room stereo, however, the kids and their mom came back from a bike ride and found him in the middle of grabbing their electronics. Chandler was pretty nonchalant as he described the unexpected audience, and his spontaneous decision to grab Wanda Sue and drag her into the kitchen, beat her and then strangle her. One of the two kids had run into the kitchen to save his mommy while Wanda Sue was still in the midst of her final death throes. She grabbed his little hand and held on tight, so Chandler took the large blade and severed his grasp above his wrist. The kid was screaming his head off so Chandler slit the kid's throat to shut him up. The older boy saw what happened and ran toward the front door. Chandler recounted how he ran after him and accidentally stabbed himself in the hand. This made him angry so he stabbed the older kid repeatedly, leaving the knife in the kid's back.

Before Chandler had completely finished describing the Patterson murders, he suddenly began rambling about murderous details that were clearly outside the realm of the Patterson case. The twelve-year-old boy began one sentence talking about the Patterson home, but ended it discussing blood, guts and gore that were not by any stretch of the imagination involved in the case. Several detectives at the table shook their heads before rolling their eyes, apparently imagining that closing the Patterson case might suddenly be sullied by an insanity defense. The only one of the detectives at the table to hear Chandler's otherwise nonsensical words and process them was Detective Brown—who was stunned beyond words to hear this twelve- year-old describe nearly word-for-word details taken from his cheat sheet documenting the Robinson murder. The facts Chandler described were only known by someone involved in the crime or involved in the investigation as they had never been publicized. It was unthinkable to Detective Brown that Chandler could have killed Mrs. Robinson jus a few days after his eleventh birthday. But, according to the details flowing out of Chandler's mouth, he was a very precocious and criminally advanced twelve-year-old, as he had no problem recounting his first killing and showed little to no remorse for what he had done.

Chandler's mother sat and listened to the grisly recount with tears flowing down her mascara-stained cheeks. With Chandler still seated right next to her, she began profusely apologizing to the detectives, and repeatedly explained that Chandler was not her biological child. She shared more information than was otherwise necessary, beginning with the fact that Chandler was actually her meth-addicted younger sister's child, who was killed in a car wreck after a night of binge drinking. Chandler's "mother" sat across from Detective Brown, crying uncontrollably, unable or unwilling to let go of the opportunity to share her unfortunate burden with another human—even if it were under these horrible circumstances. She rambled on about Chandler's father being a high school football player who never accepted responsibility as a father, and how Chandler had become the source of many arguments in her first marriage. Her first husband left her, most likely as a result of Chandler's incorrigible behavior. Even after remarrying and having two biological boys of her own, her family wasn't able to bond the way it would have if Chandler wasn't forced upon her, and his presence in their home was the basis of constant drama. Chandler's "mother" continued crying throughout the conversation, but by the end, Detective Brown was fairly certain that her tears were shed more for her own life misfortunes rather than what had become to Chandler.

Detective Brown listened as Mrs. Craig gathered her wits together and lucidly stated that she was rather unsurprised that Chandler was involved in another burglary, but she was absolutely mortified that he admitted to killing four people in their small town. With that, the woman who'd raised Chandler Craig stood up, told the detectives that she presumed she would never see her "son" again, and left without so much as a farewell.

Chapter 2

Due to his age, Chandler Craig had the law on his side. Wyoming statutes allowed juvenile courts exclusive jurisdiction in all cases in which a minor who had not attained the age of thirteen years was alleged to have committed a felony punishable by imprisonment for more than six months. The premise behind the law was that youth under thirteen did not know the difference between right and wrong. Frankly, very few violent felonies were committed by youth at this tender age. Had Chandler been thirteen when the crimes had occurred, then he could have been tried as an adult. The law in Wyoming was controversial, and, as such, provided a legal loophole for young violent criminals. For Chandler, this was fortunate because according to Wyoming state law, all that the court could do was hold him in a juvenile facility until his twenty-first birthday. Thus, after four brutal murders, he would serve nine years and be a free man with a clean slate. Juvenile records were sealed at age twenty-one.

The notion that Chandler Craig would only serve nine years for killing her entire family infuriated Carolyn Patterson, as well as many other citizens of Wyoming. The loophole in the law made front-page headlines in local and national newspapers for months, and eventually caught the attention of the U.S. Department of Justice. An investigation ensued wherein commissions argued whether Wyoming's "Outlaw" Juvenile Justice Act was in compliance with federal law. Any changes made to Wyoming's law would not be retroactive, allowing Chandler Craig's release regardless of any new laws in effect. He was a juvenile serial killer who made his debut prior to turning thirteen, and his actions, under the law at the time, were akin to a plea of not guilty by reason of mental incompetence. Thus, the sentencing judge at the time ordered that Chandler undergo intense psychological therapy during his nine year stay at the juvenile detention facility in Casper, Wyoming.

As years of litigation ensued regarding the constitutionality of Wyoming's juvenile laws, Chandler served his time for the crimes of murder in cell 201 of the juvenile facility. After four years in "Juvi," as they called it, he'd developed a reputation for good behavior among the guards and a reputation as a bad-ass among the other juveniles. He was the only youth at the facility who had killed someone.

The facility's only problem with Chandler was that he refused mental health treatment as was ordered by the judge at sentencing. On the strict advice of his lawyers, Chandler claimed that psychological interviews violated his Fifth Amendment rights. When this issue was brought up before a judicial review board, Chandler's court-appointed attorneys argued that a psychiatric examination might result in Chandler being placed in a psychiatric facility for a commitment beyond his twenty-first birthday. Despite efforts by the county attorney to force psychiatric intervention, Chandler adamantly refused.

Chandler was able to convince the staff that he was a model student at the juvenile facility, earning a high school equivalent diploma. He was even allowed to take online satellite college courses, participate in sports such as soccer, football and baseball, and was even allowed to make a rap video for his visual arts class–a musical which included threatening lyrics and glorified violent images. The staff was displeased when the rap video appeared on YouTube because the lyrics of the song focused on a son who hated his father so much that he killed him and dismembered him and, piece by piece, ate his organs during a cookout with pals. The video was extreme in its imagery, causing a major uproar regarding inmates and a reduction in online privileges.

When Carolyn Patterson learned of Chandler's special treatment at the facility and his continued disregard for the mental health treatment he was supposed to get while serving time for murder, she commenced a campaign to stop the favorable treatment, enforce the judge's order that he undergo psychiatric treatment, and postpone his upcoming release, which, at this point, was only two years away. The campaign garnered local and national attention, drawing into question once again the legality of a system which could allow a serial killer to go free, without any counseling or intervention, essentially giving back to society a cold-blooded killer who would quite possibly kill again.

The growing campaign quickly gained momentum, and the victims' families were hopeful that something was going to be done this time. The citizens of Wyoming made it quite clear that they did not want a serial killer lurking in the desolate streets of their small, peaceful towns. They pummeled their local and state legislators with letters, phone calls and emails.

Unfortunately, the combined issues of the constitutionality of laws, federalism, Fifth Amendment rights and privileges, and mental health court orders were complex, and put together in one lawsuit, tripped the best of legal minds. As such, on May 26, Chandler Craig's twenty-first birthday, much to the chagrin of Carolyn Patterson, he was released a free man. Mrs. Patterson was present on his release day along with many others who had protested the freedom of a cold-blooded murderer. News media recorded the event and as microphones were shoved toward Chandler, he seemed to enjoy the media splash.

As he took his first few steps of freedom, he thought back on his time at the detention facility. He remembered the first few months when he had to prove to the older guys that he was man enough not to be messed with. He allowed his cellmate to use a broken off pencil to carve 6-2-101 in his left arm, which was a reference to the first degree murder statute in the state. Prison life was monotonous and to avoid boredom, Chandler entertained himself by reading books on hunting and wilderness survival. He dreamed of the day that he would be released and his promise to himself that he would avenge the man who was responsible for Chandler's life behind bars. As he walked away, he reminded himself of his promises.

Carolyn Patterson sadly watched as he walked away from the juvenile facility, realizing that there was no one there to greet the boy who had killed her family. Had his family given up on him? Carolyn had heard that his "mom" and "step-father" divorced soon after Chandler's case was publicized, and she had since lost track of his family. She knew that it was unwise for her to do so, but she nevertheless gathered the courage to breach the media circle and approach him and remind him that she had not given up her fight to see that he remain incarcerated for the rest of his life. She tucked an envelope inside his backpack which she hoped that he would open soon and encouraged him to study the photographs in the envelope to remind him that the people he killed were her only human connection to this world.

Chandler laughed in her face and told her to get over it.

Carolyn Patterson felt a ball of fury forming in her stomach–fury that had been churning over many years. "What comes around, goes around," was all that she could muster. She had hoped that this day would never come and if it did, she intended to say so much more, but her words were choked with the pain of the past. As the tears formed in her eyes, she watched him turn and walk away.

Chandler Craig couldn't wait to show the world how he'd outsmarted them. Now, a tall man with long dark hair, light blue eyes, dimpled cheeks and a physically fit body, he hopped on a Greyhound bus heading south on I- 25 to Colorado. He had unfinished business to attend to.

Carolyn Patterson patiently started her Chevy Impala and followed the Greyhound bus as it headed south through Medicine Bow National Forest. She, too, had unfinished business.

Chapter 3

Twenty is a good number. It carries with it a certain sense of dedication, commitment, and entitlement. It had been twenty years since *The Fabulous Five,* as they jokingly referred to themselves, had graduated from the University of Colorado at Boulder and had vowed to never let a year go by without a girls' only weekend. They met, as planned, at The Sink, a Boulder institution on the Hill, home to the renowned Sinkburger and "Tappy Hour," featuring Guinness draft.

It had been twenty years since they'd thrown their graduation caps into the air and headed to their favorite bar near Pearl Street in downtown Boulder where the promise had been made over pitchers of beer and kamikaze shots. Every year they kept their promise and had met in different cities–sometimes in honor of a wedding, or a birth of a child, or a parent's funeral. Sometimes, they just enjoyed a getaway. This year was one of those years–an end-of-the summer getaway without the stress of an event. The five women would be staying in a cabin in the Boulder Mountains and planned to hike, eat good food, drink fine wine, laugh, cry, and relax. On Sunday, they'd agreed to help close down the cabin for the winter.

Unfortunately, *The Five* would add an eighth activity: begging for their lives.

* * *

Mary MacIntosh, the organizer of *The Fabulous Five,* was the first to arrive at the tavern in Boulder, dressed in her favorite faded blue jeans, an olive green tank top and flip flops. She had grown up in Boulder but was presently an attorney in northern Wyoming. After graduation, she attempted to join the police academy, but after learning that she loathed holding a gun, decided to pursue a different career in law by attending law school. Tall and athletic, with long auburn hair, big brown eyes and a wide smile, Mac had made a name for herself among the Wyoming legal community. She'd handled just about every type of case thrown her way, including a CEO accused of murder, a famous rodeo cowboy whose land had been destroyed by a methane gas company, and, most recently, a little boy whose mother had been accused of trying to poison him. Every case she handled changed her in some way, but the biggest change in her life happened a year prior when she married a born-in-the-saddle cowboy named Wyatt Anderson. Mac was the last of the five friends to marry, and she was still adjusting to life on the ranch and the fact that she and her new husband lived a few hundred feet from his parent's ranch house. This was her first weekend away from Wyatt since their wedding, and Mac was rather excited to have some time and space to herself. Wyatt was busy with late summer ranching obligations, and Mac had just finished a lengthy trial. The timing could not have been better for her to steal away. The summer cabin where the *The Fab Five* were staying had belonged to her family since 1899 and it was her turn to board it up for the winter. It was a lot of work for one person, but she anticipated that it would pass quickly with the aid of her friends.

"Still can't believe you married a cowboy," a familiar, husky voice announced from behind. Mac turned to see Hesta Knotingham, her five-foot- six, opinionated and edgy friend standing behind her barstool. Hesta's Louis Vuitton bag hung at her side, complimented by expensive blue jeans, designer stilettos, and a cigarette in hand.

"Still can't believe you smoke," Mac joked as she stood and gave her friend a warm embrace. "Put that thing out before we get kicked out of here." Hesta huffed and rolled her brown eyes while dropping the cigarette to the wooden floor and smashing it with her Jimmy Choo high heel. "How's the publishing world treating you? You look great, by the way."

Hesta softened a bit, nearly smiled, and filled Mac in on her life. She still lived on the Upper East Side and was now the top dealmaker at Gold Publishing Group. She made big money, worked long hours, and still complained more than anyone Mac had ever known. "John is still in the picture. God knows why. He still isn't published, despite my connections, and I still refuse to support him so he continues to live off his mother's trust fund. That woman is a witch with a capital B."

Mac knew better than to ask if they were ever going to start a family. They'd been married for over ten years and his laziness, coupled with her anger, made it clear that God was blessing them with infertility. Mac reminded herself of Hesta's memorable quote some years prior: "Children are for people who can't entertain themselves." At the time, Mac laughed out loud, assuming that Hesta was joking. Over time, Mac realized the seriousness of her friend's comment.

"When's Rema due in?" Hesta asked as she saddled up to the bar and ordered an apple-cinnamon martini. Rema Setliff lived in Denver with her husband Scott, who was a former Denver Broncos wide receiver. Rema was a triathlete and trained in Boulder five days a week. Mac knew that Rema would be the last to arrive because she told Mac that she would meet them at the cabin, as she was on a twenty-mile training run, followed by a three mile swim and a fifty-mile bike ride up and down the steep canyon trail. Despite her rigorous training, she'd never made it to the big leagues, and her age was certainly not in her favor at this point. She was in fantastic shape, but the years of training out in the Rocky Mountain sun had taken their toll and her skin looked aged and leathery. She'd recently emailed Mac and informed her that she was switching from triathlons to ultramarathon running—and would compete in a one hundred mile race soon. Mac wondered what Rema was running from? She too had no children and spent little time with her quite handsome and accomplished husband.

As Hesta's drink arrived, a voice boomed from the entrance to the bar, "Make that two!" Melanie yelled. Mac and Hesta turned to greet Melanie Dylan, a hemp eco-clothing designer who lived in Berkeley and was married to an estate, tax and water rights attorney. Melanie was petite and muscular, with a short, no-fuss hairstyle, blue eyes and the freckles of youth. Her bright smile and flamboyance lit up the room as she bounded over to the bar wearing tan shorts, a t-shirt, and running shoes. She hugged her friends with the warmth of summer.

"Let me show you pictures of Charlie and William!" she beamed, as she took a long pull off Hesta's martini and then reached into her wallet to retrieve recent photos of her two boys, ages eight and six, both clad in matching soccer uniforms and toothless grins. "Aren't they adorable? Charlie is the fastest on his team and William can kick the ball farther than his older brother." Mac and Hesta smiled as they listened to their friend fill them in on her life. The clothing business had recently boomed and now she was designing men's, women's and children's clothing and to her surprise, the children's line was the most successful. Michael, her husband, had just made partner in his law firm, and life was good.

"Let me see your pictures," a fourth voice called. It was Patti Cherney, a former math teacher who lived in Boise and was married to Bob, also a former teacher who'd changed career paths into real estate. They had three teenaged boys and Patti exchanged photos of her awkward-looking family. Patti had been attractive when they were in college, but in recent years had put on some weight across her middle and she dressed like a frumpy housewife, wearing stretchy shorts and an oversized smock. In the photo, however, the formerly fat and balding Bob had transformed into a slim and fit man.

"How did Bob grow his hair back?" Hesta asked.

"Started with transplants and ended with some drugs. I don't ask anymore. I need a drink."

Aside from Mac, who was the designated driver, the women coddled cocktails and caught up on small talk before loading into Mac's SUV. They had a thirty minute drive up the zigzag mountain road through the canyon that supplied Boulder residents with all the outdoor adventure one could desire. The gorgeous Flatirons provided an epic rock climbing experience, while the hiking and biking trails adjacent to the road meandered their way up to the quaint hippie town of Nederland.

"The 60's are alive and well, apparently," Melanie said, as the four women glanced at the co-op produce market and adjacent head shop in Nederland. "This place hasn't changed much since we were in college."

"You should open a store here," Hesta joked. "Hemp appears to be chief with the locals." Melanie offered a half-hearted laugh. Her clothes did sell here and they also were quite successful in a few stores in Boulder. She was proud of this fact but was not one to brag.

"Nose-blown glassworks," Patti said. "What in the world . . . "?

"Actually, we'll have to come back here tomorrow," Mac interrupted. "The lady who makes this stuff is incredible, if you can get beyond the incredible amount of armpit hair that sticks out of her smock. You will be amazed by the originality and beauty of her craft. If you watch her blow glass, you will want to laugh and cry at the same time. Her lamps are world famous."

They window-shopped on their way to the local market, joking about the past and their frequent visits to Mac's cabin while in college. "Get plenty of fruit and veggies," Mac called out to Melanie, as they split up the grocery shopping list. "Rema is a vegetarian still."

"Wine is made of fruit. Does that count?" Melanie replied, as she spun her cart toward the produce section of the small market.

Two hundred dollars later and with a full load of food and wine, they piled back into Mac's car and drove into the wilderness beyond Eldora, to Mac's family cabin called the "Kilkenny-Kerry."

"Before we unload, we have to say hi to Old Misses Nellie Monlock," Mac said.

"She's still *alive*?" Hesta remarked. "She was nearly eighty the last time we were here."

"She's ninety-three and still makes the most potent blueberry brandy on the planet. She's still sharp as a tack and will drink you under the table," Mac said. It was true. Nellie had spent her summers in the mountains of Colorado for the past fifty years and her cabin was only three hundred yards away from the Kilkenny-Kerry. Mac's grandmother Ruthie was Nellie's summer friend, and their bond was unbreakable, until Mac's grandmother passed away. On her deathbed, Mac promised to visit Nellie every summer. Mac kept her word.

Nellie opened her cabin door and squealed in delight to see Mac and her college friends. She immediately invited them into her cozy cabin and shuffled over to shut off the T.V. She snatched five shot glasses from her kitchen cupboard and cracked open a label-less bottle. The women exchanged winks as they watched her shaking hand pour a dark and thick liquid into the glasses. Nellie offered each of them a glass, raised hers in the air, and toasted to a long life filled with life-long friends. She was the first to toss back the brandy and refill her glass.

"Now, ladies, what are your plans this weekend?" Nellie asked, her five-foot-eight frame bent over slightly with osteoporosis. She wore a floral smock dress and blue hand-knit house slippers. What was left of her gray hair pulled back into a tight bun at the nape of her neck.

"Drink, laugh, hike, and complain about our husbands," Mac joked.

"You haven't been married long enough to complain," Nellie shot back. "And by the time you get to my age, you'll wish that you complained less and loved more."

Mac smiled at Nellie. She never said a negative word about anyone.

"What are you working on these days?" Mac asked.

Nellie smiled and pulled up a basket full of knitted baby caps. "I knit one a day for the newborns at Boulder General. Nicole, my neighbor up the road, takes them down for me once a week."

"They are beautiful," Patti offered.

"My hands aren't what they used to be," Nellie said. "My arthritis limits me to one a day. I used to be able to do a cap and a blanket a day." Nellie examined her crippled hands for a moment. "My eyes aren't much better. I used to read a novel a week, and then, last year, my glaucoma became quite debilitating. The large print books weren't even an option. But Nicole brings me books on tape from the Boulder Library and I simply love them. My favorites are the old Agatha Christie short stories and the Nancy Drew mysteries. I like some modern day sleuths, but nothing compares to the old ones."

Mac was saddened to see Nellie's health failing. Nellie was the most independent woman Mac had ever known. The thought of her not being able to drive herself up and down the canyon reminded Mac of her own grandmother's demise. Mac had spent every summer in these mountains with her grandmother and Nellie. It occurred to her that this chapter of her life might be coming to a close soon.

After two shot glasses apiece, the women gave Nellie loving hugs and staggered back to Mac's cabin, promising to return the next day for a happy hour rendezvous with Nellie.

* * *

The Kilkenny-Kerry had been in Mac's family for over one hundred years and carried with it the charm and character of a memoir. Mac's great grandparents on her father's side were from Kerry County and Kilkenny County, Ireland. Mac's father died when she was a young girl, so her heritage was somewhat unclear. This cabin was Mac's only link to her father and it was an incredible treasure in the forested Rocky Mountains near the Fourth of July trailhead, where Mac came every summer to hike the Arapaho Pass Trail to the Continental Divide.

The property consisted of five structures constructed from Jeffrey pine logs that were stained dark brown, each log interspersed with white cement chinking. The window frames were painted cherry red and outlined in an Irish Kelly green. The main cabin, which had been added onto several times over the century, consisted of a main entry room, three bedrooms, a living room, kitchen, and dining room. The garage, which had two large wooden doors, opened wide enough to house an old Model-T Ford during the day, but now provided storage room for the shutters and other maintenance equipment. The garage also had a sizeable work bench and even a spare bedroom in the rear, which had its own separate entrance, for the occasion when large parties spent the night. The bathhouse was its own structure and adjacent thereto was the woodshed.

The women built a large fire from the wood hauled in from the woodshed and unpacked and made up the hundred-year-old double bunk beds. As they opened the windows to usher in the fresh mountain air, they heard a knock at the side door. In unison, they all yelled, "Rema!" expecting their ultramarathon running friend to have finally exercised her way up to nine thousand feet, where the air was thin and the training made the athletes strong. Patti, who was in the kitchen, went to the screen door and was surprised to see the face of a handsome young man on the other side. Melanie met up with Patti and together, in their trusting fashion, greeted the man.

"Excuse me but can you help me out?" he started out, his dirty dreadlocks pulled into a short pony tail behind his ears, revealing crisp blue eyes and suntanned cheeks. He appeared to be in his early twenties and wore a stained t-shirt and frayed blue jeans. His hiking boots were two generations older than he appeared. "I somehow got off the trail at Devil's Thumb Pass and my food supplies are like really low. I was with this massive group of really cool people and it's a total drag that I'm not going to be able to find them before it gets dark. We're on a thirty-day pack trip and my wallet is locked in my car at the East Portal Trailhead, where we set out on the trek. I don't have money or food, and was wondering if you wouldn't mind helping a fellow Wyoming-ian in need?"

By this time, Mac and Hesta had joined Patti and Melanie, and together the women quickly agreed to offer food to the lost stranger.

"How'd you know we're from Wyoming?" Hesta asked, being a suspicious New Yorker.

"License plates on your car are from Wyoming. I made a guess."

Mac nodded at Hesta to alleviate her friend's paranoia.

"You need to wait outside," Hesta said. "We'll throw something together for you."

The young man shrugged his shoulders and nodded, and waited on the back step.

"He's cute," Patti said, sheepishly giggling like a school girl.

"Girls weekend," Hesta said. "No men allowed."

"Think of the fun we could have," Melanie playfully teased. Mac laughed but shook her head, silently agreeing with Hesta.

"I need some fun in my boring life," Patti continued. "Bob certainly doesn't provide any."

"Bob looks better than I remember," Hesta said.

"He lost forty pounds, had hair plugs, and has taken up tennis. Guess that's what guys do when they're having an affair with one of their former students who happens to play tennis." Patti's eyes welled with tears as she described the disintegration of her marriage. She talked while sloppily applying peanut butter to bread, an act she'd performed a thousand times while raising her three boys.

"Are you sure?" Mac asked. "Maybe it's just his career change. Going from being a high school math teacher to a real estate agent is a big transition. Image is everything in real estate. Maybe he is just trying to look the part."

Patti grabbed the grape jelly and plunged it on top of the peanut butter. "Mac, you've been married less than a year. I've been married nearly twenty. Wives know when their husbands cheat. Not only are all the signs there, but he is gone all the time and uses ridiculous excuses. He gets text messages constantly and he now drives a sports car. Real estate agents don't drive sports cars. His clients have to meet him at the houses he shows. His car is for dates. So is his new body. He works out every morning at the racquet club. She works out there too before playing tennis."

Patti stuffed the two sandwiches into a bag and handed them to Melanie. "I'm so sorry," Melanie said, as she gave her friend a much-needed hug. "Husbands are a pain in the butt. We all should have done what we agreed to do in college: live in a commune together and get artificial insemination. We could have avoided a lot of heartache."

Hesta, who'd been opening a bottle of Cabernet Sauvignon while the food assembly line was in the works, offered each of her three friends a glass of wine. The four of them toasted, "Women Who Don't Need Men," clanged glasses and drank to their *Fabulous Five* motto. As they turned around, they saw Rema standing in the doorway, looking sweaty and exhausted.

"Rema," they yelled! "Did you run up here?" Rema did not say a word. Her lower lip was trembling and her eyes were wide.

"Are you okay?" Mac asked, thinking that her friend had once again over-exerted herself physically. It was not uncommon for Rema to work out so hard that she threw up or collapsed.

Just then, the young man appeared in the doorway behind Rema. Hesta let out a high-pitched gasp.

Quickly thinking, Melanie shoved the sack toward the man. "Here's some sandwiches, chips and a few bottles of water. Do you want anything else before you go?"

The handsome man smiled, but did not answer right away.

Hesta looked him over closely. His eyes were set too close together, like that of a wild boar and his nose prevailed too sharply between his narrow eyes. Yet it was his smile—more so of a leer or smirk—that gave Hesta the chills. She stared him down and took a step in his direction with the authority of a city woman unafraid of posturing. He took a step back, tucked the sack under his arm and sneered.

"No, man. I'm out. See ya."

Chapter 4

Rema looked suspiciously at her four friends as she stood shaking in the dining room of the cabin. Her short dark hair was hidden under her Nike running cap and her lean, muscular legs trembled. She stood five feet four and weighed one hundred pounds on a good day. Exercising eight to ten hours a day will produce such results. Her black shorts clung to her sweaty thighs and her wet pink jog bra showed flat nipples and little else. Not an ounce of body fat or femininity showed on this woman who was clearly on a mission. The mission was still a mystery to her four best friends.

Patti offered a glass of wine, but Rema declined. Her training regime did not include alcohol. Instead, she removed her fanny pack–her only belongings for the weekend -- and stripped naked in front of her friends. Without adieu, she fished out a dry jog bra and a clean pair of running shorts and reassembled herself in the only apparel she wore presently.

"Who was that guy?" Rema asked. "He gave me the creeps."

"Some random guy who got lost from his camping group," Patti offered, almost defensively. "We made him some food and sent him on his way."

"You would have preferred to straddle him in a bunk bed," Hesta teased.

Mac stepped in. "I'll show you around. Do you remember this place? We haven't been here as a group since college. How sad is that?

Mac took Rema on the cabin tour. "It was built by my great grandparents in 1899. It has been added on over the years, but the main cabin remains in its original state." Mac showed off the old-fashioned kitchen stove, which was now surrounded by a microwave, coffee pot, toaster, and crepe maker. After pointing out the master bedroom that had belonged to "Gram," she took Rema by the hand to the main living room which was majestically framed in stained pine with a stone fireplace surrounded by century-old rocking chairs and tables. Each item of furniture was neatly covered with an original Navajo throw rug, adding comfort, color and originality to each piece. A uniquely carved Cramer upright piano offered its devotion to the comfortable room, along with a green marbled Radiola tuner circa 1920s. Shelves of Hemingway, Hawthorne, Edgar Allan Poe, Richard Harding Davis, and Dickens lined the walls, framed by a retired F. Howard & Co. Grandfather clock, rifles, deer heads, religious statues, and needlepoint artwork.

"Everyone already claimed their rooms. I have Gram's room, Mel and Hesta have the double bunks off the second sitting room, and you will be with Patti in the single bunks on the right. As you can imagine, Patti already unpacked. Not sure if there's much room left in the dresser."

"I didn't bring anything except the clothes on my back and what I ran up here in."

Mac shot Rema a look of surprise. "Toothbrush? Personal amenities?"

"I travel light these days."

"Good thing I brought sheets for your bed. Didn't know I'd be your mommy for the weekend." Mac nudged Rema as she made this flippant comment, but not completely without intent.

"I'll probably just spend the night with you guys and then take off in the morning. I need to get a fifty miler in tomorrow."

"Rema, this is our weekend together. Can't you put your training off a day or two so that we can have time together? We're planning a nice hike tomorrow–that will be good exercise, and then we're going to go hippy shopping in Nederland. It will be fun. Your body could use a break. It can't be good to train this hard every day. You look like you're about to collapse. Tonight I'm going to build a giant fire in the fireplace and we're going to drink wine, eat junk and catch up. You need it, my friend. I don't care what you're wearing."

Rema looked like a cornered wolf, searching for a way out of a hunter's snare. "Uh, we'll see how I feel in the morning," was all that she'd commit to. Mac was frustrated, but not surprised. This had become the norm.

Rema could not be in one place for more than twelve hours before she bolted, literally, on foot, for days, weeks, or months at a time. The woman was running from something. Nevertheless, Mac fluffed the pillow on the top bunk, grabbed her friend by the hand, and escorted her back into the kitchen where she promptly forced a glass of wine into Rema's hand and shoved a guacamole-laden chip into Rema's mouth. Rema smiled, gobbled the chip, swigged the wine, and toasted to friendship.

At nine thousand feet elevation, after three bottles of fine Cab, a meal of only heavy appetizers, a warm fire, and endless talk, *The Fabulous Five* climbed into bed at midnight on September 4th with that certain fiery feeling of love that comes with twenty years of support, respect, kindness, acceptance and caring.

* * *

Brewing strong coffee was one of Mac's finest attributes, and the smell of espresso permeated the century-old cabin by seven-thirty. Mac and Hesta sat on the porch in their pajamas and drank the brew, while Patti and Mel slept off their overindulgences. Rema had been running for hours, presumptively. She was long gone by the time Mac rose with dawn's first light.

By eight, Mel and Patti joined the ladies on the porch and to their collective surprise, Rema returned by eight thirty, with a mere twenty miles of running under her belt.

"I'm taking a day off to spend with my friends," Rema proudly announced as she sprinted through the wooden archway at the perimeter of the front yard to the cabin. Mac smiled at her friend. Rema, about to smile back, squinted at the gang in sudden astonishment, noting that they were all adorned in their pajamas. "We're hiking to the Divide, right?"

Hesta lit a cigarette and laughed at her exercised-obsessed friend. "Yes, doll. That was the deal. You run a marathon. We drink coffee. We follow you up the ridiculously muddy trail to the top of the universe where I fall to my death from lack of oxygen. Wasn't that what we agreed to last night or was that the wine talking?"

Patti looked at Hesta with antipathy. "You'll die from smoking. I'll die from a heart attack. I'm fifty pounds heavier than our college days. I feel like shit. I look like a pig. I used to be cute. What happened?" Patti stretched her pajama top away from her belly, shaking her head at herself in aversion.

"If I didn't smoke," Hesta offered, "I'd be heavy too."

"Stop," said Mel, the eternal optimist. "Ladies, every day counts. Quit smoking. Quit eating the crap. Quit complaining. Start moving." Mel jumped out of her chair and ran inside the cabin, emerging a few seconds later with a fabric tote bag in her hand. "I brought all of you hemp-only hiking clothes, in like colors. We will all match and look cute while being environmentally correct. If we all die on the hike, we will at least go out in style."

"Good," Hesta said. "'Cuz all I can think about this morning is death.

Mac's family has about fifty crucifixes all over this cabin. It's like walking through the Sutton wing of the Louvre. Why do you Catholics like to look at a dead guy hanging from a cross?"

"Four of my great aunts were nuns, Hesta," Mac said, shrugging her shoulders. "They worshipped Mary and they prayed a lot up here. Sorry that you're offended by a little 'religion.'"

"I'm not offended. It's just disturbing. Why focus so much on a dismembered man hanging from wood? We have been molded in history by focusing on mayhem. What is our fascination with the cruelty of death?"

Mac knew that a philosophical discussion was brewing. She decided that it would be best to continue the discussion during the long hike. "Remind me to show you the Jesus tree on the hike, then," Mac said, winking to Hesta. The two of them had a long history of great religious debates. It would never end. It would never offend. It would simply exist. And, in certain friendships, that's perfectly fine.

With religious symbols safely at bay in the cabin, five women in matching clothes, backpacks, and hiking shoes locked the Kilkenny-Kerry and headed west to the Fourth of July Trailhead. On their way, they stopped at a family friend's cabin to say hello.

"Max? Nicole? Anyone home?" Mac asked as she stepped over the knee-high wooden fence surrounding a modern-looking A-frame cabin. A couple emerged from their vegetable garden and warmly greeted Mac. Mac had known them for decades, and in fact, Max and Nicole Barbosi looked after the Kilkenny-Kerry in the winter season when the cabin was closed and boarded up.

"Headed to the top?" Nicole asked as she pushed her long bangs out of her eyes with her dirt-stained hand. She was a petite yet muscular woman in her mid-fifties who taught first grade at the elementary school in Nederland.

"If Hesta doesn't keel over first," Mac offered. "How have you two been?"

"Good. The same. Not much changes up here," Max said. Max was of medium height and build with sandy blonde hair and large blue eyes. He worked construction part time in the mountains while attending to his doctorate degree in political science at Boulder.

After exchanging small talk, Mac paused for a moment, thinking of whether to say anything to Nicole and Max about the wayward hiker that had appeared at the cabin door the previous night. She decided to share. "We had something a little strange happen last night. We were in the kitchen making dinner when a disheveled guy appeared at the side door asking for food. He said that he got separated from his hiking group. He was a little weird looking."

"This is hippie central, Mac," Max offered. "Like I said, nothing's changed. That sort of thing happens all the time up here. Nothing to worry about."

"He had sinister eyes," Rema said. "Gave me the chills and I run into all sorts of folks on the trails up here."

"Had you already been to Nellie's before this guy showed up?" Nicole asked with a grin. "I suspect the blueberry brandy had you off-kilter. That stuff is a certified hallucinogenic."

Mac laughed with her friends. Nicole was probably right.

On a more serious note, Max said, "Don't be so sure. We did have that gruesome murder here over Memorial Day weekend."

"True," Nicole agreed. "I forgot about it, as ridiculous as that might seem. There was this skateboarding festival in town and some of the kids took their after-party up near the ski area and this woman turned up missing on that Friday night."

"They found her Sunday morning dismembered and stuffed in Hefty bags about a half mile from the ski area," Max finished. "The crime remains unsolved."

"Did authorities release information on the lady? Was she a local?" Mac asked. In all the time that Mac had been coming to the Nederland area, she'd never heard of much crime. On occasion, a cabin was broken into, but it wasn't a regular occurrence.

"She wasn't local," Nicole said. "I don't remember what the police disclosed about her. I'm not sure that they know much about her, to be honest. It was a big deal for a few weeks and people were freaked out, but it's been pretty quiet up here the rest of the summer, so the buzz has died down a bit."

"Stick together on your hike," Max warned. "And don't get stuck at the top when the thunderstorm rolls in this afternoon."

They exchanged goodbyes and agreed to meet on Monday morning to close the cabin for the winter. Max was great help in closing up the large wooden shutters on each window and covering the two chimneys with mesh and metal. Nicole always helped remove and store the priceless Navajos and cover the windows with plastic on the inside to keep the snow from snaking in during the winter blizzards.

The five ladies waved and then proceeded to hike, talk, laugh, and, not surprisingly, some ventured to complain their way to twelve thousand feet in elevation. The trail itself zigzagged up the face of what used to be gold and silver mining camps from a century prior. The view of the valley beyond showcased adventurers in their hot air balloons cascading over the majestic pine and aspen trees. Many of the wildflowers remained in bloom despite the late season due to the heavy moisture the preceding spring. Water trickled down the falls casting a net of rainbows over the valley floor.

"See the Jacob's Ladder?" Melanie said, pointing to a beautiful blue flower on the side of the path. "The purple ones are called River Beauty. My favorites are the Forget-me-Nots."

Melanie, Mac and Rema, who were all in excellent shape, led the way, keeping the conversation lively. Hesta and Patti struggled with each grueling step, suffering the blight of inert health.

As they crested the snow-capped destination, the five women sat at the top of the world enjoying their picnic lunch. Hesta, of course, slipped a cigarette in her mouth in celebration of health and fresh air. Rema snapped it out of her mouth before she could make the match catch light.

"This proves addiction. No oxygen at twelve thousand feet and you still need a joint."

"It's not a joint, you moron. I haven't smoked pot in years."

"Too bad for you," Patti said, with a hint of sparkle in her eye.

Mac looked sideways at her straight-laced school teacher friend.

"What? Why are you all looking at me?"

No one responded.

Patti pulled out a small, tightly rolled package. "Medicinal. I have a prescription. It's for . . . pain."

"I support all variations of hemp," Mel said with a loud laugh. She grabbed Hesta's lighter and lit the joint. Within a few minutes, the joint was gone and the five friends from every hue of socio-economic background were laughing hysterically at nothing much at all.

"The clouds are rolling in," Mac said abruptly. "We need to get down before lightning strikes and the rain falls."

"Too late," Patti offered. Rain spittles were landing on her chubby cheeks and a flash lit up the sky.

"I hope we make it back alive," Hesta said, without even realizing the significance of her light-handed comment. "I can't die in hemp clothes and hiking shoes. New York would never forgive me."

Chapter 5

"My God, I never thought I'd see the Kilkenny sign again," Patti shouted as the five soaking wet, exhausted women rounded the corner of the dirt road leading to the cabin. The rain had picked up considerably toward the end of the hike as had the lightning, which was harrowing in its proximity and velocity as it cracked thunder overhead. Their legs and shoes were covered in mud as they ran toward the side entrance of the cabin. "I'm first for the shower," Patti announced.

Patti sat on the stone planter outside the cabin entrance and peeled off her muddy hiking shoes and socks. She proceeded into the cabin, retrieved her change of clothes and then marched past the four women who were removing their footwear. The shower room was a small cabin to the right of the main lodge and it contained an old fashioned claw tub with a shower, toilet and sink. Patti stripped off her dirty hemp shirt and spandex exercise pants and was relieved that the mirror above the sink was tiny and did not allow a visual of her fat belly and thighs. She turned on the shower and melted into the heat of the water as she rinsed and soaped herself. She could no longer hear the chatter of her friends outside and assumed that they'd gone in to make hot tea or margaritas, or both.

Showering in the mountains during a storm was romantic to Patti and she wished that she had romance in her life. She was quite certain that her husband had romance in his life and this made her pensive and sad. She didn't blame Bob for not wanting to look at her naked body. She hated looking at herself. She had a cute face still, with large blue eyes, rosy cheeks with short, layered blond hair. If she could only lose the weight, she'd be attractive.

As her mood sunk, a loud crack of thunder jolted her from her thoughts. Patti turned off the shower and reached outside the curtain for her towel, which was hung on a hook by the wooden door. She tugged on the cotton towel but it appeared to be caught on the hook. Patti jostled the plastic shower curtain open.

The young man who'd asked for sandwiches the night prior was standing in the shower room holding her towel. Patti was so stunned that it took her a second to realize that she should scream. He had an evil smirk, the stance of a violent man, and a knife to justify both.

"Scream and I'll kill you before you take a second breath."

Patti thought about the emails she'd read about how to avoid being a victim of a violent crime. She thought that she was supposed to scream as loud as she could and take him off guard by throwing something or knocking him down. She inhaled for the scream, but as she did, he shoved the towel in her mouth and knocked her backwards into the tub. She hit her head hard on the porcelain as she fell and her naked body sprawled within the slippery tub. She scrambled to get a grip on the side of the tub to pull herself up, but as she tried to alight herself, he pushed again hard. She tried to kick him in the groin but missed, grazing his thigh. He climbed in the tub on top of her and shoved his knee into her abdomen. Patti could not wiggle free and was certain that he was going to rape her. She remembered reading somewhere that it is better to cooperate with a rape and survive than to fight it and anger the assailant, or was she supposed to fight the assailant as hard as possible so that he'd give up? She couldn't remember the survival rules. She tried to bring her knee up to buck him off of her, but he quickly flipped her onto her stomach and shoved his knee into her spine, which caused a sharp pain to shoot down her legs. He snapped her head back and tied the towel around her mouth and then tied her hands behind her back with part of an extension cord that used to connect the radiator to the bath house wall. With the strength of an ox, he jerked her body out of the tub with one arm.

Patti struggled onto her feet. Her legs felt wobbly and her hands were bound tightly behind her.

"We're going on a little walk. Make a peep and I'll cut your tongue out with this," he said, showing her the large kitchen butcher knife that he'd placed on the bathroom sink. He placed the knife to her neck and marched her naked body out of the shower house and into the wood shed next door.

There was no light in the wood shed, only stacks of chopped, splintery wood and a long table with a Shepard vise and a large ax. He shoved her into the wood pile sending dozens of logs tumbling down on top of her. With her hands tied behind her back, she could not defend herself from the pummeling of the splintered wood. She felt pieces of wood pierce her flesh yet she could not yell out in pain.

"Stop your whimpering," he scolded. "You have no idea what pain is."

He was quiet for a moment and then gave Patti another shove. A piece of wood wedged further into her skin and she let out another moan.

"When I was three, my asshole stepdad's two sons took me down into the basement and kicked and hit me until I had bruises everywhere. When I cried, they hit me in the head with a brick. They told me if I let out another whimper, they were going to bash my skull in. They took two planks from my step-dad's workshop and made a makeshift cross with them. They tied me to the cross and left me there in the dark. They hardly even got into trouble when my mom found me there. She was too afraid of the bastard to stand up for me. Those brats told her that they were practicing Sunday school and my step-dad told my mom that she was getting what she deserved for making them go to church. So, don't even cry to me about pain."

Patti wanted to say something to this man—to acknowledge his anger. She'd worked with enough troubled kids to know that the one thing they needed most was a voice. This boy—man, was a hurt child. She thought that she could calm him down if only she could talk to him and listen. She moaned again, but this time in an attempt to speak with him.

"I told you to shut up," he said.

Patti complied.

"Crawl up there," he demanded, motioning towards the wooden work bench. Patti did as best she could with her portly belly and arms tied behind her back. He made her lie on her stomach. He untied her from behind and re- positioned her hands above her head, hog-tying her to the vise by clamping it down as tightly as he could. Patti screamed in pain, but her shrieks were muffled by the towel. She could feel him lurk over her as if deciding what to do next.

Patti felt the cold tip of a blade gently scroll up and down her spine. Was he deciding where to sever her spinal cord? Patti thought of her boys and how much she would miss them. She was so excited about her girls' weekend that she'd barely said goodbye to her teenage boys. Not that they would have noticed, but she now wished she had told them how much she loved them.

She thought of Bob too. She wished they had parted on better terms. She left him a nasty voicemail prior to boarding the plane, demanding that he stop seeing the "hussy" or she'd hire a divorce lawyer.

The man leaned over and whispered to her slowly and ominously, "Perhaps your husband hired me to kill you" as he teased the cold blade of the knife up and down the soft curves of her neck. Patti shivered with fear, and was fighting hard to maintain consciousness as every neurotransmitter in her body neared its maximum capacity. "Or perhaps, one of your lady friends has a husband who . . ."–he let this voice slowly drag on before he finished in a husky whisper, "would rather be single, shall we say? I'll let you convince me that it wasn't your husband who is the lecherous beast."

Patti sensed that this man wasn't done taunting her, but this was the last thing that she registered from him before she lost the fight and completely blacked out.

Chapter 6

"What in the hell is she doing in there? Shaving her legs?" Mel was second in line for a shower and had already finished two margaritas. "If I wait any longer, I'll be too tipsy to wash my hair standing up."

"Don't you remember how long it took Patti to do her 'Farrah Fawcett' hairdo back in college?" Rema scoffed. "It drove me nuts! We all had to share one bathroom, but she used it eighty percent of the time. She would use that stupid curling iron and curl every piece of her hair and by the time she was done with the second side, the first side's curls were falling out, so she'd start over. Then she'd fog the entire place up with hairspray. Talk about leaving a carbon footprint."

Melanie was suddenly filled with memories of Patti's bathroom hogging. The issue hadn't really affected Melanie so much, as she'd always worn her hair in a simple, short style, but she recalled many arguments among Hesta, Mac and Patti about whose turn it was to use the bathroom. Then they invoked the kitchen timer rule, which was regularly violated. Then they invoked the "shower in the bathroom, primp in your bedroom" rule, which was fallible due to poor lighting and a lack of electrical outlets. They settled on the "leave the bathroom door open and shower" rule so that one could shower while others got ready. This rule worked for Rema and Melanie only. Patti complained that her hair would not hold any curl with the shower's humidity. Mac complained that she simply was not able to blow dry her thick hair with the shower on. Hesta complained about privacy, citing a tad too much personal information to support her position with regard to shower practices and procedures. Despite all their frustratingly different grooming practices, the ladies had been able to work through it and work it out.

Mel smiled, reflecting on the longevity of their friendships and negotiations, as she reached over to gather up her hemp sweat suit and begin her trek on over toward the shower house.

* * *

Mel was surprised to see the shower door was still open when she arrived, and a tad more surprised to see that Patti was not inside. The shower had been used, as it was wet, but Patti's soiled clothes were still lumped in a ball on the stool next to the shower. "What the hell?" Mel said out loud to none one in particular, and turned her direction back towards the shower's entrance half expecting to find her friend outside running around naked in the rain. For a split second, she smiled at the thought of running around naked, because that was certainly something she or Hesta would have done in college. The smile dropped quickly when she realized that this was not something that Patti would have ever done either with Mel and Hesta, or by herself. No, that was just not Patti.

Mel grabbed the flashlight that hung over the bathroom mirror and walked down the cement stone pathway that led from the bathhouse towards the main cabin. She called out Patti's name, but there was no answer. A loud crash of thunder reverberated throughout the canyon, and sent a chill down Mel's spine. "Maybe she went back into the cabin using the front door?" she questioned herself out loud. The main cabin had three entrances–the original front door that no one used; the side door into the eating area and kitchen that everyone used, and a back door into Gram's bedroom, which was only used by whomever was staying in Gram's room. Mel knew that the main cabin door was open and unlocked so that the cabin could air out, so technically, it was possible that Patti walked the long route to go around the cabin and enter into it through the front, and was currently dressing in her bedroom. Perhaps she had remembered the bathroom negotiations just as Melanie had, and was trying hard to follow their old college rules regarding hogging the bathroom. Yeah, and monkeys might fly outta my ass, Mel thought to herself. Patti's extra girth certainly hadn't gone unnoticed by Melanie, and the extra distance it took for her to gain entry into the cabin in this manner was highly unlikely. Melanie didn't like the way she was thinking, so she corrected her negative train of thought and presumed that Patti was in the cabin getting dressed for dinner.

The sudden chill in the air helped pull Mel's mind off of Patti's current whereabouts, and made her consider how delicious a hot shower would be. Patti was a big girl, she could fend for herself. Melanie wasn't going to continue to treat this trip like she had brought her family with her, and she was governing over her friends like she did to her eight-year-old Charlie or her six-year-old William. Dammit, this trip was about letting loose and having fun, and after all, that shower wasn't going to remain vacant for much longer.

When Melanie returned to the bathhouse she reattached the flashlight to the magnetic strip above the bathroom mirror before letting her running shorts slide off of her and fall to the ground at her feet. She reached her hand into the stall to turn on the left knob of the shower so she could get the water to start heating up, but she quickly remembered that the knobs were switched. She reached over and turned on the right knob full blast, and was rewarded by the heat of the water gracing her bare hand. Steam quickly filled the room, as the evening air temperature quickly dropped, and when Melanie turned her attention back towards the mirror above the sin to assess whether she needed a shampoo, she was unable to see her reflection through all the steam fogging up the mirror. After she wiped down the mirror with her hand and assessed her hair's overall condition, she decided to forego washing it this time. Her hair was damp from the rain still, so she decided that it could wait another day and get rejuvenated in the morning by the simple addition of some hair gel to spike it.

As Melanie turned around to close the door so that she could remove her top and panties, the door to the bathroom suddenly slammed closed. She didn't immediately process this unexpected motion, because she thought she was all alone in the bathroom and so the door closing by itself simply didn't make any sense. Mel was momentarily stunned, with her head cocked slightly to the left and her eyes wide open in shock. She remained frozen in a state of confusion until the face of the lost biker suddenly registered somehow deep within the confines of her subconscious, and startled her out of her reveries. Mel's eyes regained focus and she turned her attention towards the stranger in her midst–the stranger with a wicked grin on his face and an even more wicked butcher knife in his hand.

Mel's instinct to fight or flee set in, and she lunged at the man with all of her five foot four frame. For a brief moment, she felt somewhat hopeful as her arms were wailing and landing several decent hits on the man, but that sensation was fleeting as suddenly Mel realized that the butcher knife has sliced through her left shoulder, and she quickly dropped down onto both of her knees. She heard the sound of her flesh tearing as he ripped the knife out of her and she could feel the warm blood drip down her arm and onto her legs. She quickly put her hands over her head in a defensive move, trying to protect herself from what she anticipated would be an imminent yet fatal blow. Visions of Charlie and William flooded her mind, and she was overwhelmed with the realization that she might never see them again. She would not die without a fight.

He kicked her backwards and grabbed her by the jaw. "Not a sound," he said.

She flung her arms and legs at him, trying to strike him in the eyes and in the groin.

He slapped her hard across the face and then punched her in the mouth, sending blood squirting. "I knew you'd be the one who'd end up being a pain in the ass." He tied a hand towel around her mouth and jerked her around backward by wrenching her arms behind her back. Her shoulder wound oozed blood as he used a part of what looked like an electrical cord to tie her hands together. "Walk or I'll slit your throat."

He shoved her in the direction of the garage, which was an independent wooden structure to the right of the shower cabin. The garage had two large wooden doors that opened outward. It was stained dark brown to match the main cabin and had a large window framed in red with a large green wooden shutter in front. The garage housed all the maintenance and repair tools for the century-old cabin, including wooden shutters for winter, paint, stain, rakes, gas cans, a lawn mower, and tools. The man dragged her inside the garage and shoved her to the ground. She landed sideways onto her injured shoulder, sending a spray of blood into the air. He kicked her in the left leg twice before dragging her by the neck to the thick pine log that served as the support for the roof structure. The man pulled her into a seated position and used a rope from the work bench to tie her midsection to the log. Her legs were uncomfortably twisted on the cement floor, but he had tied her so tightly to the post that she could not readjust them.

Melanie squirmed in protest and tried to scream but the towel was shoved deep into her mouth, muffling all noise.

"You are as big of a sniveler as your fat friend. Knock it off or I'll slit you from ear to ear–which is something that I'm not impartial to, honey. Let me tell you that the last time I slit someone's throat, I watched as the blood shot out of her neck and straight up into the air. It was like a water fountain. Only red. Her head wobbled back and forth after she hit the ground. I thought it would snap off. That would have been something." The man laughed to himself out loud, sending a pall of horror into Melanie's brain.

The full moon shone brightly through the garage window and Melanie could not stop herself from looking into the man's vacant eyes. She silently wondered how such an attractive face could be so cold and evil. She watched him as he picked through the old cans and containers on the work bench. He hummed to himself, as if torturing people was something he did regularly and with pleasure. She thought of her two little boys and wondered if this monster in front of her had ever been a darling eight-year-old. Was it possible that her boys could turn out to be like this fiend? She worried about that from time to time. Her eldest son Charlie was very impulsive and had a mean streak. He had to win every game at all costs and would cheat to succeed. He often bullied his little brother into letting him get his way and would throw huge tantrums when his attempts at persuasion were unsuccessful. Melanie took him to a child psychologist regarding his anger management and impulsiveness. She was told that he would grow out of it, but most first born boys grew up with the notion that they were more important than others. It was up to her to make Charlie understand that every voice counts and that his needs were no greater than other children's needs. She had been trying to work with Charlie, but when she visited the school during recess, she noticed that he still had to win every game and he did not share empathy or consideration of others. Was this how the man wielding the knife in front of her grew up? Would her little Charlie become this man someday? Melanie was immobilized both physically and emotionally, and she could do nothing but think as she watched the monster tinker about in the garage. Her mind kept wandering, and she couldn't help herself from racing through tons of fleeting memories that all seemed completely unrelated to the life or death struggle at hand. As she watched him take glee in his twisted and macabre plans, she wondered how he ended up this way. She prayed that her sons would never cross the path of whatever it was that caused this man to turn into such an animal.

The man's cruel voice suddenly jolted Melanie from her reverie.

"I wasn't born mean," he said, as if he could read her mind, and Melanie looked back at him in surprise as if signaling that he had correctly interpreted her thoughts. "My real dad took off when I was a baby. My mom married a piece of crap coalminer with two other shit-for-brains kids and he beat my mom up all the time. He used to knock me around too. My mom was such a fucking weakling. She never stood up to that asshole and when she tried to, he'd smack her into next Tuesday. That's when she started heavy on the meth and whatever else she could get her skinny little fingers on. Before she was hooked, she used to come and watch me play sports and stuff. But once she got strung out, the only thing that mattered to her anymore were her drugs and staying an arm's distance from that piece-of-crap husband." The man stopped for a moment, pausing as if reliving a moment only he could see. A smile broke across his soft and youthful lips, making him look even younger than he was. He slowly turned his attention back to Mel. "My asshole step-dad is one of the reasons I ended up here. He lived up the road from here about a mile. I killed him yesterday."

Mel could not believe his lack of empathy. He spoke as if he were telling a ghost story. He not only voiced no remorse for his actions, but he actually appeared to revel in them.

"The other reason I'm here is because one of your husbands hired me to kill one of you. It will be up to you to convince me that it isn't your husband who wants you dead."

Melanie glared at this monster before her. Did he expect her to believe that Michael would hire someone to kill her? Her husband was an upstanding attorney and the father of her two boys. They lived happily in a suburban California neighborhood, he was a gentle man with a kind spirit, and there was simply no way in hell that Michael would do such a thing. Mel thought of her four friends' husbands, and contemplated whether any of them could make what this man was saying a remote possibility. Bob was apparently cheating on Patti. Hesta loathed John. Scott and Rema had not been seen together in the same room for a decade—he was too busy playing golf or performing some function for his former team, the Denver Broncos. Rema was too busy running. Mac had only been married a year to Wyatt and everything she'd seen this far appeared idyllic in their relationship, but wasn't the first year of marriage often the hardest? Mel personally thought that Mac had very little in common with Wyatt, so technically, they were fair game as well.

The man walked closer to her with the knife in hand. He traced the line of her jaw with the blade. "Nasty slice you have in your shoulder. I bet it hurts. I'll bandage it up for you nice and tightly to keep you alive . . . for a little longer, at least," he said as he taunted her with his undeniable upper hand in their obvious power struggle. "But if you try to free yourself, which I suppose you will, I'm pretty confident that you'll die from blood loss before you ever get even one of your muscled little legs free from your binds. Come to think of it, I'm thinking I might rather enjoy watching you try to free yourself."

Melanie considered his words. He circled around the post she was tied to as he spoke.

"I'm pretty good at restraint when I want to be," the stranger said mockingly. "I have a lot of practice, you see. When I was a wee pup, I had to restrain myself from killing my step-dad and his asshole sons practically every single day. Now, don't get me wrong—I did allow myself to indulge in quite detailed fantasies of myself actually engaging in the act," the man chuckled to himself. "And I was quite clever. I rarely killed them the same way twice, but every time I killed them, it was always painful—and they always died looking into my eyes and begging me to put them out of their misery. Crying to me, apologizing to me, blubbering to me like fools, as they drowned in their own blood and guts and gore, but mainly pain, pain, pain." The stranger's eyes focused in on Melanie again. "Unfortunately, my mom finally got the courage to divorce the mother fucker. Too bad really. I wasn't sad to see him go, but it would have been fun to watch him die in agony back then. Luckily, I got the chance yesterday to fulfill my fantasies and kill him in the most hideous way."

The stranger laughed out loud again as he gathered up some rusted old tools from the work bench and headed toward the door. "Well, I'm off to see the wizard. There's no place like home."

The minute the garage doors banged shut, Mel began wiggling her hands, in a desperate bid to free herself. No jerk was going to prevent her from mothering her two sons. No way. No how. Melanie kept frantically moving beneath her restraints, oblivious to the stranger's warning about bleeding out, insistent that she was a fighter and wouldn't let anyone get the better of her. That is, until she began to cry.

Chapter 7

Hesta had the patience of a typical New Yorker. She was the first one to notice that neither Patti nor Mel had returned from the shower room after more than sufficient time, and she was the first one to voice her objection with the imposition it had on the rest of the group. After nearly a half hour, Hesta stood up from and announced, "Well, I think our two friends have decided to lather each other up in the shower, and I'm not about to miss out on good lesbo sex. I'm going to join them."

Mac and Rema let out a roar of laughter at the notion of Patti and Mel having sex. "As if," Rema said. "Patti was a virgin when she married Bob and from all accounts, has reverted back to virginity. And Mel and Michael are as in love as they were at grad school in Berkeley. Now, I can certainly see you enjoying a little bit of 'lesbo sex' as you call it, Hesta, but good luck trying to convince one of them to join you. Cheers!" With that, Rema raised her third margarita and clanked glasses with Mac.

Hesta flipped Rema off as she backed out of the kitchen, smiling, and headed towards the shower.

Hesta could hear the water running as she crossed the short cement pathway between the main cabin and the shower house. She knocked on the door and said, "Hey ladies, let me in! I'll lather with you!"

No response.

"Rub-a-dub-dub. Hesta wants in the tub. I ain't kidding, ladies." Hesta paused a second as she stood outside the bath house, before knocking again. "C'mon gals–I'm dirty and I need a shower. If you're not coming out, at least let me come in there, get some of the residual spray while I watch you guys," she whined.

With that Hesta turned the door knob and charged in, deciding that she'd been a good girl and waited long enough and was simply going to wait no more, and still giddy from three margaritas and a long day of laughter and hiking. The shower curtain was closed preventing Hesta from seeing exactly what was going down inside the stall, yet its steam rose above the curtains and fogged the small room making it difficult to see.

She'd absolutely never considered any of her *Fab Five* friends as candidates to participate in anything even remotely similar to her recent and clearly scandalous rendezvous, and she really was kidding when she initially began teasing about a lesbian shower power session. The more she began commenting and thinking about it, however, the more she began thinking that her pals were engaging in precisely the sort of activity that Hesta herself had found quite engaging. Normally, she preferred to attach anonymity to these sorts of excursions–but, if Patti and Mel were willing, what the hell?

"Ladies?" she called out again, focusing her attention to the shower in front of her. When the door slammed from the wrong direction–behind her–Hesta was together enough to recognize the significance of this discrepancy and immediately felt terror shoot through her veins. She'd been mugged once on her way to the subway after a late night at work and being no stranger to peril, her body responded immediately. But before she could turn around and see her assailant, a hand cupped her mouth from behind and a sharp blade pressed against her throat.

"You're not so tough, are you now?" he snarled. "Your chubby little friend was so scared that she pissed herself. And your skinny friend, well, she thought she was tough, but in the end she pissed herself, too. Well, sort of. Actually, she's kind of pissing on herself right now," he whispered softly while chuckling to himself, taking only a brief pause before continuing. "At least I consider the blood pouring down her body to be synonymous with pissing herself, because in the end, she's still wetting herself, right? Tsk, tsk, if only she listened to me, darling. I warned her, but she thought she knew better, and tried to take me one-on-one in a little wrestling match." He rolled the sharp blade against her throat, seeming to size her up. "Now what about you, honey? What are you going to provide to me in the way of resistance? Are you going to put up any sort of entertainment like your friends? Or are you just a jagged tongue?"

Hesta turned her head a bit to the left sending the weight of her shoulder-length, layered bobbed hair swishing over her face. She peered at him through her peripheral vision, watching him in fear as he fantasized about what he just did to her friends and about what he planned on doing to her and the rest of the gang. She felt goose pimples forming on her arms as he took a step in her direction.

Hesta briefly thought about biting his hand, but realized that he had the knife was now pressing so hard on her jugular vein that even if she were successful, she might end up causing the knife to nick her neck and kill herself in the process. The blade had already broken her skin when she'd flipped her head to the left, and she could feel moisture on her neck.

He set his blade down on the bathroom sink so that he could tie a towel around her mouth. Hesta considered grabbing the knife for a moment, but thinking through her exit strategy, she realized that she was trapped in this small room and the thug was blocking the door. She'd have to maim or kill him in order to get out alive. And while Hesta had no doubt that she could successfully stab him, she hadn't seen enough of him yet to know what kind of shape he was in and whether a quick stab or two would be sufficient to immediately cripple him to provide her an opportunity to escape. The chance to act passed too quickly and within seconds, he had the knife back in his hands and was ordering her to turn around and put her hands together behind her back. She complied. He tied her hands together and then shoved her to the ground with force. She fell back into the water heater, ramming her shoulder blade into the red dial so hard that it punctured her skin. Pain shot through her body, but she was oblivious to it because she was focused on the fact that this animal–the wild boar as she'd monikered him when she first saw him back at the cabin the previous night–was pulling his small yet erect penis out of his pants. While any other woman might have been frozen with fear upon the realization of an impending rape, Hesta was motivated by her fierce desire and intention to avoid getting raped by this monster. She waited until he was on his knees with the weight of his body forward when she jammed her knee into his groin.

The brute yelled out in pain.

"You little bitch."

Hesta tried to knee him again, but this time, he grabbed her knee and shoved it back to the ground. He climbed on top of both her legs with his knees pressing hard into her thighs and managed to pull down her hemp hiking shorts with his left hand.

"When I'm done with you, I'm going to cut your vulva out, just like I did with that woman who followed me here," he spit out at her breathlessly and in an apparent state of anxious anticipation. He lowered his head to look down at his prize, and continued talking, but no longer was it directly aimed at Hesta. His voice appeared as forced, but quieter, almost as if he were talking to himself, when he said, "She thought that she was so clever tracking me, but it turns out that the hunter was being hunted by the prey."

Hesta didn't waste any energy trying to interpret what he meant by that statement, as she was focusing every ounce of her strength on fighting off the sexual attack. It wasn't long, however, before Hesta succumbed to sheer force, and the wild boar proceeded to have his first anger-fueled sexual experience with a woman.

Chapter 8

Mac poked her head out the side entrance to the cabin and saw that the light to the shower house was on and heard its water running. "Maybe Hesta got lucky," Mac said in a joking tone.

Mac and Rema tossed around the idea of a fourth margarita, but ended up agreeing that might not be a good idea without the benefit of some food inside of them. Mac went out to the stoned-in patio in the backyard of the cabin to start the grill while Rema remained in the kitchen slicing and dicing the vegetables and meat for the fajita feast. The rain was subsiding, and the fresh rain-soaked mountain air lifted Mac's spirits even higher than they already were. She couldn't remember feeling this good in a long time. She felt so lucky to have time with her best friends while at the same time reminiscing in her mind the many childhood memories associated with her family trips to the Kilkenny-Kerry cabin.

When Rema heard the back door slam shut, she assumed that Mac had gotten unusually lucky and was able to light the grill on her first try. Mac had warned her that it usually took a few tries to fire up the old Kamado grill, with five minute breaks in between each attempt.

"Did it work on the first time?" Rema shouted out without turning. When she didn't hear a response, Rema turned and immediately stared directly into the face of a monster–a monster she was sure she'd seen before this weekend. The split second she made direct eye contact with this beast appeared to freeze into eternity, and Rema's brain began racing through its archives searching for the source of familiarity. Was it from one of her twenty-mile morning runs? Was he a character in a television show? Had she run into him at the supermarket, the gas station, the gym . . . her mind cycled endlessly through possible sources of recall, but nothing clicked.

Somewhere deep in her subconscious, she had been face-to-face with this fiend before, but she could not place him.

As time began to slowly return to normal, Rema's eyes moved from the beast to the knife in his hand. Rema's paring knife could not compare, but she kept it behind her back hoping for a chance. She slid it into the lining of her running shorts, praying that it would not fall out.

Rema was always on high alert, thanks in large part to her long distance runs in the backwoods. It is necessary to be aware of the dangers in the wild, because the feral nature of animals would lead an otherwise isolative mountain lion on a chase to kill a runner. The uncivilized nature of a hermit would lead him to seek out a female hiker and kill her for no apparent reason. Presently, she knew that her guard would not help her.

Rema gulped loudly as she recognized fresh blood on the tip of the blade in his hand. The man was broken from the silent trance the two of them appeared to have equally engaged in from Rema's loud and instinctive swallowing, and gruffly instructed her that if she yelled, he would kill her on the spot. He was very routine and straight to the point when he grabbed her arms and escorted her through the main living room of the cabin and into one of the back bedrooms and tied her crucifixion-style to the end of the single bunk bed. He was focused on his task at hand, and did not engage in any discussion with her until he made sure that she was securely fastened.

Rema had not put up a fight, recognizing the danger from the second she spotted it. She lay splayed across the bed, with each of her arms tied crossways the bed onto each of the top bunk's bed posts, and both her feet to the bed frame below. Her body hung freely forward and within no time at all, she had lost all feeling in her hands and forearms.

The man broke the silence when he told Rema as he had the women before her the reason for his appearance. He was noticeably less cocky and arrogant this go around, but Rema clearly had no way of knowing this, nor any way to interpret what, if any, significance this might have. In comparison to how he treated the others, he treated Rema compassionately.

Rema looked deep into the stranger's eyes. The familiarity was striking. While her conscious mind wasn't able to draw upon the specific memory that connected her to this man, her subconscious mind clearly already had it all figured out. As soon as Rema settled down into her bindings and looked back towards the evil lurking amongst her, she was startled t her herself suddenly blurt out one word.

"Scott."

Chapter 9

Mac had been mugged at gunpoint in her law office in Jackson Hole ten years ago. The investigating officer admonished her that had it not been for her boss's entrance into the office in the middle of the assault, Mac would likely be dead because she had responded to her armed assailant with force. The lesson was learned: if the man has a weapon, don't piss him off.

When the mountain man confronted her on the back patio with a large, bloody knife, Mac therefore did exactly as she was told to do and allowed him to gag her and then tie her to Gram's bed. He did not hurt her; she was well aware, however, judging by his chattiness, that he had cut, raped, and battered all of her friends. Mac realized that if there were any hopes of her saving not only herself but her friends, she would be forced to use her brains and not her brawn.

Mac immediately began to think through her options, and the first thought to pop into her head was to consider whether or not they had any advantages. There were five of them against what she presumed was one man. He did not appear to have backup–and that was clearly an advantage. Another advantage was that Gram stayed at this cabin alone many times over the thirty years she'd been widowed, and had ensured a stable communication system was set up through both her local network of neighbors and a secure telephone system. Unless a storm knocked out power, Mac knew that Gram had ensured that the telephone in this place was guaranteed to be operable year round. In addition to the landline, Gram's friends in Nederland always looked out for her when she stayed. Gram had passed away eight years ago, but the friendships remained, and every time Mac visited the cabin, her neighbors stopped by to check on her and invite her over for a drink.

But Mac knew for every good thing she had going for her, there were just as many–if not more–obvious and potentially devastatingly gruesome negatives dancing in front of her face. For one, Mac was certain that she had little time, and for another, she was equally less likely to have any opportunities available to her to exploit to her advantage. At this point, Mac surely couldn't trust the word of a madman so Mac did not even know whether her friends were alive, and if so, whether they urgently needed medical attention. Even if she could free herself from bondage, she had no idea whether she could flee to get help. And if their captor had been able to locate Gram's deeply rooted landline, none of their cell phones had service this high in the mountains.

While running through all of these pluses and minuses, so to speak, Mac was persistently jiggling her wrists in an effort to loosen the tether that bound her. Eventually, she began considering the brute's stated motive. *One of your husbands hired me to kill one of you. It will be up to you to convince me that it wasn't your husband who wants you dead.* Was this true, or just the sick mind game of a brutal and twisted man?

Mac had fallen in love with and married Wyatt a year ago. Wyatt was a gentle and kind cowboy who would not deliberately hurt any living thing. He'd lived on a ranch all his life and used "horse whispering" as a technique to train horses. Granted, they'd gotten into a slight argument prior to her departure for this girls' weekend, but it was rare that they argued. The fight wasn't that big of a deal, really. Mac was feeling the squeeze of living on the ranch in close proximity to Wyatt's parents and had suggested that they look at buying their own place closer to town. Wyatt overreacted to her suggestion, in her opinion. He suggested that if she was that unhappy living and sharing his life on the ranch, then perhaps their union had been a mistake. Out of pure defensiveness, Mac told Wyatt that she agreed, but she didn't mean it at the time, and she certainly didn't mean it now that a few days had passed. *Honestly, it was just a silly fight*, Mac thought to herself. *Wyatt would never do anything to hurt me.*

But then, her mind started to wander as she struggled with the ropes around her wrists. Wyatt was a loner. Maybe he was unhappy with her. Maybe he felt trapped. And she had dated Wyatt's brother for a long time before she ultimately married him. Maybe Wyatt was harboring resentment toward her for having an intimate relationship with Greg. Wyatt and Greg had never really been on good terms and to the best of her knowledge, really never had made much progress in mending old childhood wounds. Maybe Wyatt had a change of heart and wanted to get rid of Mac the easy way?

Stop it! Mac told herself. This is exactly what the brute wanted her to do—start doubting her security. If her foundation started to crumble, this monster would win. She was not going to let that happen. After all, she reassured herself, if what the monster said was true, it couldn't possibly be set up so quickly. Her first real spat with Wyatt had only happened recently and surely couldn't have given Wyatt sufficient time to put together such an intricate plan.

Mac hoped that her analysis was correct, but she couldn't be sure.

* * *

As soon as Patti heard the wet, crunching footsteps heading in her direction, she immediately pulled her naked legs to her chest. She was cold and wet and covered with splinters from the woodshed. Every time she moved a muscle, another sliver of wood pierced her flesh. Fresh tears ran down her cheeks. With each closing footstep, she prepared herself to hear that it was Bob who wanted her dead and that her assailant had come to make good on his word.

That bastard! Patti mouthed through the towel that had grown wet from her saliva. Bob was the obvious perpetrator of this conspiracy to get her out of the picture so that he could live freely with his new girlfriend. An inconvenient death in the Rocky Mountains would free Bob from the pain and agony of a messy divorce in their small Idaho town. If he wanted out of their marriage the normal way, he'd end up getting the short end of the stick from a Mormon family law judge and with his adulterous ways and his newfound riches in the real estate world, he would have to pay Patti a king's ransom in spousal support. Yes, Patti was sure that Bob was behind this scheme. And she was certain that she had only a few seconds left in this world. And now because of her and her messed up home life all of her closest friends were in harms way, too. She began to sob as the door to the woodshed opened and the beam of the flashlight blinded her.

"Time for us to chat," the man said.

Patti could only see the outline of his body, and she was surprised to notice that his voice sounded very much like Bob's. Perhaps it was this familiarity in his voice that touched upon something deep within Patti, and touched a part of her that she was never able to make contact with herself despite years of therapy and counseling, but Patti suddenly felt the "fight" response for the first time in her life. In every other circumstance prior to this, Patti always responded by choosing "flight," and had swallowed her pride (along with most everything in the kitchen cupboards) when put in these situations. Patti was overcome with deep ceded, recessed, anger. She was angry that she allowed her husband to treat her with utter disrespect. She was also angry that she allowed herself to mollify her feelings with comfort food instead of standing up for herself. *He's not going to get his way this easily.* She realized that for the first time in her life she was about to fight back.

Chapter 10

As soon as Melanie could see the headlights of a car approaching through the crack in the garage doors she tried to scream as loud as she could, but little noise escaped her bound lips. She fought hard to try to free herself, but eventually resigned herself to the fact that the only thing she was accomplishing was resurrecting the bleeding gash on her arm. Hey, look on the right side of things, kid—at least you're not leaking blood anymore, she teased herself. The fact that the blood flow had subsided over the last hour was undoubtedly an excellent turn of events, and the newly tinged hemorrhage-stained red to her hemp shirt was irrefutable proof of this. She forced herself to relax, taking deep and calming breaths. Bleeding to death was not an option.

She listened intently to all the sounds around her, trying to gauge as much information as possible with the limited tools available to her. Her ears perked as she suddenly noticed the sound of tires approaching, and her spirits both soared and tensed simultaneously. Would this be potential help, or could this be the perpetrator returning to inflict more pain? As the sound of the car tires continued past the cabin and beyond, deflation settled in. Mel's attempt at pumping herself up and psyching herself out of her current predicament was failing miserably as she realized that she'd missed the opportunity for help.

As Mel felt herself start to succumb to the emotions of failure, she realized she needed to desperately find something to distract herself from beating herself up over a missed opportunity. Situations such as this did not happen every day and there was no way she would hold herself accountable for pausing to reflect upon whether the sounds she heard were predatory or otherwise. She began to furtively direct her attention to the room around her, focusing on every microscopic element specifically in front of her. This would not only prevent her from a downward emotional spiral, but this would also provide her with additional knowledge concerning the extent of danger she was facing.

She had actually been avoiding the simple act of inventorying the garage because she didn't want to deal with what her eyes might discover, and deal with undeniable proof that she was in a chamber of torture. The look in the madman's eyes when he tied her to the post assured her that he would take great pleasure in whatever method it was that he chose to kill her, and she feared seeing evidence of his chosen mode in front of her here in the garage.

As Melanie's eyes slowly adjusted and moved around the dusty, confined area, she couldn't help but notice that nearly every tool or gadget in the garage was old and rusted. To her right she saw the work bench, fitted with an operable hand vise. On the bench was a sledge hammer and a cleaned out old Bush's Baked Beans can full of rusty nails. Melanie stopped her mental surveillance to note the benefits her surroundings actually had for her, as well, and that if she were at any point able to free herself, she could smash him over the head with the sledge hammer and then tie him to the vise. She continued dreaming up an escape scenario, which had her then removing his shoes and then spreading nails over the garage floor so that he could not get away without stepping on nails. Melanie's thoughts turned positive as she began to think of various ways in which the inventory of the garage could work to her advantage, and came up with a variety of scenarios in which she could successfully escape and rescue her friends.

But each flash of hope Mel had didn't last long. Dammit, something always happened to cause doubt to start creeping back in.

As she continued her inventory of the garage, she noted an old Puerto Rican jug of rum that was now affixed with a label indicating it was filled with paint thinner, and a corroded two-handled lathe. Was that a bark stripper hung on the wall adjacent to the garage doors? That would be an excellent tool of torture. And let's not overlook the branding iron dangling from the rafters overhead. Is that a chainsaw? Could the chain be any more heavily oxidized?

Melanie was doing what Melanie did in times of crisis. Her melodramatic, sarcastic personality overtook her.

"Look at that hack saw!" she said out loud to herself. Her jaw was aching because she had been working diligently on gnawing the towel in her mouth. "Name that tool," she joked to herself. Shovel. Rake. No, make that four rakes. Spade. Axe. Tree saw. Log saw.

"Stop. Stop it," she mouthed to herself.

She took a deep breath–the kind that she practiced in yoga class three times a week. She could see that she was doing herself no good by engaging in negative thoughts, so she decided to engage in the type of positive thinking she often did when she was at home or at work. She flogged her mind with happy thoughts of her wedding day. Michael was so handsome, in that boyish sort of way, standing in his white tuxedo under the trellised archway at his parents' Menlo Park home. The wedding had been attended by the elite Palo Alto crowd–his mother pleased that Melanie hadn't embarrassed anyone with her homemade gown made of natural fibers.

Mel used up the quick happiness associated with her wedding day and immediately moved on to another happy thought. She remembered signing her first lease for HempCo Designs. She thought of the day when she learned that she was pregnant with Charlie. And the moment she brought William home from the hospital–and how disappointed Charlie was that William couldn't talk or play. She remembered taking the boys to work with her when they were little, and then transitioning them into preschool.

Suddenly, Mel started to wonder whether Michael would ever do anything to contravene these happy moments. They had a good friendship. They co-parented the boys well. True, she was a better athlete and more competitive with the boys and their soccer. But Michael didn't have time to coach a soccer team, while she did. And Michael didn't have time to help them with school projects. Mel did. Her company had been doing so well that she was able to hire a project manager to attend to the daily glitches, allowing her the time and opportunity to manage the company from a more hands-off standpoint, focusing on the larger corporate vision and network of relationships. And this also allowed her more time with the boys.

Michael, on the other hand, was working more hours than ever before as a water rights, land use and taxation specialist. Water in California had become a more litigated issue and Michael had just achieved partner status at his firm. The water rights field was narrow in terms of legal expertise, and it seemed like the competition for business had increased over the last seven years. Michael's partners expected that he would have a large book of business by now, and the fact that he didn't have a sizeable client base made him very uneasy about his future with his firm. His taxation business was the only book that brought a steady revenue source to the firm, yet he disliked this area of law and was having problems with his biggest client.

Mel had apparently not realized the extent of this problem with Michael, because when he began discussing it with her recently, she'd responded by flippantly teasing that he could always come and work for her if need be. Her company had more and more disputes regarding patent infringement issues, and she figured that an attorney seasoned in the fine print of client rights would easily transfer water rights to hemp invention rights.

Either this suggestion was not well timed, or is never a good thing for a wife to mention to a husband in the midst of troubles at work, because Michael ended up both offended and furious. She had no intention of upsetting him, but truth be told, she made twice as much money as he did and worked half the hours. If he worked for her, she figured that they'd both be able to spend more time with the boys. While Melanie clearly had no idea of the depth of Michael's wounds when making her light hearted statement, financially, it was a sound one and should not have resulted in the type of emotional response that it did.

Perhaps Michael did not want more family time after all.

* * *

Hesta's thin frame lay shaking on the cold floor of the bath house. For the first time in nearly twenty-five years, she did not crave a cigarette. In fact, the mere thought of smoking repulsed her. What was exceedingly more repulsive right now, however, was the mental image she couldn't erase from her brain of the whack job who had tried to rape her. She could not etch out the image of the seething anger burned into his face as he tried repeatedly to enter her with his withering ductile penis, only to have the anger grow fiercer with each failed attempt at penetration. Had he been able to rape her, perhaps he would not have been compelled to mutilate her, but his inability to perform clearly infuriated him to the point of no return. With the expertise of a surgeon, he circumcised her with his knife, excising her clitoris with the flick of the razor without regards to pain or bleeding. The pain Hesta experienced was without a doubt the most excruciating of her life, both physically and mentally. She had no idea what his intentions were with regards to the knife, or just when he intended to stop using it.

As the blood pooled around her bottom it lay dormant and eventually grew sticky. The pain was immediate and incessant, and radiated from between her legs throughout her body. She grew confused, unsure of what was real and what was imaginary, and whether this might perhaps–hopefully–be just some ugly nightmare from which she'd awake? She hoped amongst hopes that this was nothing more than coming back to her in a dream and haunting her subconscious, but that she would wake up and it would all be over.

Hesta fought off the pain and the delirium by attempting to force her mind to contemplate facts entirely outside of her recent disfigurement. She began running her mind over the possibilities involving her own husband, and whether he could possibly have had it within himself to have hired this horrible man to come to the cabin this weekend to kill her. That was the question weighing most heavily on her mind. It was no secret in the publishing world that John Knotingham was a first class drug addict loser. He ran in the elite upper crust society as a result of his mother's money, which she herself had acquired only after marrying into when she hooked up with an elderly steel mogul. Maria Knotingham must have been quite astute, because story has it that she made quick inventory of the mogul's needs, and immediately figured out a way to fill those needs–and then some–within a few months time. The prenuptial agreement was standard, but it did not exclude inheritance to natural born children, so Maria made it her full time business to increase all likelihood of progeny. John was born within a year, and, fortunately for him (or Maria, depending on with whom you spoke), just fourteen months before his birth father's death. Maria inherited old money, and John inherited his mother's manipulative personality.

Hesta, through gasps of pain, tried to shrug away the memory of the old hag, but then again—dammit, John got all his manipulative ways through her, and Hesta just wasn't able to wave the old bitch from her thoughts.

Maria's sly ways had been fine-tuned over the years and her disdain for Hesta was a published fact. Fortunately, Hesta's rise up the corporate ladder within Gold Publishing Group allowed her ammunition for retaliation in the social circles and, whenever possible, Hesta took it upon herself to edit any detail regarding Maria's public and private persona. Of course, Hesta was well aware that the warfare between her and her mother-in-law weighed heavily on John. Perhaps this was the only thing that bothered John, as he had been in the process of writing his debut novel for over a decade, but had not been able to document much more than three chapters. John holed himself up in their Upper Eastside apartment most days, allegedly working on this debut novel's manuscript, but when he went out into the social circles each night, Hesta saw that he made little, if any, progress in his writing. She assumed that John had plenty of lovers that distracted him from his daytime writing, presumably both male and female. Hesta believed this because for one, John showed no interest in her whatsoever, and another being that he would never be one to limit himself to just one option when her grew up with a mother telling him he could have whatever he wanted whenever he wanted—why would his selection of a partner be any different?

John made it clear that he had no interest in divorce. Hesta made great money, and John could not depend upon inheritance from his spendthrift mother. If he displeased his mother for any reason, she quickly threatened to write him out of her will. Such stringent demands made it unfeasible and impractical for John to divorce Hesta.

Reviewing everything in her marriage leading up until this point, she realized that John had every reason to want her dead. It was really quite simple, and if it worked out the way it apparently was intended, would be rather successful for him. Hesta knew this all to be true. She knew that John had ample motive to want her dead. He believed that he would inherit all of the money that she had worked so hard to attain. He thought that he would no longer be financially dependent upon his wife or his mom. In his mind, he would be a free man.

Chapter 11

Rema Setliff was hanging crucifixion style, just like the statue of Jesus that hung above the doorway to the single bunk bedroom. For the first several hours, all she could think about was her training and how this creep was keeping her from her standard forty-mile Sunday run. She had not hydrated properly if she didn't get out of here soon she might not be able to compete in her next race. Over time, it dawned on her that she was being completely irrational, but it was hard for her to alter her rigorous way of thinking now. Training is what she'd turned herself into. Training is what she'd become. Training is all she did anymore. All she thought about was training. She lived it, ate it, drank it, and breathed it. Nothing else mattered to her.

"What is wrong with me?" she asked herself in a muffled, gagged voice.

She thought about the answer to her rhetorical question. She was unemployed and had been for the past ten years. She had no children and no meaningful relationships in her life, including with anyone within her own family. The only friendships that she maintained were the Fab Five, and other ultramarathon runners. Her relationship with her husband, Scott, was estranged, so she couldn't even consider her husband as a confidant.

Rema's thoughts turned towards her husband momentarily, reflecting upon their unusual marital arrangements. While it was true that they were married in the technical sense of the word, that was as far as the relationship went. They rarely saw one another, and the fact that Scott was a former Denver Broncos wide receiver meant that he maintained a great body which furthered their distance; the demand for his attention was always high within the community, especially considering that he went out of his way to become politically involved in their local scene. Despite his retirement from the game, he seemed to always be in a meeting or on his way to some charity event. Whether he was actually on his way to a charity event, or just using that as an excuse to get a piece of ass here or there was anyone's guess. After all, it was common knowledge that he had girlfriends on the side, and he was rarely without an entourage of young people who stroked his ego. Rema didn't like Scott much and really didn't care whether he had extramarital affairs. She had little interest in Scott's mental or physical persona, and wasn't really looking to fill the gap that he presented with anyone else. Her only interest was running.

Rema's review of her unusual relationship with Scott made her contemplate what her captor had taunted her with earlier, and considered whether it could possibly be true. If so, she wasn't sure whether Scott could be the culprit, and whether he would feel the need to lower himself to the point of actually hiring someone to kill her. Granted, their relationship totally lacked any emotion, and she was sure he'd be totally fine with her being dead, but similarly, he had absolutely nothing to gain by her death, either. He lived his life the way he wanted without any repercussions from her, so why would he give a shit whether she were dead?

Rema tried to consider whether there were any potential motives for murder present in their marriage that she might be too quickly glossing over. Perhaps she wasn't appreciating the level of disgust he had for her obsession with regard to training? He had gone out of his way to make clear his annoyance with her compulsive training schedule, but she just couldn't see that being the basis for homicide. Could it be money? Did Scott want a divorce but not want to part with half his fortune? Rema figured that they were worth at least five million dollars, but Scott's ability to earn was diminishing over time, as he was getting older and not likely to be sought as a sportscaster much longer. Network contracts were difficult to negotiate and he'd been quoted recently making some controversial comments on the air. Perhaps he was insecure about his future earnings potential and wanted to lock in his options?

What if the emotionless Scott had actually been able to warm up to someone, and Rema was now standing in the way of his true love? Scott had mentioned that he'd always wanted children, but his traveling and her training had always prevented them from doing anything about it. At this point, Rema wasn't quite sure whether she was actually even able to physically reproduce given her obsessive physical schedule, which had stopped her from getting her period several years ago. What if he found someone who both wanted and was able to give those children to him? That would be something to potentially make him consider what this thug who'd kidnapped them had suggested.

Ultimately, Rema didn't think that Scott would resort to murder. No reason made sense at all, but none of this did. And the more she thought about it, the more she realized that perhaps she really just didn't know her husband as well as she thought she did. The longer that she hung in this crucifixion position, the more she realized how little she knew and how anything was possible. She grunted as she began to recall their initial introduction to one another, back in the day in Boulder, when he was the star football player and she was running track and field. He noticed her running the steps of Folsom Field when he was practicing with his team and asked her for a date. They dated throughout college, but it wasn't a secret that he was a playboy when the team was on the road. She married him the summer before he was drafted into the NFL, with the understanding that he would be gone much of the time. Rema decided to stay at Boulder and finish undergrad, get her masters, and train with the hopes that she could somehow get her times down low enough to qualify for the Olympics.

When it became readily apparent that she was not fast enough to make the Olympic track and field team, she decided that her only hope was longer distances. She set her sites on this goal and it never left her crosshairs. Scott's career was never very interesting to her, despite his successes. He invited her to every game in nearby Denver, but she usually made an excuse not to attend. Over time, those invitations grew less frequent, which was just fine with Rema. Perhaps he harbored resentment toward her for not being the typical NFL wife. Perhaps this derision had developed into scorn. Perhaps Scott did hire this creep to kill her.

Rema slung her head forward as Jesus likely did at his time of death. She said a quick prayer that God would give her the strength to get one of her hands free so that she could reach into the waistband of her running shorts and retrieve the knife that she stashed there. Regardless of how she found her motivation, Rema was determined not to die. Right now, the reason for that last ditch effort was her never-ending dream of becoming the next infamous ultramarathon runner. No asshole was going to string her up like a rack of meat and kill all her dreams at once.

* * *

Mac had quickly ruled out the possibility that Wyatt would hire someone to kill her. What she hadn't been able to rule out, however, was the fear that Greg, who was Wyatt's brother and her former lover, had masqueraded himself as her husband and contracted a murder for hire. She and Greg had not parted on good terms. Greg had tried to poison her to stop her from finding out about a methamphetamine drug trafficking story that he had been covering. Of course, this ended their relationship. Greg and Wyatt loathed each other. What better way to get back at both of them?

Mac looked up to the ceiling of her grandmother's bedroom. She wondered how many times Gram had laid on this bed praying for something. What would her grandmother do in a situation like this? She was a smart, independent woman who would not have allowed her own fears to get in the way of solving a problem. Gram would have considered the motive of the individual for sure, but she would have spent most of her time and energy determining how to get out of the bad situation. Mac decided to follow suit. She looked around the bedroom to see what she could use to her advantage. For one thing, she had her own private entrance to the cabin. If Mac could free herself, she could escape without the freak knowing it—at least for a short time—and get help from Max and Nicole who lived less than a quarter mile away.

Mac ruled out the possibility of escape as she determined that the freakish criminal had bound her extremely well to the bedpost, and her bonds were simply too tight for her to loosen. Instead of giving up or giving in, Mac quickly surveyed the room around her looking for some other device that could be used for her own benefit. Next to the window was an old Singer sewing machine, just up against a French door which was bolted shut. Next to the French door was a nightstand and adjacent to the queen-sized bed was a closet. There really wasn't much else, as Gram kept the room sparsely decorated and minimal in accessories. Mac tilted her head back and lifted her eyes up towards the ceiling in momentary pause looking for internal guidance from above. She looked around her, but felt the urge to look back above her for some unknown reason. All Mac saw above her was the light bulb overhead.

It took a moment for it to process, but Mac finally had her "A ha!" moment. The light was operated mainly by the switch near the door, but also had an overhead pull string so that Gram could turn off the light without getting out of bed. If she could arch her back into a back bend, perhaps she could snag it between her knees. If only she'd kept up on yoga. It would have paid off at this point. Mac was in excellent physical shape, but not terribly flexible. Nevertheless, she would give it a try.

She wedged her feet as close together as possible and jammed her heels into the footboard, which wobbled and squeaked under pressure. She would have to be quiet, she knew, which would prove difficult with a fifty- year-old bed frame.

Next, she pushed the heels of her hands against the headboard and gave a push. Fortunately, the headboard was wedged tightly against the wall of the cabin and would provide good support. With both hands and feet in proper position, she pushed hard, using her stomach and back muscles to hoist herself up. To her amazement, she was able to do a backbend. It was not pretty, and it was not comfortable, but it was manageable. To get enough elevation to get the pull string in between her knees, she had to arch her back just slightly higher and lean her weight toward her hands.

Mac strained as hard as she could to hold this position while trying to clamp the slender white string. Her first try was a near success, but she accidentally nudged the string too quickly and it spun in circles around her knees. She had to hold her position and wait until the string stopped spinning. When it finally came to rest, she lunged at it again. This time she caught it. She gently lowered her body while squeezing tightly with her knees, pulling the string down and clicking off the light bulb. She let up a bit and then lowered herself again, clicking the bulb back on. She repeated this procedure and clicked the light off.

Mac waited a minute and then repeated the sequence. She hoped that Max and Nicole would notice.

And then she heard stomping footsteps heading toward Gram's bedroom door.

Chapter 12

Nellie Monlock sat alone in her cabin and watched the late evening news. The thunderstorms had since quieted and she breathed in the mountain air made fresh from the rain. As she finished the last few stitches on her second knitted baby cap of the day, she couldn't help but feel the pang of disappointment in Mac. Nellie had been looking forward all day to an afternoon visit from the hikers and they had forgotten about her.

Nellie thought about Mac–whom she considered her adopted granddaughter. Had Mac changed since she'd married that cowboy? Nellie wondered if it were true. Mac had been coming to the Kilkenny-Kerry for over forty years and had never missed a day of visiting Nellie. What was different about today?

Nellie looked at the framed needlepoint art that hung above her television. Mac had made it for her one summer when she was here with Gram. It read:

"Old wood to burn, Old wine to drink, Old friends to trust, Old books to read. With mirth and laughter, let Old wrinkles come."

Nellie suddenly became overcome with worry. What if something had happened on the hike? It was a long way up to the Continental Divide and due to the late spring storms this year, there were reports that there was still some snow up there. What if one of the five ladies had fallen and been injured and they had no cell service to contact anyone for help?

After pondering the situation for some time, Nellie was convinced that something was wrong. At age ninety-three, she knew better than to try to walk in the dark to Mac's cabin. One thing was resolute in her mind–at first dawn's light, she would take hold of her cane and make her way down to the Kilkenny-Kerry and check on her beloved Mac.

* * *

It had been quiet outside for a long time. The wind had died down and the thunder had ceased. There were no more raindrops splattering on the old shingle roof.

Patti knew that something terrible had happened to both Melanie and Hesta. The wood shed and the bath house were less than eight feet from one another, and she heard the attack on Melanie not long after he'd clamped Patti's arm in the hand vise and left her splintered in the dark and cold of the wood shed. By the sound of the attack on Mel, he'd taken her down the dirt driveway toward the garage. By the sound of what happened with Hesta, Patti figured that she was still in the bath house. If only there was a way to communicate with her friends—to see if they were okay. The gag in her mouth was so tight that she could hardly make gurgling noises. She wanted to yell out, but she couldn't.

Every time Patti moved even a centimeter, another splinter of wood shed itself from the old workbench and into her skin. Her arms were numb. Her body was cold. She was miserable and afraid, but the misery was turning into a new feeling—a feeling Patti had not experienced enough in her life. She was growing angry. She was angry that this beast had abused her. She was angry that Bob had abused her. She was angry that her three sons took her for granted and treated her like their servant. She was angry most of all at herself for letting these men in her life take advantage of her kindness and generosity.

"To hell with them," Patti said to herself.

She used her weak and flabby stomach muscles to lift her fat thighs up in the air and with all the rage she could muster, she kicked on the wooden door with all of her might. The door shook with a loud thud and she heard something crash on the ground outside. Patti remembered the bird house that hung above the wood shed door. Mac made that bird house when she was a little girl and bragged that it had stood the test of severe Colorado winters. Patti felt a brief pang of guilt and then corrected herself. She knew that her friend would not care under the circumstances. Patti pulled her legs up and pounded the door again. Powered by anger, she pulverized the door over and over again until it sprang off its old rusted hinges.

A charge of cold air stroked Patti's body, causing goose bumps to form on her naked pink flesh. She knew that her only hope was to free herself from the hand vise and run to Max and Nicole's house.

Patti wriggled her wrists, realizing that the coldness of the air was working in her favor. Her hands had shrunk a bit and, for the first time in a long time, Patti felt hope. She was capable of doing something about her predicament. She did not have to lay back and take the mistreatment any more. She felt empowered to take control of her life. Why hadn't she done this long ago? Why hadn't she told Bob to 'go to hell' when she suspected that he was cheating? Why hadn't she put her foot down with the boys when they tried to manipulate her?

And then she heard the crunching of gravel and the footsteps coming her way. All hope and new-found strength left as quickly as it came.

"What the fuck have you done, Fatty Patti?"

The monster knew her name.

Under the moonlit sky, Patti saw the bloody hack saw in his right hand and she immediately assumed the worst.

"You have a little more fight in you than I thought. That's good. See, I figured you were one of those wimpy chicks that just cry and let bad things happen to you. It's a relief to see that you got a little more to you."

The man paced back and forth in the darkness, strategizing his next move. Patti's anxiety rose with each pump of her heart beat.

"When I was in jail, there was this little guy who everyone assumed was a Betty because he looked like a pansy-ass. But he was a mouthy little shit and he wouldn't back down from a fight. I left him alone for the most part. I liked the fact that he didn't let the bullies take advantage of his weakness. Looks like you've got a little fight left in you."

Patti was dumbfounded that this animal was speaking in full sentences to her. Did he actually have a grain of compassion in his body?

"Your friend Melanie is not doing too great. You and I are going to visit her in the garage. That's where this hack saw comes into play. We're going to do a little science experiment with your courage and her aggression."

Chapter 13

Melanie started crying the moment she heard him fiddling with the padlock on the garage doors.

"Brought you some company," he said.

Melanie lifted her dirty and tear-stained face as she watched her bound and naked friend being escorted into the torture chamber.

Patti's eyes grew wild when she saw Melanie tied to the center garage post, a pool of blood encasing her. The man pushed Patti to the floor next to her friend.

"Eenie, Meenie, Miney, Mo," he said, using the hack saw to point back and forth to each woman as he spoke. The saw was pointed at Melanie when he stopped with the nursery rhyme. "Guess you are it." He walked over to her and pulled her clenched fist to cement floor. He pulled her pinky finger out flat and slammed the saw down on it. Melanie's entire body tweaked in pain as her finger was severed from her left hand. Patti nearly fainted as she watched in horror.

"I have a picture frame at the cabin made out of my step-dad's severed fingers. Decided that Melanie's finger would be the start of a new frame," he said as he shoved Patti through the door into the bedroom adjacent to the garage. He turned on the overhead light briefly so that he could tie her to the footboard of the double bed frame.

Mac's family had converted a portion of the garage into an additional bedroom some years back to accompany large family reunions at the cabin. The bedroom had single bunk beds and a double bed all within small living quarters. The room was decorated in cowboy bedding and had rope around the molding to give it a western look.

The floor had a stained piece of carpet over the old linoleum floor and Patti's naked bottom rested on the carpet.

"I'm going to starve Patti for a week or two so that her skin loosens up. Then I'm going to skin her alive and use her skin to upholster some old chairs."

Patti gasped for air. She felt a panic attack coming on.

"I have mastered the art of using human skin for all sorts of home decorating. Skin also makes fascinating jewelry."

The monster peeked around the corner to get Mel's attention for his next statement.

"Skulls make nice bowls. And ashtrays."

Mel did not even raise her head. He had spent the previous half hour telling his life story of pain and torture and had explained, in gruesome detail, the people he had killed and what he had done with their corpses.

"Your friend Hesta has a nice vulva. I cut it out. I plan to paint it silver like I did with the lady I killed at the ski area. I have this nice little box that I keep vulvas in. I call it 'The Vulva Box'." He laughed out loud with his lips curled back in a sort of a snarl.

"I must be on my way, ladies. No, don't get up. I can see myself to the door. I have a lot of work to do before sunup." He laughed to himself in a mocking way.

With that, he turned off the bedroom light and shut the double wooden doors to the garage. Patti winced as she heard the padlock click. Melanie did not react this time. She reserved what was left of her spirit to pray for her two little boys. She forced herself out of the moment in time and put herself into their bedrooms. She pictured Charlie asleep in his blue wooden bed. The wallpaper in his room was that of a sports theme and a large soccer ball rug served to warm his feet when he awoke in the mornings. Mel pictured him holding his favorite dolphin stuffed animal, dreaming of his Sunday soccer game.

She then focused on her sweet baby William, fast asleep in his red race car bed. Her mind painted a picture of him holding on to his star-shaped soft fluffy, happily dreaming of his flag football game.

She thought of Michael tucking both boys in. She knew that he loved being a father and enjoyed the time when she was not there and he had the boys all to himself. Maybe that is what he wanted full time? He was very frustrated at work and wanted to move to Montana or Washington. He wanted to work for an eco-friendly environmental firm, or better yet–start his own company. He wasn't interested in practicing law for the rest of his life. The problem was Melanie. She did not want to move. She loved her neighborhood and her neighbors and the kids' school. Her company was less than five miles from home and she was able to be there for the boys more than most working moms. She did not want to change their life, even if it meant that Michael was not happy in his work.

If they divorced, which Michael had recently suggested in a moment of anger, she reminded him that a divorce lawyer told her that he would not be able to move the kids out of the state without the prior approval of a court.

Of course Melanie was not being truthful to her husband. She had not seen an attorney, but said so in a moment of anger. She knew the law from speaking to women at work who faced custody battles. Michael's response to her statement was pure shock. She knew that she hurt his feelings, but was too selfish to admit that she lied to him.

But Michael didn't know that. And in Michael's mind, if Melanie was out of the picture, he could move wherever he wanted.

* * *

Mac heard footsteps coming toward Gram's room so she stopped flicking the light on and off.

"Sending out a signal, were you?" he said to her. "You think someone around here is going to see a light go on and off and come running to save you and your friends? Not a chance."

Mac recoiled at the sight of the hammer in his bloody right hand and the Hills Bros. Coffee can in the other. She'd seen that can many times in the garage and knew that it contained old rusty nails.

"Guess we'd better pin you down so that you can't reach the rope," he said with a disdainful laugh. "It would be easier to cut the rope, but not as much fun."

Mac noticed his icy blue eyes and his baby face. How could such an attractive man be so cruel? In her mind, cold-hearted killers looked like Charles Manson or John Wayne Gacy. This kid looked like any other hippie- style college kid educated in Boulder. The difference, she supposed, was the ghastly gleam in his eyes when he was about to do something horrific–like nail her to the bed.

Chapter 14

Rema Setliff had never taken guff off anyone. When bullied as a kid for being the shortest on the block, she retaliated by becoming the fastest runner in town and mastering mind games like "ding-dong ditch" and hide- and-seek. She was steadfast in her determination to be the best in everything—whether it be scholastics or athletics. With her sheer determination, she made it happen.

When she met Scott in college, he was attracted to her because of her stalwart attitude—and her nonchalant reaction to him. Most women flocked to him and pursued him with gusto. He was the stud on campus after all. Rema admired him for his physical attributes, but also acknowledged the fact that he worked hard in school to get a good education. He did not rely on his football scholarship to coast through school. He actually sought the most out of his education by attending class every day and putting in the effort to get good grades. She liked his determination to succeed. She shared that determination.

She had no interest in him romantically when they first met. His magnetism drew her in, but her self-discipline kept her safely at bay. She didn't have time to get involved with a Casanova. It was Scott that pursued her with resolve, yet Rema had the fortitude to ignore him longer than any other woman had managed. This, of course, intrigued Scott to no end. The more interest Scott showed, the more determined Rema was to snub him, which in turn, intrigued Scott even more. In her mind, she was resurrecting a game of 'hide and seek' from youth.

It was this same kind of determination that allowed Rema to keep her cool when the freak sauntered into the bunk bed room and slapped her hard across the face. She was still hanging, crucifix-style from the bed.

Her arms had long since gone numb and her legs were swollen with lactic acid and blood. She had run over fifty miles in the two days preceding this monster's arrival at the cabin and it was common practice for her to elevate her legs by the end of the day to allow the lactic acid to dissipate and her muscles to relax. Being hung to a bed like Jesus wasn't helping the healing process at all.

But for once in her life, Rema wasn't worried about tomorrow's run. When the "hostage crisis" started, she knew that they'd overtake this bastard and her running plans would resume. After being held captive for several hours, and after his last visit when he'd cut off her left earlobe "for the handle to his new ashtray," she realized that running wasn't even remotely on her list of priorities, and survival was now her main objective.

When he walked into her room and slapped her, she quickly regained her decorum and, through her gag, asked his name. He understood her question.

"I go by Craig," he said.

She nodded. She studied his t-shirt, which she recognized as a concert shirt from a Red Rocks performance by Neil Young. He watched her as she studied him.

"I didn't go to this concert, if that is what you're wondering. I was locked up at the time, but apparently my stepfather went. This is his shirt. He was wearing it when I found him in a cabin up the road."

Rema immediately knew that his story was not going to have a happy or pleasant ending.

He gestured with his index finger and made a slicing motion across his neck. He smiled and said, "The bastard was an asshole to me when I was a kid. I swore to myself that I'd find him someday and repay my debt of gratitude for always making me feel like a 'red-headed stepchild,' which is what he used to call me. He told me that I was stupid and lazy and wouldn't amount to anything. I told him that I'd kill him someday. Well, turns out that we were both right."

Craig paced the bedroom, mumbling to himself for a few seconds, as if he was trying to remember his train of thought.

"I'm stupid and lazy 'cuz I've been locked up for nearly ten years. Just a few days ago, I arrived at his home unannounced. He didn't have a clue who I was. Hasn't seen me since I was a kid. I introduced myself at the same time that I slit his throat and cut off his lips. Lips are great for wind chimes. You use them opposite the whistle chimes to balance the weight. When I'm done bleaching his skull, I will use it for a cereal bowl."

Craig drew his lips back into an evil grin. Rema felt like he was trying to intimidate her with his evil stories and it made her angry, but she was helpless with no way of telling him what she thought of his grotesque and manipulative ways. She wished she could tune him out, but he kept on talking.

"See, he destroyed my self-confidence and my ability to reason. So, now I'm returning the favor. I fried his brains with butter and salt, added wedges of his heart, and ate some of it for dinner last night. The sandwiches you and your friends made for me were nice, don't get me wrong, but I'm on a high protein diet."

Rema's stomach turned at the thought of human brains in a frying pan. It was at that moment that she realized that this young man's depth of vengeance had no boundary. He'd probably never been taught how to cope with disappointment and anger. His anger had grown to fury and rage and had been fueled without constraint.

"I don't blame you," Rema said, regaining her composure as quickly as she could. "I'd do the same thing." Her words were mumbled through the dishtowel that had been stuffed in her mouth and tied tightly around her head, but he seemed to understand.

"You're lying. No one carves out someone else's brains and heart and fries them up for supper."

"Jeffrey Dahmer. Edward Gain. David Berkowitz. Thomas Hamilton." Rema was trying to think of more, but that was the best she could do.

"Serial killers," he said.

Rema nodded.

Craig stopped pacing and turned toward her and said in a deep and evil tone, "I'm not a serial killer."

Rema shook her head up and down again.

"No, I'm not. Serial killers just kill for the sake of killing. They don't even care who their victims are."

Rema shook her head from side to side.

"I kill for revenge."

Rema shrugged her shoulders. "You don't have any reason for revenge against me or my friends, but here you are," she garbled.

The man threw his head back as he laughed out loud. "How well do you know your friends?"

Chapter 15

The Nederland Police Department was located in the Caribou Shopping Center and by all accounts could be described as modern day-Andy Griffith's Mayberry R.F.D. Until recently, not much by way of criminal activity occurred in this peaceful mountain community. The police force addressed marijuana use with a wink and a nod and focused mainly on driving under the influence, especially those heading down the winding highway from Nederland into Boulder. Otherwise, serving as an officer for the NPD was a fairly laid back and enjoyable assignment.

Last year, there was a murder-suicide in a cabin just outside of town and a string of burglaries in mostly unoccupied summer homes. Earlier in the year during the snow season, a young man went "postal" at the Eldora Ski Area and began shooting into a crowd of snowboarders who were drinking beer at the end of their day on the slopes. Two young men were killed and a few others were injured. The man was apprehended by the NPD and taken into custody in Boulder.

Recently, there was an unsolved report of a woman who'd driven her car with Wyoming plates to a ski area where a party was ongoing after a local skateboarding contest. The woman's car was found, along with her purse and parts of her remains in a suitcase, but portions of her body were never found. The case remained open, but the clues had been sparse. No one at the party appeared to know the woman. Her driver's license listed her as Carolyn Patterson from Douglas, Wyoming. Investigators determined that she had no living relatives and the police have no idea what a woman in her mid-sixties was doing at a party where the average age in attendance was twenty-four.

Other than these recent crimes, the quaint mountain community remained peaceful and serene. Folks enjoyed a lifestyle of hiking and biking and other outdoor activities. Neighbors looked after neighbors. Conversations at the local coffee house centered around who had summitted Long's Peak or Chief's Head. Folks bragged about drinking escapades at Nedfest or Frozen Dead Guy Days. The more civilized residents collected flowers and were thrilled with an arrangement consisting of Jacob's Ladder, Beard Tongue and Indian Paintbrush. The Garden Tour was prime time to the botanists.

Fall was lurking and despite the late spring and short summer, the aspens were ebbing into hues of gold and ginger and crimson. Summer cabins were being shored up for winter and vacationers were making their way back home.

It had been an unusual year in Nederland—one which local residents would never forget.

* * *

Mac heard the sound of hammering on the window above Gram's bed, but she couldn't gather the strength to pull her head backward to look overhead to see what was going on. Her hands had been nailed to the headboard and it sickened her to see her own blood staining the bedspread that reminded her so much of her grandmother. The pain was excruciating to the point of nausea, and moving even the slightest caused a throbbing pain in her hands and up each arm.

Mac heard the wooden shutters on the bedroom window close and then she heard the metal latch bar clang into the latch thong, locking the shutters in place. Mac was very familiar with this sound, as every summer she came to the Kilkenny-Kerry to close the cabin for the winter. Part of the process included closing all the red clapboard shutters and locking them into place with the latch bars, and then covering all the west-facing windows with tar paper to keep the snow from drifting in over the winter.

Mac then heard the man come around to the west side of Gram's bedroom and latch the shutters on that window. She heard this procedure repeat itself about two dozen times over the next half hour and with each latch thong clanging into place, she knew that she was one nail closer to being sealed into the cabin for good. This would be her coffin. He was closing them in for the winter.

Mac had been holding out hope that Max and Nicole would stop by and notice that something was desperately wrong at the cabin. However, if they arrived to find the shutters closed and the latch bars in place, they might assume that Mac and her friends had closed down the cabin ahead of schedule and had left for the season. It would likely not occur to them that the five ladies were being held prisoners inside and that once the latch bars were down, there was absolutely no way to get out. Mac felt the tears drip down the outside corners of her eyes and stream their way into her long auburn hair. She would never see her husband again. She would never see her brother or her mother or her step-siblings. She would never see Pam and Megan, her office staff who'd become like family. She would not be able to say good-bye to her foster boy, Levi, whom she'd saved from a mother who suffered from mental health issues. And she would not get to say good-bye to her faithful cat, Ted.

How could this happen? How could one deranged man ruin so many lives with his depravity?

And then she thought of Columbine High School and the fact that two boys could maliciously kill and maim students for no apparent reason. She thought of her former client, Gil, and his insatiable thirst for killing prostitutes. And then she remembered Joseph Atkins, whom Mac did a research paper about for one of her college psychology classes. Joseph had been adopted as a toddler, and as an adult came back to his childhood home and killed the man who adopted him, as well as a thirteen-year-old neighbor. Mac followed the case through the appellate process and remembered that Joseph was put to death by lethal injection. Mac also thought of the Son of Sam—David Berkowitz—who was also adopted by a nice family who took good care of him, but for whatever reason, David was a bully with a mean streak and he took to the streets to shoot and kill many women.

Mac thought about the man who was busy sealing her into a winter coffin. Had he been adopted? Was his childhood so horrible that he'd lost all feelings toward humans? She thought about what he had been doing to her four friends. Every time he came to visit her in Gram's room, he bragged as to what he'd done to them, but Mac couldn't allow herself to believe what he was saying. She had to stay strong mentally. She knew that he was trying to break her down psychologically.

When she heard his footsteps coming back into the cabin, through the kitchen and toward Gram's bedroom, she realized that he was winning the battle. She could feel her stomach churning and panic rose in her veins.

"Time for you to visit the girls," he said. "I like Rema. She might be spared. The rest of you are a bunch of weaklings. You remind me of my mom."

Mac squinted at him, not sure how to react.

"I'm thinking that this is gonna hurt a little. I can't say that I've ever pulled a nail out of someone's skin when they're still alive. Used to do it to animals when I was a kid, and cats especially would make this howling sound that you can't believe. Dogs were different. They'd jerk real hard and nearly rip their paw off just to get free. Are you more like a cat or a dog, I wonder?

I'm thinking you are a cat person."

He reached toward Mac's hand with the claw of the hammer and jammed it hastily into her skin. Mac winced in pain and would have bit through her bottom lip had it not been for a dishtowel in her mouth. He jerked the nail out of the bedpost causing a spurt of blood to spray over Gram's blue bedspread. He walked around the room to the other side of the bed and repeated his procedure. Mac's bloodied arms fell limp to each side of the double bed. She inhaled deeply to maintain composure and wanted desperately to pummel him with her freed hands, but the throbbing pain was far too great for such a feat.

"My name is Craig," he said in a conversational tone as he helped Mac to her feet. "I think you should go by your real name of Mary. It is a nice name. Mac sounds like a cheap hamburger. You are too pretty for that."

Mac shot him a sideways glance. He knew her name. What else did he know about her? Did Wyatt tell him her real name? Or was it Greg?

He fashioned her arms behind her back and loosely tied the bleeding limbs together and then he slipped his hand into the crook of her arm, as if they were going on a date. Mac wondered if this was the first time this man had ever touched another human in a courteous fashion. His accounting of his past had led her to believe that he had never experienced love.

"Thank you," she whispered.

"For what?"

"For helping me."

Craig glared at her and then scoffed.

"You don't get it."

Chapter 16

On the walk from the cabin toward the garage, Mac looked at the clear night sky and saw the stars winking at her. She said a silent prayer toward heaven in hopes that one of the winking stars was her grandmother watching over her. "Please, Gram," Mac said in her head, "send help." At that precise moment, a shooting star zipped like a bullet over Longs Peak and vanished like a spirit.

Mac looked back down the long driveway, wondering if any of the neighbors were awake. She was uncertain of the time, but figured that it must be around three or four in the morning based on the stillness of the air and the darkness of the sky. As they walked, she glanced back at the main cabin, noting that all of the windows had been bolted down for winter. Craig had even nailed the tar paper to the western side of the cabin for winter snow protection. How did he know to do this? Her heart sunk, accepting the notion that Max and Nicole would assume that she'd closed the cabin herself and that she didn't need their assistance. Mac looked down the long driveway and noted in dismay that her car was missing. It made her wonder whether he had an accomplice. She had not heard other voices, but realized that perhaps he had a buddy who was attending to her friends in the garage while he was taking care of business in the main cabin. How could one man torture five women, close up a cabin and dispose of a car within a few hours?

They walked along the flagstone path from the main cabin toward the garage. As they passed by the bath house, Mac thought of the many summers that she and her siblings and cousins dragged a large metal bucket from the woodshed and filled it with well water from the red hand pump in front of the bathhouse. They would make "soup" using a variety of wild flowers and grasses from the acre of land they owned. It was dark now, but through the moonlight, Mac could make out the bell shape of the red handle. The well itself was next to it and was covered with wooden planks. If only she could shove this creep sideways about ten feet so that he could fall through the planks and into the water supply.

As they continued their journey toward the garage, the flagstone path ended and the dirt driveway began. As Craig fiddled with the padlock to the garage doors, Mac had a fleeting desire to run. She knew the area well and she was certain that she could get to Max and Nicole's house. He must have sensed her desire to flee because he immediately grabbed her by the hair and shoved her against the garage double door.

"Don't even think about it. You'll have this axe through your shoulder blades before you get to the end of the driveway if you try."

She fought back the tears of frustration and pain as he swung open the doors to her great-grandfather's garage and in it, bloodied and hog-tied to the ridgepole, was her friend Melanie. Across from Mel and clamped to the work bench vise grip dangled Hesta, dried blood stained like lava flow between her legs. Around the corner and within eyesight, tied to the guest bedroom footboard, was a naked and bruised Patti. The only one missing was Rema.

Mac winced in pain when the monster pulled down the old hydraulic tire inflator and wedged it between her bound, bloodied, crucified hands and hoisted her by a rope to the ceiling rafter. The nails were still lodged into her palms. Any movement was excruciating.

"Give me a minute, ladies," he said to no one in particular. "I have to get the skinny one and then we will all have a little party together in here. With the cabin all bolted up and your car neatly tucked away behind a cabin on the trailhead, no one will come looking for you for a few days. By then, death will be your only hope.

* * *

Rema's survival mechanism was to run away whenever times got tough. Therefore, it was impossible to explain her actions when she was finally able to free herself.

Once she wiggled her left hand free from the rope that secured her to the bunk bed, she reached back into the waistband of her running shorts and removed the paring knife that she'd hidden. She cut the rope to her right hand and prepared to run for help. In a moment of panic, however, and knowing that she only had a split second to get away and get help for her friends, and upon hearing the monster coming back into the main cabin, she darted into the double bunk bedroom. She crawled up into the hidden storage closet above the wood paneling and pulled the door closed with the draw string.

Rema knew that the secret storage compartment existed from the times that she'd helped Mac close the cabin in the past. The family kept the heirloom Navajo blankets stored in this secret compartment so that if anyone ever broke into the cabin, the priceless blankets would not be stolen. She knew that there was a flashlight up in the rafters of the storage area. Other than a large wooden chest and a flashlight, there was nothing else there to sustain her.

In her mind, it was safer to be hidden away than to run to safety. Being that running was her best attribute, hiding seemed counter-intuitive. But she'd heard the man bolt down the windows and doors and figured that the only way out was through the side entrance. She also figured that the man was guarding the side entrance and that if she tried to run out that way, he'd kill her. So, she hoisted herself up into the hidden compartment, closed the wood paneled door with the draw string, and submerged herself into the bowels of darkness.

Within a few minutes, her eyes adjusted to the darkness and her olfactory senses adjusted to the stank, moldy smell of closed-in air. She soon realized that there was a small beam of light coming through a tiny chinking gap between the cross poles and the gable near where the main cabin chimney stood. Rema inched her way over to the flagstone chimney to see if there was a way out of this nightmare.

* * *

When he returned to fetch Rema from the back bedroom, all he found was a rope still affixed to the left bedpost and the cut threads of the rope from the right bedpost.

"Fuck!" he yelled. "Where the fuck did you go, you skinny little bitch?"

From Rema's position almost directly above, she could hear his voice. She remained statue-like and held her breath.

"Come out, come out, wherever you are. I won't hurt you."

Rema slowly pushed air out of her nose and silently sucked in the stale air. "I know that you're still here. There is no way out. I cut the phone

lines so you can't call for help. If you make it easy and show yourself, I won't hurt you. I'm going to be watching every movement in this place. Come out voluntarily and you and I will have something to talk about. If you make me find you, consider yourself dead."

Rema assumed that she was dead either way.

Chapter 17

Nellie Monlock sensed something terrible when she awoke with the cresting of first morning light. She had not slept well at all worrying about Mac and her friends. Nellie had always had a sixth sense about her, yet she had not learned in her ninety-three when not to question it. One day when her daughter was in grade school, Nellie was home tending to the ironing. All of the sudden, Nellie was overwhelmed with the feeling that her daughter was hurt and needed medical attention. Nellie called for an ambulance before she sprinted down Main Street in Garden City, Kansas, and into her daughter's school yard. As she neared the school, Nellie learned that her daughter had just fallen from the second story fire escape during a routine fire drill and had fractured her skull. Nellie's daughter lived to tell the tale, and never knew that her mother had sensed the injury before it occurred. Nellie had many of these premonitions over the years and had learned that God had granted her special grace in that regard, and knew that questioning God's grace was a bad idea. Nevertheless, she often second-guessed herself when feeling that something was amiss.

She arose and massaged her arthritic knees before standing at the foot of her bed. She dressed in yesterday's clothes, swallowed her pills with a glass of Knott's Apple Juice, and took hold of her walking cane. It was getting increasingly more difficult to navigate the seven rickety wooden plank steps that led to the doorway of her cabin, but with sheer determination, she hobbled down them slowly and steadily.

Nellie shuffled up the dirt road two hundred feet until she saw the Kilkenny-Kerry cabin. Much to her surprise, all the winter shutters were drawn and the latch bars were locked in place. Mac's car was gone and the place appeared closed for the season. Nellie kept shuffling closer to the cabin to get a better look at the place. As she hobbled up the uneven driveway, she noticed strange dragging marks in the dirt. Maybe Mac's friend had one of those new rolling suitcases and she dragged it to the car, Nellie thought to herself. Oddly, however, near the tracks on the ground appeared to be drops of blood or some other dark substance.

Nellie was not a petite woman. In fact, in her day–a day before she developed osteoporosis–she stood five foot nine and weighed one hundred fifty pounds. She had always been stout and that fact did not change as she aged. She remained strong like most good German women, but her knees and ankles hurt quite a bit when she walked. Bending over to pick something up had become quite a chore, so she opted not to closely examine the stains on the driveway. Instead, she continued her journey toward the main cabin.

She had always had a key to the cabin, and over the years when locks were changed, she was usually the first non-family member to get a copy. Max and Nicole had a key as well. It was important for neighbors to look after neighbors in this remote part of the Rockies, and this was why Nellie was so concerned about Mac's whereabouts. When Mac was at the cabin, she checked in with Nellie every day, no matter what. It was neighborly and it was tradition.

Nellie let herself in with her key and immediately noticed that something was amiss. First, when Mac closed down the cabin in the fall, she put everything away in its designated place. All food was removed. All linens were taken home for cleaning. All the windows were covered with plastic from the inside to keep moisture out. All electricity and water was turned off in the pump house. Nellie noticed that none of these things had been completed. In fact, some lights were on.

She walked into Gram's room and took a look around. How many hundreds of times had she and Gram sat on the patio adjacent to Gram's bedroom and sipped on an afternoon toddy while reminiscing about days gone by? She knew Gram's room like the back of her hand and noticed something seemingly peculiar. There was a dark stain on the light blue bedspread that had covered Gram's bed for thirty years. In fact, there was a dark stain under both posts of the headboard, and there appeared to be holes in the white wood of the bed frame. Nellie took a closer look and thought that these might be blood stains. Or was it red wine? Nellie knew that Mac loved her Cabernet. It was possible that Mac and the girls had been a little clumsy in their consumption. And, oddly, Mac's travel bag was still on the floor in the bedroom.

She surveyed the rest of the room and all else appeared to be in place, including the statue of the Blessed Virgin Mary holding baby Jesus in her arms. Nellie said a quick prayer to Mary before continuing on through the cabin.

The main sitting room appeared intact and nothing seemed out of the ordinary, other than the fact that the priceless Navajo rugs were still on the floor and hanging from the walls. Nellie knew how much Gram loved those rugs and had made strict storage instructions for them during the winter season. They were supposed to be wrapped and stored in the crawl space above the larger bunk beds in the first bedroom off the main entrance.

Nellie continued on into the second bedroom. Again, she noticed a small pool of red stain at the foot of the small bunk bed. There was also a rope tied to one of the top bunks. The second bedroom had nothing in it but for one travel bag that remained closed and zipped.

Perhaps the ladies had decided to go on an overnight trip to Rocky Mountain National Park the night prior. Nellie thought it out of the ordinary, but it was certainly possible. It didn't explain why the shutters were closed and bolted down, but it did offer a reasonable solution. A trip to Estes Park and the old Stanley Hotel was always a fun excursion from Nederland. It would explain why Mac's car was missing.

Nellie decided that she would put her sixth sense on hold for a day and rely on the reasonableness of a side trip to the Park. She decided to stop worrying so much. She would go back to her cabin and occupy herself with knitting for another day and look forward to Mac's return. She let herself out the front door of the cabin and walked down the flagstone path, under the Kilkenny-Kerry sign, and back down the road to her shanty a quarter mile away.

* * *

"You did good, ladies. Real good," the man said to the four women bound and tied in the garage. "I told you that I'd kill you if you made a peep and I meant it. You were nice and quiet when the little old lady came by. I thought about going after the octogenarian to kill her. I might put that on my to-do list for tomorrow."

Mac gave the man a deep, scornful look at the mention of harming Nellie. Mac had never wanted to kill anyone in her life, until now. When she was training for the police academy years back, the one thing that kept her from advancing in the program was her adamant dislike for guns and her heightened aversion to killing another human in the course of duty. Now, faced with the situation at hand, if she were offered a loaded revolver, she was certain that she had the courage and anger to aim at this fiend and pull the trigger. Armed only with intellect and a background in psychology, she decided that her only option was tact–until she and her friends came up with another plan.

"Where are you from?" Mac garbled through the gag in her mouth.

To her surprise, the man untied the gag.

"Nowhere. I'm a man with no country, as they say."

"Everyone is from somewhere. You said that you were in prison in Wyoming. Is that were you are from? You must have done something in Wyoming in order to be in prison there."

Craig sat down crossed legged on the cement floor of the garage and put down the axe in front of him. His torn and stained 501 Levi's were frayed with white thread at the knee. He pulled on the fray with his thumb and index finger as he spoke. Mac perceived confusion in his face as he contemplated the question.

"I killed some people there."

Craig looked at Mac with his plain speak, searching for her reaction.

"I assumed as much. Was it your family?"

"Nope. I would've, but I got caught first."

"Is that where you grew up?" Mac sensed his hesitation. She did not want to antagonize him, so she decided that she'd consume him in conversation to distract him. "I grew up in Colorado. Boulder to be exact. I love it here. I've been coming to this cabin all my life. My great-grandfather bought it in 1930. It was just the main room then, I think. It was built in 1899. During the Great Depression, my great-grandfather's business did okay, so he had some money. He brought his family here for a vacation and they fell in love with the area. So, he bought the small cabin and added on to it year after year."

Mac inventoried her friends, hoping that they understood why she was befriending this fiend. Melanie sat motionless. Hesta looked provoked like any good New Yorker might. Patti, to Mac's amazement, looked maddened–like she was ready to fight. Mac decided to keep talking as long as he would allow.

"See that bark stripper over there on the wall?" Mac continued, motioning with her head to the eastern wall of the garage, "I watched my grandfather and uncles use it to strip the bark off pine trees that they'd cut down near the Fourth of July trailhead and drag down here. They built this garage with those logs. Nowadays you'd probably get in trouble for cutting on National Forest land, but back then, I imagine that it must have been okay or my grandfather would not have done it. He was one of those straight-and-narrow kind of guys. Federal Judge in this state. And see that Tom Moore Colonel Claro cigar box on that shelf?" Mac said, nodding toward the shelf of supplies across from where Craig was sitting. "I remember riding in my dad's car over to Estes Park one day and he was smoking one of those cigars. I must have been about twelve or so, because when we got to Grand Lake, which is where we had picnics in the Park, I tried to smoke a little of it when he wasn't looking. I threw up all the way back home."

"Mac," Patti said, interrupting. Mac ignored her friend and kept on talking.

"And see that Bush's Baked Beans can–?"

"Aren't you curious as to which of your husbands hired me to kill you?" Craig interrupted with a flat tone.

Mac said nothing. She looked around at her friends who seemed equally impassive. She then said something peculiar. "The thing I like most about Wyoming is the friendly people. No matter what town I'm driving in, people wave at me as if they've known me all my life. I think that is a great thing. Did that ever happen to you when you were in Wyoming?"

The man uncrossed his legs and it appeared that he was going to stand up. Mac wanted to distract him and keep him still as long as possible. She continued talking.

"When you were in prison, could you see out any windows? Could you see any sage grouse flying in the fall? Could you see trees? My favorite tree in Wyoming is–"

"Yes, I could see trees, you dumb ass. But let's get back on topic. Who votes that it was Patti's husband that wants her dead?"

Mac heard Patti let out a whimper from the back bedroom. Mac knew that she needed to be strong for her friend. "I don't believe that any of our husbands wants us dead and I'm quite certain that none of our husbands know you. I think you made that up just for your own entertainment."

Craig appeared fascinated by Mac's statement. It was possible that he smirked slightly at her and as certain as the moon draws water, he seemed baited by her proclamation.

"Take me for instance," Mac continued, suddenly finding strength, "my husband and I have been married a very short time. We are happy and he would never cause me harm. He is a peaceful man."

"Most split ups happen early on. Bet you have nothin' in common," Craig said, as he absent-mindedly stood and reached up for the ancient roto rooter than hung above the garage doors. "Bet that you are trying to change somethin' about him and he doesn't like it much."

Craig took the tip of the rusted rotto rooter and poked it into Mac's leg. It didn't hurt, yet, so Mac restrained her glare to the extent possible.

"See, women like you never shut up and they never are satisfied with what men have to offer. My guess is that you like him alright, but that you were getting too old to find a husband and all of your friends were married and you were starting to think that no one would ever marry you so you picked the closest guy around and got hitched. He probably didn't see it coming and went along for the ride and once the dust settled and he realized that you were a pain in the ass, he decided to get rid of you."

Craig took the rooter and started slowly turning it into Mac's leg as he spoke.

"You think you have the right to control your husband. Wyatt's his name, right? Well, maybe Wyatt don't like you telling him what to wear or how to act or where to live."

His words bore through her with more pain than the rooter. He *knew* Wyatt's name. He *knew* that Wyatt didn't like when she suggested that he wear something other than "country." He *knew* that Wyatt resented the fact that she wanted to move closer to town. *Oh God. It was Wyatt. Wyatt wanted her dead.*

Chapter 18

Max arose with the sun each day and greeted the world by taking his Labrador, Jimmy, on a run to Lost Lake. Jimmy whined beside Max and Nicole's bedside until Max's shoes were tied and they were out in the fresh morning air. Jimmy was off leash during their trek and happily marked his usual spots along the five-mile loop and otherwise kept Max company. Sometimes they would happen upon a moose or a fox, but most of the time, they enjoyed the peace and serenity of deer feeding upon dewy grass and the sounds of meadowlarks and blue jays.

Jimmy wasn't the smartest dog in the world and was pretty much afraid of his own shadow. Max had never considered the notion that Jimmy could protect him against the forces of nature and it was this thought that caused Max great surprise when Jimmy darted off the trail toward Old Man Lee's rickety cabin.

"Come, Jimmy," Max said, following loosely behind as Jimmy sniffed his way up to the wobbly fence surrounding the property. Max noted the abundance of "Keep Out" signs tacked to the fence and detected a foul odor permeating the place. "Old Man Lee lives like a pig," Max said out loud to his dog. "Let's go."

Max whistled and Jimmy turned in his direction to see that his owner had pulled a treat out of his pocket. Never one to miss an opportunity to eat, Jimmy bounded in Max's direction. As soon as he took the treat from Max's hand, he headed back towards the cabin. This time, Max followed further up the trail, but not without a tense feeling. As he caught up to his dog, he sensed an edginess that he hadn't felt in years. He'd heard rumors about Old Man Lee's hard-core drinking and his proclivity to shoot anything close to his property line and Max was not in the mood to confront the long barrel of a shotgun this morning. He grabbed a hold of Jimmy's collar and affixed the leash that he brought with him on the daily run but rarely used. Max pulled his dog away from Old Man Lee's place and back on to the path of the trailhead. Jimmy trotted with his owner toward Lost Lake, but every so often turned back in the direction of the old man's cabin. Had Max looked back to Jimmy's line of vision, he would have seen the back end of Mac's car parked on the southeastern edge of Old Man Lee's property.

* * *

Melanie was relieved that her friends had joined her in the garage because it took her mind off focusing solely on what method of torture awaited them next. But seeing Mac with nails through her hands dangling from the rafter made her stomach turn. Despite this, Mac seemed to have plenty of fight left in her. Of all of them, Melanie was certain that Mac was the toughest, both mentally and physically. Rema was the most physically fit, but Melanie was sure that if pushed too far, Rema would fold. Mac would fold only when she had shed her last drop of blood. This bought some hope to Melanie.

More disturbing perhaps was the vision of Hesta. Her thin frame slumped in an awkward pose and with her legs slightly open, Melanie could see the effect of castration. Hesta had not made a sound since she had her hands restrained by the vise. She wanted so much to hold Hesta in her arms and assure her that this would end soon but Melanie suspected that she would never have the chance.

As Melanie reveled in her own misery, the man turned toward her with a beckoning look. With sudden swiftness, he swiped the gag from her mouth and spoke, reminding her that if she screamed, he'd kill them all before the sound of her voice reached the neighbor's ears.

"Michael, right?"

Melanie looked at Craig with confusion. She nodded, struggling to find her voice.

"Think he'd want to hang a vacancy sign in the marriage department?" Craig asked, mockery sliding off his tongue like butter.

Mel shook her head slightly, her short blond hair swishing as she moved. Almost a tone of embarrassment, she spoke. "Michael loves our family. He would never do anything to break us up. He wouldn't do it to Charlie and William."

"Sure about that?"

Mel nodded. Her deep blue eyes and freckled nose made her look like a little girl being questioned by the school principal.

"What'd you think Mac?" Craig asked. "Do you believe this farce?"

"What farce?" Mac asked with a tone of derision. "The farce that a family can be happy? Just because you grew up in a crappy household doesn't mean that the rest of the world did. Mel and Michael have been happily married for a long time. They are very supportive of each other. That's what makes them happy. Your mom was selfish and left you to go partying. Your aunt was nice enough to take you in. But she was stupid enough to allow terrible men into her life and that made your life suck. You can't remain mad at the world for your own–"

"Shut up," Craig interrupted. "You don't know shit about shit." He looked out the window again, keeping a keen eye on the cabin, watching for Rema.

"I know what you told me."

"Maybe I was lying."

"Maybe you were. Maybe you weren't. All I know is that you are a very angry person and that if you could channel your feelings in a positive way, you could be a very productive person. You are nice looking and have gifts from God like everyone else–"

"God? You've got to be kidding me. You think that there is a *God*?"

"Yes, I do. So do the rest of my friends here," Mac said, and then suddenly felt the need to retract her statement. Hesta did not proclaim a faith, but at the present moment, didn't seem compelled to interject her agnostic ways.

"Well, that's your problem if you think that there is some savior out there who is going to get you out of this."

"I didn't say that," Mac firmly stated. She took a deep breath and focused her thoughts. "Just because we believe in God doesn't mean that we don't believe that bad things can happen to people who believe in God. Bad things happen to good people every day and most of these good people believe in some form of God or faith in a higher being. But I suppose it is worth saying that most serial killers don't believe in God."

Craig looked sideways at Mac and then cocked his head to the side. "You girls like to talk about serial killers, don't you?"

Mac pressed her lips together in contemplation and then nodded slightly. Her auburn curls fell loosely in front of her face as she spoke. Melanie watched her in awestruck horror, mesmerized by the tributaries of blood that continued to flow from Mac's hands down her forearms, now almost reaching her stretched biceps. "I knew another serial killer once. Met him in my line of work. I found out a lot about them during that time. Even went to the F.B.I. lab in Virginia to learn more about them."

"Like what?" Craig asked. His interest in the subject was obviously piqued.

"I learned a lot of things. One thing that many serial killers have in common is that they are adopted. The theory is that adopted children often feel different and uncomfortable around others. They are often bullies as young kids and suffer from attachment disorders. They often reveal feelings of hatred toward others—even if the folks around them treat the adopted child very well. They often feel persecuted. And in the end, most of these feelings funnel down to the notion that they feel rejected by their natural mother or father—or both. Maybe you feel this way?" Mac knew by the look Melanie shot her that it was a bold statement. Hesta even looked up for the first time.

"They asked me all that shit when I was supposed to do psycho testing at Juvi. I never answered them directly. It was more fun to take those docs on round-a-bout discussions and never answer the question. Watching their frustration was a lot of fun. Have you ever—"

"Answer it now," Mac suggested, her tone more pleading than demanding.

"No. See, I'm running the show and the question posed at this interrogation is why Michael would hire me to kill sweet little Melanie over here," Craig said, moving past Hesta while speaking. He reached up above the paint thinners that were stored in Puerto Rico Rum jugs and grabbed hold of an old branding iron as he spoke. Cob webs rained down from the rafters as he pulled his latest weapon into both hands. "I think I need to refresh your memory on the game we're playing. *You* need to convince *me* that it wasn't your husband who hired me to kill you. Don't go spouting off about happily ever after. It doesn't exist. One of you has a dude who wants a "re-do," but doesn't want to go through the pain and suffering of a divorce. See how it was explained to me is that divorce lawyers charge more than corporate lawyers and the wife gets half of the assets. If the wife dies 'accidentally,' then the husband doesn't have to pay for the divorce lawyer and he gets to keep the assets and the life insurance. Win-win-win. Ding-ding-ding." Craig snickered at his own jab at humor. "Wish I could build a fire in here to heat up this poker. I'd love to brand Patti's fat ass."

"Michael isn't that happy with me right now," Mel said. "He hates his job and wants to move to Washington. I refuse to consider the notion. We're at a stalemate, as they say. When I left for the airport, he told me to think long and hard about our commitment over this weekend and he was going to do the same. We've talked about divorce. I've been in denial for a while. Saying it out loud somehow makes it more real, and I'm just not ready to cope. I love my business and my neighborhood and my kids' school. I don't want to change. I'm happy. The boys are happy. I think that Michael should suck it up until the boys are in college."

"See what I mean?" Craig said, moving closer to Melanie. "She doesn't give a shit what her husband wants. And you think that this is happily ever after."

"What's in Washington?" Hesta said, her voice rough like sandpaper. Her head hung low to the ground as she spoke.

"I'm not sure, to tell you the truth," Melanie admitted. "I've been pretty closed-minded about the discussion. He's mentioned the fact that there are more favorable laws for water rights attorneys there and that he is sick of the battle in California. Outside of that, I guess I haven't heard his motive."

"You always did get your way Mel," Hesta said.

"She's right," Patti's voice floated in from the garage bedroom. "You never listen to the other person's side of the story."

Patti and Mel were roommates for one year in college and had a number of disagreements about issues that none of the others deemed terribly pertinent. Patti found the disagreements to have enough merit to move into the small bedroom in the basement of the house *The Five* shared, just to have some separation from Melanie and the arguments. The house itself was two blocks from Pearl Street and was enshrouded by an enormous oak tree. The style was that of bungalow and the rooms were tiny, allowing one master bedroom, shared by two, and three tiny singles. The basement was in reality a cellar with a staircase that pulled down from the kitchen floor. It was dark and dank and by all accounts creepy, but Patti preferred creepy to confrontations about how to hang shirts in a closet and stack jeans on a shelf and whether shampoo should stand cap up or cap down and if one was allowed to read in bed while the other was trying to sleep.

"That's unfair, Patti. I listen," Mel said in her own defense. "I just don't think that Michael's reasons are good enough to uproot a family."

"What if the tides were changed?" Hesta asked. "What if your hemp business was in the tank and the only market where you could capitalize was in the Pacific Northwest? What if you wanted to move there for your business? Would the analysis change?"

Mel sucked in a breath and let it out slowly. "Maybe. But that's not the case. My business brings in the lion's share of our income. That's why my business should trump his."

"See what I mean," Patti huffed. "You're always right. No matter what. I don't blame him for contemplating a divorce. He probably feels that he doesn't have a voice in the relationship. I certainly know how that feels and I can assure you that over time, it doesn't feel good at all. Michael has always let you run the show."

"Not true."

"Who chose the house?" Patti asked.

"Well, I did, but he liked it."

"Who chose the boy's names?"

"That's not fair. We always agreed to name them after our fathers."
"Your father first, right? What if William had been a girl?"

"Look Patti, I know that I'm stubborn, okay? I know that I can be difficult to live with. But I know that Michael wasn't really serious about divorce."

"Divorce wasn't the request," Craig chimed in.

Chapter 19

"Bob is more likely to want you out of the picture than Michael," Melanie said with a hint of disdain. "You said that he's having an affair. And now that he's making the big bucks in real estate, he probably doesn't want you to get half of his commissions."

Uncomfortable silence haunted the garage for a few seconds until they heard a sniffle from the garage bedroom. Patti often cried first and talked later. Mac assumed that the tears were flowing and that Patti would sink into her habitual depression.

"Even if Bob is having an affair, which I'm not sure about, he would never be so cowardly as to hire some thug to kill me. I've told him many times that if he wants out, the front door is wide open."

"You'd never say that," Melanie retorted. "You're too pleasing to say that. It's more likely that you'd cry and promise him that you'll change so that he's happier. Truth is though, instead of taking care of yourself and making yourself more attractive to him so that he's not out chasing tail, you pour yourself into a tub of Ben & Jerry's and whimper. Then you pamper those boys of yours to the point of nausea because it is a distraction to the truth that is staring you in the mirror. And the truth is–"

"Okay, Mel. She gets it," Mac said.

"Yeah, I get it," Patti shouted back. "I'm sick and tired of getting it. I'm sick and tired of being the one who gives in on every argument. I'm sick of being taken advantage of by my husband and my children and my parents and my friends. Everyone thinks that they can walk all over me because I'm nice and pleasant and genial. Well, that's the old Patti. I can be as objectionable as anyone else. I just choose not to be. It is a choice."

"So is taking care of yourself," Melanie interjected.

"You know, Mel, not everyone has the genetics to weigh one hundred and two pounds their entire life."

"It's not genetics, Patti. I work out every morning before the kids get out of bed. Even when I'm exhausted or it's bad weather or I'm cramping and starting my period, I get myself out of bed and go to the gym. It's called discipline. I care what I look like and I care to be a good example to my children. I want them to make healthy eating choices and how can they if every time the chips are down, I'm scarfing food?"

"Well we all know that you are perfect, Mel. You've been telling us that for twenty-some years."

"Ladies. Stop it," Mac said.

"Patti is right," Hesta said. "Rema and Melanie are both experts on being experts. Look at this fucking shirt I'm wearing. We all have to match to take a hike, for Christ's sake. And look at Rema. She can't even spend an hour with us before she has to take off and run one hundred miles uphill. Talk about self-centered."

Mac threw back her head in panic. "Where is Rema?" she asked Craig. "What did you do with her?"

Craig snickered while tapping the branding iron into his left hand. He had no intention of letting them know that he could not find her. The question reminded him that he needed to check the main cabin once more for her. It had been nearly a half hour since he'd united the four in the garage. He set down the branding iron on the work bench above Hesta and reached into his tan hiking shorts pocket to retrieve an item.

"Here is a part of her," Craig said. "Earlobes make good handles for things. Coffee cups, for example. I was thinking about taking a picture of the five of you and making a picture frame out of your earlobes."

"Copycat," Mac snorted. "Jeffrey Dahmer beat you to it. You need to be more original."

"Original isn't as important as you think. Quantity is a much bigger factor when it comes to the fame and fortune of murder."

"Not really," Mac interjected, more out of a desire to stop her friends from arguing than anything else. "I think that being original is more interesting."

"Guess we'll focus on you then," Craig said. "Wyatt's not too wild about you right now. Cowboys like to take care of business the old-fashioned way. Let's see if we can find an original way to make me famous with you as the victim. Lots to choose from in here," he said, picking up the branding iron again. "Cowboys brand the baby lambs every year, right?"

Mac was sorry that she stepped in. She'd already thought through the issues with Wyatt and was not hopeful that a discussion with her friends about the subject would be fruitful. In her mind, it was more important to figure out if Rema was safe. Why would he leave her alone in the cabin? He'd gone back to get her, he'd said, but came back alone and agitated. Maybe she bolted away from him and he couldn't catch her! If that was the case, surely she would have gone straight to Max and Nicole's house and they would have the police here by now. It didn't make sense.

"Why is Wyatt unhappy?" Hesta asked. "You never tell us anything. You always act like everything is just fine and we have to find out from a killer that it is not."

Mac understood Hesta's sudden mood change. The woman smoked a pack of cigarettes a day, sometimes more, and was probably craving her drug of choice.

"The only thing you two have in common is Greg. I think marrying Wyatt was a big mistake. You can't marry your ex-boyfriend's brother and expect that everything will be peachy-keen."

"Hesta, I fell in love with him and he with me. We have a foster son that we help take care of. We do have things in common and we care very much about each other."

"Is that why you keep in touch with Greg?" Melanie chimed in. "That can't help things."

"I haven't heard from Greg in a long time. And anyway, he is my brother-in-law. I'm sure that you keep in touch with in-laws. It's not abnormal."

"It is when you slept with him for two years."

"Mel, I know that it wasn't textbook, but it is what it is. Wyatt does not begrudge me for having a relationship with Greg. Wyatt and Greg barely speak to one another."

"No doubt," Patti chimed in. "How could Greg even look Wyatt in the eye? Greg was still in love with you when you two got married. It was painfully obvious at the wedding."

"He was only there a few hours," Mac said in her defense. "You didn't even talk to him."

"I didn't have to," Patti said. "It was obvious to all of us that he was in too much pain to stick around."

"Greg can't stick around for anything," Mac said, tensing in tone. "He was never there for me. His career with National Geographic was more important to him than our relationship. The time clock was ticking. Was I supposed to wait forever for him to decide whether he could make a commitment to me?"

"You still love him," Hesta said. "You couldn't take your eyes off him at the wedding. I'm sure that Wyatt noticed. He's just far too much of a gentleman to make a fuss."

"Or far too disinterested to care," Patti spat. "He didn't hardly even talk to us at the wedding, and it was the first time we'd met him. You'd think that he'd want to meet and get to know his bride's friends. Instead, he occupied himself most of the time by talking to his parents. He lives right next to them, for crying out loud. He sees them every day, yet he didn't make the effort to get to know your family and friends. That tells me that he's not too committed to the relationship."

"He's a quiet man, that's all," Mac said. She knew that she sounded self-protective, but that was the best she could do. Her friends were right. She was embarrassed at the wedding when Wyatt kept to himself and made little effort to get to know her family and friends. She tried to justify it in her mind by telling herself that he was a shy man, but the truth is that he was not shy around people that he shared common interests. When people arrived at the ranch for horse training, he went out of his way to greet them and get to know them. Folks traveled from all over the United States to have Butch and Wyatt Anderson work with their horses. Butch was certainly more outgoing than Wyatt, but Wyatt would make a great effort to make conversation. Granted, most of the conversation concerned horses or ranching, but that is what interested Wyatt most and that is what he knew most about. He'd never been to college and, frankly, had never lived anywhere but the ranch. He was comfortable there. He was in his zone.

But he could have gone out of his zone to make everyone more comfortable–for her sake. Mac thought about this issue many a night. Wyatt rarely wanted to go into town for a nice dinner or a drink with friends. Mac's law practice was in the center of the small town of Sheridan and the success of her practice involved social connections. She was a member of the Rotary Club and often attended Elk's Club events. She worked out at the YMCA so that she could meet people. She went to happy hour at the Mint Bar with her staff from time to time, and served on the board of the Thorne Rider Foundation.

Wyatt never attended any of these events with her.

"Maybe you are right," she finally admitted with helpless resolve. "Maybe we aren't a good match." The words escaped Mac's lips too quickly and she felt like an anchor had befallen her. In truth, she wasn't sure whether they were a good match, but was anyone ever sure of such a thing? Wasn't there always something about a relationship that caused doubt?

As she spoke, a faint line of sunlight shone through the crack between the two large garage doors. In a moment of silence, she watched the light move and change the position of its trajectory. In that fleeting moment, she saw the darting shadow of a hummingbird flit around the garage door, and somehow this restored her strength. Her arms ached from the piercing wounds and her body throbbed from hanging in a painful position, but her tenacity toward survival suddenly kicked in.

"Wyatt is not your guy," she said to Craig. "Even if Wyatt was unhappy, he would take care of business himself. He would never hire the likes of you to do his dirty work. That, for sure, is what I know."

* * *

Rema sat motionless in the attic, contemplating the thought that she was hiding in an inescapable tomb. She could not afford to make a sound; otherwise he would find her and kill her. But doing nothing was worse than death to Rema. She would rather die trying to escape than die a coward.

Presently, the real issue was whether to attempt to flee out the side entrance of the cabin and risk the high probability that Craig would intercept her versus trying to see if there was enough space around the chimney screen to crawl onto the roof and jump. She doubted that the space would be adequate to fit her petite frame, but she remembered closing the cabin a few years prior and the necessity of installing a large metal plate over the area to prevent snow leakage. In any event, sliding over toward the chimney would require noise, and noise would attract attention.

She sat still for the time being and contemplated her relationship with Scott. There was no doubt in her mind that he had numerous extramarital affairs over the course of seventeen years of marriage. When he played in the NFL, it was common knowledge that most of the players had an assemblage of women in each city. Some of the wives traveled with their husbands from game to game just to keep an eye on things. Rema, of course, could not afford to travel with Scott. It would interfere with her training schedule. She rarely had time to even watch a quarter of a game, and only did so when she was forced to attend.

Hesta had attended more of Scott's games than Rema had, which was always of interest to Rema. Hesta was not a sports fan, by any means. In fact, she disparaged Scott constantly in college and made it perfectly clear to her friends that she strongly disapproved of professional athletes. "Most of them are thugs who'd otherwise be serving jail terms but for their sport," she would frequently say.

But when the Broncos played in the New England area, Hesta made the effort to attend the games. Rema assumed that it was a networking ploy in the publishing world to attend large media events as often as possible. But recently when she was Googling race results from the Pikes Peak run, she accidentally clicked on Scott's email account and noticed an email to Scott from Hesta. The message was brief yet confusing. It simply said, "Six days and counting."

Chapter 20

Hesta Knotingham was the most opinionated woman Mac had ever known and Hesta used her opinions and attitude to her fullest advantage while fighting her way up the editorial food chain in the publishing world. Never had Hesta stifled her opinion when reporting a story and never had she kept her view to herself for an op-ed piece. Hesta was really good at covering the angles of a story while slanting the spin to fit her opinion on the subject. Ever since they were united in the garage, Hesta had offered very little commentary about their circumstances. This prompted Mac to pull Hesta into the conversation; more than anything else, Mac wanted to make sure that her friend was okay.

"Think John has anything to do with this?" Mac asked.

Hesta pulled her head up only slightly before allowing it to plummet back down. Mac saw Hesta pull in a deep breath and hold it steady, as if her thoughts floated mid-breath.

"John's too lazy to coordinate an organized killing," Hesta said.

Mac was relieved to hear the sarcasm in Hesta's tone.

"He would acquire your interest in Gold Publishing Group and then he could publish his crap fiction," Mac offered as a motive.

Hesta half laughed. "You think I'm that stupid? His bitch of a mom insisted on a pre-nup so that I couldn't inherit any part of his trust fund if we ever got divorced. When that happened, I should have insisted that it be mutual so that he could inherit nothing from me, but I wasn't as sophisticated back then with financial matters."

"So what happens if you die?" Mac asked. She hated to be boorish, but Hesta's parents were older when they had her and had died nearly a decade ago. She was an only child.

"It goes to you four."

Mac considered this for a moment. It was news to her.

"Why didn't you tell me?" Mac said.

Hesta was quiet for a moment before answering. She raised her head a few inches and said, "Because friendship shouldn't be based on opportunity. I didn't tell you because I wanted our friendship to remain real. I thought that if you knew, you might go the extra mile to keep our bond alive."

"Does anyone know about this?" Mac asked.

"My estate planner does."

"I mean, do any of us know? Melanie, did you know?"

Melanie shook her head in the negative.

"Patti?" Mac called out. "Are you hearing this?"

Patti said, "Uh-uh."

"Does Rema know?" Mac pressed.

Hesta was once again quiet, as if contemplating how to answer. "I did not tell Rema."

Mac considered Hesta's word choice. *She* had not told Rema. Did that mean that someone else could have told Rema, or was Mac reading too much into the statement? After all, Hesta was in great pain after the vulgar acts committed against her by this monster. Mac decided not to press the subject. Nevertheless, Mac was consumed with the possibility that one of the husbands knew about the arrangement and had hired this thug to kill Hesta so that his wife could inherit one-fourth of her sizeable estate. Mac imagined that Gold Publishing was worth somewhere in the range of two million dollars. After estate costs and burial fees, each stood to inherit close to a half- million dollars. This was certainly motive to kill. But if this was the case, why was Craig monkeying around with them? He could have simply killed Hesta and been on his merry way.

The counter argument could be that Craig did not want any witnesses to the crime and after toying around with his sadistic cat-and-mouse games, he intended to kill them all. But, Mac thought to herself, if he did this, then the inheritance argument would fail because if all were dead, and it would not be hard to prove who died in what order, none of the women's husbands would inherit anything, and, therefore, the husband would be left out in the cold. If one of the husbands challenged the forensics on who died in what order, he would obviously look suspect.

Sometimes Mac hated her lawyering instinct, but she could not help but think about these various scenarios. It did not make sense to her that one of their husbands randomly hired Craig to kill one of them. There had to be some connection. But what was it?

"Hesta?" Mac said. "Is there something that you're not telling us?"

Hesta remained silent.

"Hesta?" Melanie chimed in. "Please!"

Mac saw tears dropping from Hesta's face, splashing silently onto the cement floor. She heard her friend draw in a stifled breath as the floodgates opened.

"I've d-d-done a terrible thing," Hesta said before bursting into sobs.

Mac looked at Melanie in bewilderment.

From the garage bedroom, Patti's voice boomed, "What have you *done?*"

Hesta let out a colossal cry and in the midst of it all, blurted, "I'm having an affair with Scott."

"Scott who?" Melanie said.

"Scott *Setliff?*" Mac shrieked. "Rema's *husband?*"

Hesta sobbed uncontrollably. All she could manage was a bob of the head. "For how long?" Mac asked.

"How did it start?" Melanie said.

"Why in the *hell* would you pick him, Hesta? You loathe professional athletes," Patti said.

Hesta remained silent.

"How could you do this to your friend?" Melanie asked. "Rema trusts you."

"Outrageous," Craig said, somewhat bewildered and amused in tone. "You're not even the one I'm supposed to kill, but I just might kill you anyhow for being a cold-hearted bitch. And I'm not the kind of guy who needs a reason to kill."

Chapter 21

Max both understood and adhered to the Nederland's motto of "live and let live." He was not one to meddle in anyone else's affairs and was not the type to complain about the manner in which a fellow landowner maintained his or her property. Granted, his home was a fixture on the Garden Tour and he strongly supported the notion that well kept property helped build pride in the community, but this alone was not enough for him to complain about the down-at-heel sorts who allowed rubbish to pile up.

Notwithstanding this axiom, Max was bothered by his dog's reaction to Old Man Lee's place. The place looked terrible and it smelled worse than a trash dump.

He told Nicole of his experience while hiking to Lost Lake and her response, as he predicted, was to leave well enough alone. Nicole believed even more so in the adage of minding one's own business and was certainly not in favor of engaging in any sort of neighborhood awareness with the old man. Personally, he gave her the creeps. Every time she saw the old goat in town, he gave her a crusty look and once even pointed a finger gun at her and motioned as if pulling the trigger. She'd never so much as spoken to the man before and had certainly never done anything to overtly offend him, so the gesture seemed flagrant and vicious to the peace-loving throw-back-to-the- sixties Nicole.

Max, however, could not leave well enough alone. He decided to take a drive into town and have a light discussion with Pat Redley, Deputy Marshall of Nederland. "Red," as townsfolk referred to him, was a tall, fit red-haired man in his sixties with plenty of experience on patrol in Denver and happily in semi-retirement in this sleepy town. Other than monthly town council meetings and bi-monthly court duty, he was rarely called upon for action. His reserve officers handled any public disturbance calls, and he otherwise attended to the important business of fly fishing and hiking.

When he got there, Max explained his concerns in great detail. Red, who was sitting with his feet up on his desk while busily tying flies for his afternoon summit with trout, listened carefully to the accounting of Jimmy's bizarre reaction to Old Man Lee's property. Red shook his head from time to time, taking inventory of the situation, promising Max that he'd have one of his officers make a home visit—in a neighborly fashion.

"Better have your officer have back-up," Max suggested. "Old Man Lee is known to shoot first and ask questions later."

"I'm well aware of his tendencies," Red responded, still spell-bound in his effort to loop his knot perfectly. "He's getting' on in age, Max, and he's bound to gain speed in paranoia. But now that you mention it, I haven't seen him in town for a few days and I certainly haven't had as many complaints of him flippin' tourists the bird, so you may well be right. Maybe the Old Man flew the coop in his sleep and his rotting corpse is stinkin' up the neighborhood. I'll be sure to let you know what my guys find out. I'm all but done for the day here. Got some union contracts to negotiate this afternoon, if you know what I mean."

Max knew exactly the union to which Red referred—a school of rainbow trout on Willow Creek that had been eluding Red for some time. The contract would involve the hook on the end of the fly he was busily tying.

* * *

Nellie Monlock had been watching the main road all morning, hoping to see Mac's SUV bouncing up the pot-hole riddled dirt road. She certainly had learned the value of patience in her ninety-three years, but somehow today, her patience was wearing thin. She decided to venture back to the Kilkenny-Kerry once more to see if, by chance, Mac had driven by when she was otherwise engaged. Even if Mac and her friends were not back from Estes, she thought to herself, the least she could do was gather up the Navajos and get them folded nicely and ready for winter storage. This alone would keep her occupied for an hour or so and would make the time go by more quickly.

Nellie once again negotiated the steps down from her cabin porch and slowly made her way westward up the lane to the Kilkenny-Kerry. Under any other circumstances, she would have shuffled up the driveway and entered through the customary side door. But following her sixth sense, she decided to walk past the cabin on the main road and quietly navigate the uneven ground of the back lot behind the cabin so that she could enter through Gram's private patio door. She used her key to unlock the deadbolt and made her way into Gram's bedroom.

Nellie took another mental inventory of the room in which Gram had slept for so many summer nights and felt a wave of uneasiness. Something was not right, and Nellie knew it. She stooped over to pick up Gram's favorite Navajo Germantown Serape, which was a fabulous pattern of gray, black and red diamond patterns, shaped in a cascading pattern toward the center figure, which looked like a warrior dancing, if one viewed it lengthwise, but also could have been two mountain peaks, if viewed widthwise. Gram loved the design and often remarked to Nellie how she adored the artisan's ability to use shapes mysteriously so that the center focus of the blanket was subject to interpretation.

Nellie carefully folded the blanket and carried it with her into the main sitting room in the center of the cabin. This room was filled with antique furnishings, including a piano, clocks, radios, and books, but what really set this room apart from any other cabin with antiquities was the colorful display of Navajos. Double saddle blankets covered the backs of each chair in splashing pattern of reds, greens, yellows and blacks. Classic serapes hung from the walls in designs and patterns that evoked conversation. Germantown children's blankets covered the top of the piano and the strongbox coffer, illuminating the notion of possible Christian influence by the use of cross patterns.

Nellie picked up each rug carefully and folded it in the loving manner in which Gram had done so many summers past. She quietly stacked them into three piles and one by one, took each pile into the back double bunk bedroom. She looked up to see whether it was possible for her to climb the bunk bed ladder and reach the hidden storage closet, which was masterfully crafted to match the pine paneled room. She decided that it was not worth the risk of falling and breaking her hip–something she'd done seven years ago and still caused her arthritic aches and pains. But upon closer inspection, she noticed that the door was slightly ajar.

Nellie hoisted herself up the first rung of the ladder to get a better view. Oddly, the drawstring that normally lay horizontal on the wood paneling was pulled inward into the storage area. "Well, I'll be damned," Nellie said under her breath. "Only way that could have happened is if someone pulled it from the inside."

After only a split second of thought, Nellie's intuition kicked in. She climbed the second rung of the ladder and secured her footing. She would need to let go of her cane if she hoped to climb any further. She took a deep breath and grabbed tightly onto the upper bunk bed frame. "This damn thing better hold me or there will be hell to pay," she muttered out loud. She pulled herself up with all of her might and climbed to the third rung. "Whew." She repeated this sequence until she got to the sixth rung and then slowly and carefully reached with her left hand, wedging her middle finger under the cranny of the open door. She tugged very slightly and the crevice widened a bit. She pulled again until the fissure widened enough that the drawstring dropped free. Nellie pulled the door wide with the aid of the string and hollered, "Anyone in there?"

Silence permeated the double bunk bedroom. Nellie shook her head in confusion. Again she said, "Hello. Who's up there?" This time, she heard a noise.

"Nellie, is that you?" a whisper escaped from the darkness of the secret cabinet.

"Hell yes, it's me. Who's in there?"

"Rema."

"What on God's green earth are you doing up there young lady? You scared me half to pieces."

Nellie watched as a waif-like figure appeared. Dried blood decorated Rema's neck and had stained her jog bra. "Is *he* gone?"

"He who?" Nellie said.

"S-s-s-s-h-h-h." Rema sounded. "There is a bad man here and he is going to kill us."

"Oh Jesus, Mary and Joseph!" Nellie said. "Come down out of there right now!"

As Rema emerged, Nellie slowly backed herself down the ladder. When Rema silently crawled down to the ground, she turned and looked up into Nellie's wise eyes. Nellie, noticing straight away that Rema's left earlobe was missing and seeing wounds around her wrists and neck, suddenly had a change of tune.

"There is a man here. He-he-he's in the garage I think with the others. He says that he was hired by one of our husbands to kill one of us."

"Oh Good Lord," Nellie said, understanding that this was not the imagination of a woman who spent too much time running up and down mountains. "We need to get over to Max's."

"We can't leave. He'll see us and he'll kill us," Rema pleaded.

Nellie silently shuffled to the main sitting area and opened the bottom bureau drawer, pulling out what appeared to be a large rifle.

"Gramps had a run-in up here many years ago and he bought this for protection. It's loaded. Always has been. Question is: are the bullets still good after all these years?"

Chapter 22

The name Varminter meant nothing to Nellie. She was no expert in the field of shotguns. In fact, if questioned, she would not be able to identify the gauge, chamber, choke, or stock of the gun. The only important feature to her was the trigger, and she had her crooked and arthritic index finger wrapped tightly around it. Nellie remembered well the circumstances for which the gun was purchased. Gram and her spinster sister had come up to the cabin alone in 1954–something they'd done plenty of times. They often spent the month of July there visiting with friends and generally enjoying themselves without the watchful eye of the more sedate Gramps. He took the train from St. Louis and joined them for the month of August. One July evening, when Gram and her sister were enjoying a cocktail on the back patio, they heard the side door slam. When Gram poked her head inside to see who'd come to visit, she met the dark eyes of a stranger who had the appearance of tomfoolery about him. He carried with him a pistol and he brandished it in Gram's direction. Gram, having grown up in the south and schooled by her nursemaid in the importance of "takin' care of unself," grabbed her sister by the hand and ran out the back lot and down the dirt path to town. The Marshall was duly notified in descriptive detail of the intruder and he was caught shortly thereafter eating bread down by Boulder Creek. The bread was a loaf taken from Gram's kitchen and she easily identified it, him, and his gun. When Gramps learned of the situation, he promptly ordered a gun from a World War II supply post and brought it with him the next month. The gun had gone unused to this date, but Nellie was quite certain that save for rust, it would still shoot straight.

Leaving her cane behind, Nellie held the gun in her right hand and steadied herself on Rema's shoulder with her left. Together, they quietly shuffled through the sitting room of the cabin on their way toward Gram's bedroom and the back entrance. As they rounded the corner into the short hallway between Gram's bedroom and the kitchen, they heard an unsolicited greeting.

"Rema, I knew you hadn't gone far. Now I told you that if you came out of hiding when I called, that we could talk reasonably. But I also told you what would happen if you didn't. So now, you must die. And it looks like you brought a friend. She will have to go too. You'd think, Rema, being a woman of your intelligence and survival skills that you would find someone under the age of eighty to help you."

Rema was standing nearest to Craig, blocking the view of Nellie. And although Nellie was on in years and was not as nippy as she once was on her feet, she was able to lean in and grimace at the man, aim and fire with one swift motion.

"Age and intelligence go hand in hand, young man," Nellie said. "I got you on both accounts."

It wasn't that Nellie planned to fire the weapon that surprised Rema. It was the fact that Nellie intended to and managed to accomplish her goal of hitting her target with one deft shot. Craig dropped to the linoleum floor of the kitchen, screaming out in hideous barks. As he lay writhing in pain, holding his thigh to his chest, Rema carefully guided Nellie out the back door of Gram's bedroom.

"I'll get Max. Is the phone at your cabin operable?"

"Yes," Nellie yelled. She knew exactly what to do. She used the gun as a cane and made her way towards home.

* * *

Red casually listened to his two-way radio when he was unofficially off-duty and en route to his favorite fishing holes. He figured that if he heard something important, it would be taken care of by Lori, his assistant, and she'd call him to let him know that it had been handled. There were certain citizens of Nederland, however, whose character commanded prompt attention, and Nellie Monlock had achieved that status over the past fifty- some odd years. When he heard her call claiming that she had just shot an intruder at the Kilkenny-Kerry place, he knew that the trout would have to wait. Everyone in town adored Nellie as she was a fixture in the community. Had Red shuffled one of his deputies to the scene, it would have been perceived by the village as a massive display of disrespect.

Red flipped a U-turn on Highway 72 and headed back in the direction from which he came. As he sped along Boulder Creek in his weathered Jeep Cherokee, he felt a sudden sense of dread. His serene community seemed to be changing. He yearned for the good old days.

When Red first moved up the canyon and into Nederland, he found it challenging to slow down his pace. He was used to spending his time on patrol in Denver, chasing bad guys. One of the first residents that he met when he moved was Nellie. She and her husband were shopping at the hardware store and when he walked in, Nellie quickly shuffled over to greet him. When she learned that he'd just moved and that he was a single man with no woman to cook for him, she promptly insisted that he join them for dinner that evening. Red would have preferred to decline the invitation, but he had been warned by his office assistant that small communities had different social rules.

When Red showed up at Nellie's cabin, she and her husband were waiting on the outdoor porch ready to greet him. He had no more than made it up five of the seven plank stairs before Nellie shoved a glass tumbler in his hand.

"Homemade," she said.

Red did not know what he was drinking, but one sip later, he could feel the effect of something strong and sweet trailing down his throat. During the course of the evening, Nellie filled Red in on the business of the community while ensuring that he did not leave without a full stomach and a light head.

Red spent many afternoons on Nellie's porch after their first meeting. She became the mother to him that he'd lost to lung cancer many years ago. Red loved Nellie and Nellie loved Red.

He drove as fast as he could to help her.

* * *

"Did you hear that?" Mac said to her three girlfriends. "Sounded like a gunshot."

"He p-p-probably found Rema," Melanie said, her voice quivering. As her ocean-blue eyes filled with tears, she whispered, "He probably killed her."

Hesta lay silent and motionless. Mac studied her, contemplating whether she should say the words that she was thinking, but before she could make a decision, Patti spoke.

"Mission accomplished, Hesta? Are you happy now that one of your best friends is out of the picture so that you can shag her husband? You, of all people," Patti said, and then suddenly stopped mid-sentence.

They all looked up in unison as they heard the back screen door of the cabin slam shut and the sound of gravel being crushed underfoot.

"He's coming for us now," Melanie said in resignation. "If any of you survive, please tell Charlie and William that I love them. And please tell Michael that I'm sorry for being so pig-headed about moving. If it meant that I could save our family, I would move, I've decided."

"You're going to survive this. Don't think otherwise. You're stronger than this. Stay strong. We've got to stick together right now and fight off this bastard. If we are divided, he wins," Mac said. "Patti, you hear me in there? Forget about Scott and Hesta and that crap right now and focus on how we are a team. Friends for life. We are *The Five*."

"*The Four*," Patti said from the garage bedroom. "There are only four of us now."

"We don't know that. For all we know, Max came to check on us and shot the rat bastard. He probably figured out that–"

Mac stopped conjecturing mid-sentence when she heard the garage door scrape along the dirt base of the driveway. She twisted from her lynching position and witnessed the eyes of an angry cold-blooded killer. Craig dragged himself into the garage, armed with a serrated kitchen knife and a wound the size of a grapefruit through his left leg. She sucked in her breath as she stared into the gaping gunshot wound, penetrating his thigh bone and revealing fragments of tissue interspersed with what looked like black pellets.

Melanie peeked at him and then shriveled into a tight ball. She tucked her head between her legs and then quietly started chanting a prayer. Hesta did not move.

Craig dragged himself toward Hesta, sweat pouring down from his dirty, dark hair. His blue eyes pierced through her like daggers. He did not speak. He steadied himself against the workbench, cranked hard once on the hand vise that held her hands within, and then raised the jagged blade over her body.

Mac screamed out as the blade dropped. She tried to kick in his direction, but she was outside striking distance. She swung her body back and forth like a porch swing desperately trying to swipe him with her feet. The pain in her hands was excruciating.

It seemed like time stood still. The blade came crashing to the ground and bounced out of Craig's hand and onto the garage floor with a twang and then a thud. Craig's body toppled over on top of Hesta–a large handle of an axe protruding stately out of his back.

Mac turned to see her friend Rema at the doorway to the garage with her right arm outstretched.

Max was five steps behind her, gun in hand.

Chapter 23

Nellie made her record very clear for Red. "You know that if I wanted to kill him, he'd already be dead. I left the long arm of the law in your corner."

Red nodded, taking notes as Nellie spoke. She sat sipping iced tea in the comfort of the Kilkenny-Kerry living room, rocking on the chair that Gram once enjoyed. She explained how worried she'd been about Mac and the girls and how she'd come upon Rema in the hideaway space where the blankets were normally stored.

"I know you're a good shot, Nellie," Red said with chagrin. "Not questioning that you did the right thing here. Just need to know what happened so that I can write up a full report."

Nellie filled Red in on every detail while his deputies swept the cabin for evidence. And although Red was not supposed to talk about the gruesome discovery at Old Man Lee's place, he confided in her nevertheless.

"Found the Old Man in bits and pieces around the cabin, afraid to say," Red started. "Musta used a hack saw on him. Some of his parts were in the fridge. His heart was in a frying pan on the stove, part eaten, I think. Fingers were cut off, as were the toes. Could tell you more but I'm afraid it's too gruesome. Deputy Johns puked when he first set eyes on the mess over there."

Nellie listened intently, sipping on her cold drink. Although it was early, she was thinking that a shot of brandy was in order. Red explained that he'd be happy to oblige her once the report was complete and she'd signed it.

"Found parts of another corpse there too, I'm afraid," Red said. "A woman."

"That's not possible. Old Man Lee hated everyone. Wouldn't allow a sole to step foot on his property. No way in hell that he had a woman there with him. Hated women, that man did. Once we went a callin' when we was trying to organize the Garden Walk. The folks who didn't want to participate let us at least fix up their front yards a bit so that we didn't have any eye sores along the route. We, meaning Nicole, Janeen Baust, and I, approached Lee's cabin and before we got ourselves half way down his driveway, I heard a gun cock. That old buzzard was pokin' his gun out the front window and told us to get the hell off his property or he'd shoot us. Said something like, 'You women doin' the work of the devil' or something to that effect. Now I know that he had a hateful divorce and all, but that don't give him the right to treat all women like the one scorned."

Red nodded. He'd been through a nasty divorce himself and sometimes felt the same way as Old Man Lee did when it came to womenfolk, but he knew better than to engage in that conversation with Nellie. "We think it might be that woman whose car they found at the ski area."

Nellie sat quiet for a minute. "You think Old Man Lee killed her?"

"Not sure, and I ain't supposed to be talking to you 'bout it, but I know your word is good. We're thinkin' that he was killed first and she was killed after him. Not sure what the connection is."

"Think it's this Craig character?"

"I reckon."

Nellie nodded sadly. "This place isn't what it used to be, Red. Hell, I remember a day when I knew everyone in this valley. I never locked my front door–even if I went to Black Hawk for the day."

"A few bad apples, Nellie. That's all it is. Most folk around here are good people. Caring people. Peaceful people."

"Two hacked up people in a cabin and five young women gashed to Smitherines? Did you see the girls? Mac was crucified to the bed. She has holes in her hands. The girl from New York had her genitalia cut out. Caring, peaceful people? Come on, Red."

Two deputies entered the Kilkenny-Kerry and spoke privately with Red. He nodded at them and watched them walk out.

"Boulder police are on their way up the mountain. I've been instructed to rope off the place and to clear out. They're bringing the crime scene investigators up."

Nellie nodded and motioned for Red to help her out of the rocking chair. "Where'd they take Craig?"

"Boulder Community Hospital. Same place they took the five ladies. He'll be released to the jail pending arraignment at the Municipal Court once he's medically cleared."

"Medically cleared, my ass," Nellie said. "They should cut off his genitalia and hammer nails into his hands and call it good, I say." She took another sip of her iced tea before continuing. "They can ship him off to the jail without his dangly parts. My taxpayer dollars shouldn't pay for his medical care."

Red smiled at Nellie as he walked her to his Jeep. "I'll drive you home and call you if I hear anything about the girls. No nippin' on that blackberry brandy that you make until after you've signed my report, you hear?"

At nearly ninety-four, she figured she could make that judgment call by herself.

"By the way," Red said as he helped her up the steps to her cabin, "nice shot. Where'd you get that old gun? Haven't seen one of them in a long time."

"I already told you where I got that gun, you old goat."

"Just checkin'," Red said, as he tipped his hat and headed back toward town.

* * *

It had been three days since Mac and her friends had been transported by ambulance from Nederland to the Boulder Community Hospital. After receiving medical attention, all but Hesta and Melanie had been released. Patti flew back to Boise with the promise to the District Attorney that she would abide by subpoena and testify at trial, if necessary. Patti was anxious to get back to her boys and was determined that she was going to let them know that she was no longer willing to be treated like their housekeeper and taxi driver. She was their mother–and they were going to treat her with respect. Before the reunion weekend, she'd been offered a long-term substitute teaching position, which she had declined. If the position remained open, Patti intended to take it and get back into the business of being in charge of her own life. Part of taking control of her new destiny included a plan to hire a divorce lawyer and to get Bob and his girlfriend out of her hair.

Rema had also been released from the hospital and had made a similar promise to the D.A. Since she lived locally, keeping the promise would not prove difficult. She had also agreed to think over the plastic surgeon's suggestion regarding earlobe reconstruction, but she would have to wait until the wound healed. Rema wasn't overly concerned about the wound on her ear. She was, however, gravely concerned about the fact that they had never determined whether Chandler Craig had been hired by one of their husbands to kill one of them.

When Scott arrived at the hospital on the first day, none of the friends had yet spoken to Rema about his affair with Hesta. Mac felt that Hesta or Scott should be the one to tell her. Mac did tell the District Attorney, Gardner Smiley, about the affair because she felt that it could play a role in the motive for crime. While he didn't completely disregard the possibility, Gardner Smiley hinted to his belief that Chandler Craig was a serial killer from birth and that his story regarding the involvement of one of their respective husbands was a myth. Mr. Smiley filled Mac in on the details of Chandler Craig's youth and the fact that he'd killed four people in his neighborhood prior to turning thirteen. He'd had no motive other than stealing when committing those crimes in his youth–chances were that he appeared at the Kilkenny-Kerry for the sole purpose of feeding his internal desire to kill for pleasure. The District Attorney promised Mac that he'd follow up with Scott Setliff, as he would with any possible suspect or witness when prosecuting a crime, but it was clear that Scott was not a "person of interest" to law enforcement.

Mac was present in the hospital room when Scott arrived. It had been years since she had seen him and their initial greeting was awkward and contrived. Mac noticed that Scott was still very handsome with his thick sandy hair and green eyes. He walked with a slight limp from his career-ending knee injury, but otherwise, Scott Setliff looked as good as he did in college–maybe better. He approached Rema and gave her a peck on the forehead just above the bandage that surrounded her head to keep the ear patch in place. She smiled slightly at her husband. He tousled her hair.

"You must have been worried sick about Rema," Mac said to him, baiting a reaction.

"Oh, I was. Did they catch the guy?" Scott asked.

"Of course they did. Thanks to Rema. She launched a hatchet into his back."

"So he's dead?"

"No," Mac answered. "Luckily, he's just badly wounded."

"Luckily?" Scott asked.

"So he can stand trial for his crimes."

"Well, that shouldn't take long with you five as witnesses."

"No," Mac agreed, noting that he'd not lost his slick approach. "The complicated part of the trial will be proving up his accomplice."

"There was more than one guy up there?" Scott asked, slowly backing away from Rema's hospital bed.

"Maybe," Mac said. "The police are still investigating it."

"But you guys didn't see more than one guy, did you? I heard that there was only one guy."

"Who did you hear that?" Mac asked.

"It was on television," Scott said, rapidly running his fingers through his hair.

"Oh. Did the reporters mention an accomplice?" Mac pressed.

"No. They said that he killed a bunch of people in Wyoming when he was a kid and that he served his time. They said he is a serial killer and that he killed two other people in a cabin a mile away from where you guys were."

"Well, maybe the news didn't cover it because the police are still investigating leads, but the guy told us that one of our husbands hired him to kill one of us."

Mac watched Scott closely, hoping to see a reaction, but he did not react at all.

"Obviously the guy is a nut," Scott said in a flat tone.

Mac waited for a moment, letting the words hang between them for a bit.

"Obviously," Mac said, as she stood to walk out of the room. "I'm sure that the two of you have a lot to talk about so I'll leave you alone. I'm going to check on Hesta. Have you seen her yet, Scott?"

Scott looked at Mac with piercing eyes. His glare told her that he had visited Hesta prior to checking on his wife. Alliances had been established. Mac did not wait for his response before speaking again. "How was Hesta?" she asked. "Were her spirits up? She has been extremely depressed."

"She's okay," Scott said. He knew that he'd been backed into a corner and he did not like it.

"You visited her before coming to see Rema?"

"I stumbled upon her first," Scott said defensively.

"I see. That seems to happen to you a lot," Mac said as she turned and walked out of Rema's hospital room.

Chapter 24

"All rise," the bailiff announced at the Boulder Municipal Court. "Judge Brooks, presiding."

Mac had not been in the Boulder County Courthouse in a very long time. The building itself was stately and with its stone façade, fit in perfectly with the stone décor of Boulder. Mac attended undergraduate school and law school at the University of Colorado and had taken the bar examination there, fully intending to live out the rest of her life in her beloved hometown. However, jobs were tough to come by upon graduation and her current law partner, Andrew "Harry" Harrison was hiring attorneys in Jackson Hole, Wyoming. Therefore, Mac moved to Jackson after law school graduation, but still had a license to practice law in both Wyoming and Colorado. She'd always envisioned herself appearing before Judge Brooks, and was wishing more than ever that today she was the prosecuting attorney in the case of *The People vs. Chandler Craig.*

Judge Brooks entered the Boulder County courtroom in his usual fashion, cloaked in his black robe and holding a stack of files. He was a short judge with thick white hair and a good sense of humor. To compensate for his size and so that he could see over the bench and into the gallery, he sat on a large stuffed animal puppy. He often made short people jokes and was not offended when counsel teased him while at sidebar. His intellect more than made up for his lack of physical stature and it was this character trait that won him the award of presiding judge for the county.

The judge could have shuffled felony pre-trial arraignments to the newer judges on the bench, but for some reason, he'd always liked to hear the matters. They were often brief and interesting—no day a repeat of the one prior. Boulder had plenty of crime due to the fact that the city was university focused—with plenty of drunk and disorderlies along fraternity row. Misdemeanor theft and assaults and batteries were common fare for pre-trial arrangements. Serial murders were not.

Chandler Craig was wheeled into the courtroom with the assistance of two deputy sheriffs. His leg was heavily bandaged and covered by a large, black brace, propped up by the wheelchair support. Mac could not see the wound on his back where Rema had so gallantly placed the axe, but she was hopeful that it had required many stitches—at least more than she'd endured to sew up her hands.

Mac had been lucky in that there appeared to be no infection and no nerve damage to her right hand as a result of the crucifixion. With a big tetanus shot and natural healing and the assistance of physical therapy, the doctor was hopeful that she would achieve full range of motion and strength in a month or so. The left hand had not faired as well—mostly due to the damage done to it while hanging from a rafter in the cabin's garage. She had suffered some nerve and tissue damage, and whether she would ever be able to firmly grasp an object again was of concern.

Mac watched as the public defender rose to his feet and greeted his newest client. She watched Sam Barakosh, in his full five feet six inch frame reach forward and gingerly shake Chandler Craig's hand. Sam had thinning dark hair, frameless glasses and the hopes of a goatee. Mac knew him from law school—he was in the class ahead of her—but they'd never spoken and she was unsure whether he remembered her.

The district attorney, Gardner Smiley, stood across the courtroom aisle from the public defender, his six foot muscular frame well defined by his navy suit and light blue tie—a color one shade lighter than his eyes. Mac also knew of Gardner, as he was in the class behind her in law school, and she thought that they might have played together on the same intramural soccer team. She'd passed him many times running on the Boulder Creek Trail, and was aware of his athleticism. She was also unsure whether he recognized her, so before the case was called, Mac slipped into the front row and tapped him on his shoulder.

"Hi. My name is Mary MacIntosh. We went to law school together. You were in the class—"

"Hi, Mary. I remember. I saw that you are on the witness list and your name sounded familiar, so I had my investigator pull you up on our database. You've been busy since law school. Congratulations on the big methane gas case."

"Thanks. That seems like a long time ago now."

"How are your hands? The police report described the scene."

"Better. My left one hurts a lot more than the right. Worried that I might not be able to hold a ski pole this year."

"Time to become a boarder then. Don't need ski poles."

Mac smiled. She pictured Gardner as a snow boarder.

"*People versus Chandler Craig*," the bailiff called.

Gardner motioned to Mac that he needed to go.

"I think they might go for an insanity plea," Mac said to him quickly. "I hope you fight it."

Gardner nodded in agreement and then turned and faced the judge.

"How does your client plead?" Judge Brooks asked in a no-nonsense fashion.

"Your Honor," Sam Barakosh started, "I must express my sincere doubt about my client's present mental competence under the Penal Code."

Mac inhaled deeply. She was expecting an insanity defense–based on Chandler Craig's childhood plea. Chandler had mastered the system in Wyoming and had skirted the law. He'd never succumbed to the psychiatric evaluations required by his sentencing and had managed to skate through his time in Juvi and get released without truly serving hard time for killing four innocent people. The thought of him trying this tactic again made Mac's skin crawl.

Judge Brooks looked at Chandler Craig for a moment and then looked to Gardner Smiley. The judge knew Gardner very well from the number of appearances he'd had before his Honor. He could read Gardner's reaction quite clearly. "Mr. Barakosh," the judge said, "please describe the reasons for doubting the defendant's mental competence and state those reasons on the record."

"I have observed the conduct of Mr. Craig while in the holding cell prior to coming to court. He appears very confused about the proceedings against him and does not appear to clearly understand the nature of these criminal proceedings. I'm afraid that he is not going to be able to assist me in preparing his defense in this matter. He rambles on and on about the fact that his father set him up and that his father is the one responsible for him being locked up. I believe that he is delusional and his delusions are clouding his judgment.

"This conduct, coupled with some of the defendant's responses to the questions asked by me in preparing for this hearing have caused a doubt to arise in my mind about the present mental competence of Mr. Craig and I state that doubt for the record under the Colorado Penal Code."

"Mr. Barakosh," Judge Brooks said in a flat tone, "in your opinion is Mr. Craig mentally incompetent? In other words, is Mr. Craig, as a result of a mental disorder, unable to understand the nature of the charges pending against him and is he unable to assist you in the defense of the charges pending in a rational manner?"

"If the Court pleases, I have tried to interview Mr. Craig on several occasions. I have been unable to communicate with him. He seems incapable of conducting rational conversation. Not only does he state that he does not remember any recent events, when pushed in a line of questioning, he defaults to the notion that his father has whispered into his ear and has put him up to it. Now, as far as I know, Chandler Craig has never had a father. I conducted a search and determined that there was no name listed as a father on his birth certificate. From what I can gather from unsealed juvenile court records from the State of Wyoming, he was raised by his aunt. There is no mention of a father. Based on this information, coupled with the information that I have previously stated on the record, I believe that my client may well be mentally incompetent."

"Your Honor," Gardner Smiley said, "May I be heard?"

"Certainly, Mr. Smiley."

"I am readily familiar with this plea and know that under normal circumstances, witnesses do not testify and the court, as a matter of course, simply suspends the criminal proceedings and appoints a mental health expert. Prior to the court taking this matter under submission and issuing a ruling, I respectfully request that your Honor allow a witness to testify regarding Mr. Craig's mental health during the commission of the crimes pending against him."

"I object," Sam Barakosh yelled. "There is no precedent for a witness to testify under these circumstances. The testimony would be tainted with prejudice. I imagine that Mr. Smiley is attempting to call one of the alleged victims to the stand. My client has a right to due process and a right to Sixth Amendment privileges of confrontation. If he is not mentally competent, his Sixth Amendment and due process rights are being subrogated."

"Your Honor," Gardner Smiley said, "that is the most ridiculous argument I've ever heard. First of all, I don't need precedence to call a witness at arraignment. It is the Court's discretion whether to allow it. Second, counsel has the right to cross-examination. There are no Sixth Amendment or other due process violations. What counsel is worried about is that the witness is going to artfully state how poignantly competent Mr. Craig was during the commission of the crimes and counsel is worried that the Court is going to see through this mental incompetence delay and deny his request."

"Your Honor, I am deeply offended–"

"Counsel, that's enough. Mr. Smiley, as much as I would like to hear your witness, we all know that if testimony is received and I deny defense counsel's request, then whatever happens at trial will be subject to appeal, and the appellate court will overturn the possible conviction based on procedural and due process errors–whether they exist or not. Therefore, I am going to order a competency hearing and suspend the criminal proceeding in accordance with the Penal Code. I will appoint a mental health expert under the Evidence Code to help the court resolve the issue of mental incompetence. The mental health expert will prepare a full written report. The court orders that the question of mental competence of Mr. Craig be determined in a hearing under the Penal Code and that further proceedings in this case are suspended until the question of mental competence has been determined. And for the record, Mr. Barakosh, I take it from your statements to the Court that your client is at this time seeking a finding of mental incompetence to stand trial?"

"Yes."

"Then, as a matter of procedural law, I must advise you, Mr. Craig, that at this time I have expressed a doubt about your mental capacity to stand trial. I have ordered a special hearing in which a determination will be made about your ability to stand trial. If you are found mentally able to do so, the criminal proceedings will continue, meaning that the prosecution will put on a jury trial regarding the two charges of murder in the first degree, as well as the five charges of kidnapping, attempted murder, and assault and battery with great bodily injury. If you are found mentally incompetent to stand trial, you will be placed in a state hospital or other suitable facility until such time as you are mentally able to stand trial. Counsel, please approach my clerk. She will hand you a list of psychiatric examiners. Prosecution and defense each gets one choice."

Sam Barakosh and Gardner Smiley both walked swiftly to the clerk's desk. She clicked a button on her computer and then reached behind her to grab a list off her printer. She handed the list to Gardner, whom she liked a great deal more than Mr. Barakosh. Gardner held the list between them and each pointed to their respective choice for a medical expert.

The clerk circled the two choices and then handed the list to Judge Brooks. Both attorneys walked back to their desks. Sam leaned down to Chandler Craig and whispered something into his ear. Chandler, who was wearing a white button-down shirt, with his long, dark hair pulled back neatly into a ponytail, smiled an impish smile. Mac watched him closely. He was as competent as she was to stand trial. The fact that the state was about to pay medical experts somewhere around two thousand dollars for expert reports irked her. The possibility that the doctor for the defense might conclude that Chandler was incompetent sent chills up and down her spine.

"The court appoints Dr. Grayson and Dr. Witt to examine Mr. Craig and report to the court in writing their opinions about whether the defendant is competent to stand trial. Specifically, the following questions must be addressed: Is the defendant presently able to understand the nature and purpose of the proceedings taken against him? Is he presently able to comprehend his own status and condition in reference to the proceedings? Is he presently able to cooperate in a rational manner with his counsel in presenting a defense? In addition, if the doctors believe that the defendant is not competent, the following questions about the use of antipsychotic medications must be addressed: Is it medically appropriate to treat the defendant's psychiatric condition with antipsychotic medication?

"What?" Chandler Craig yelled out from his wheelchair which was positioned next to the defense table. "I'm not taking any psyche meds. They tried to drug me once before and I am not going to take them. I don't care what you—"

"I apologize, your Honor. My client is in a great deal of pain right now and is not feeling very well."

"I'd say he's competent enough to remember that he was offered antipsychotics in the past," Gardner Smiley said.

"Counsel, do not interrupt the court. I'm almost finished with these statutory orders. I'm required to put them on the record. Keep your client under wraps for a few more minutes, will you please?"

"Yes. My apologies," Sam Barakosh said, motioning to Chandler Craig to be quiet.

"Where was I?" Judge Brooks said. He read to himself for a minute and then asked his court reporter to read back the last order that he'd stated on the record. She did so. Judge Brooks readjusted his glasses and then stood to read the remaining orders. It was rumored that he had a bad back and suffered from sciatic nerve pain. Sitting on a stuffed animal all day probably didn't help matters. Standing now, he continued reading the procedures into the record.

"Based on the nature and circumstances of the charges, I'm ordering that the doctor evaluations be expedited and that the reports be prepared within five days. The case is continued to next Friday at one thirty in the afternoon for review and consideration of the doctors' findings on the question of defendant's present mental competence.

"Mr. Craig, at this review hearing you will be able to discuss with your attorney the reports filed by the doctors that I have assigned to evaluate your competence to stand trial. If you and your counsel agree with the conclusions of the reports, you may request the court to make a determination of competency based on the reports. However, if you dispute the conclusions reached by the doctors and therefore do not want the court to make a determination based solely on the reports, then the court will schedule a date for a formal competency hearing. This arraignment is continued to Friday in this courtroom. Next case."

Mac stood to leave the courtroom but when she saw the wave of reporters rushing toward the door, she decided to wait for a few minutes. Originally, she intended to take a walk down the Pearl Street Mall before returning to the hospital to visit Hesta and Melanie, but she wasn't feeling very good at the moment. Right before Chandler Craig's hearing, she had finally been able to get a hold of Wyatt to tell him what had happened. Their telephone connection was not great, but she was certain that he heard what she said. At first, he expressed great concern, but as the conversation ensued, he did not seem overly emotional about the fact that his wife had been nearly murdered. Mac explained that her car had been impounded by the police pending forensic evaluation, and that she would be staying in Boulder for the remainder of the week with her hospitalized friends. Her absence didn't seem to bother Wyatt. According to him, he was very busy on the ranch bailing hay for the winter and was quite hopeful that her hands would heel by the end of the week so that she could drive herself home.

Mac thought back on her conversation with Wyatt. Was he disappointed that she was still alive? He had not even offered to come to Boulder. In fact, only one of the five husbands had bothered to show up for one of the most horrific experiences any of them had ever endured. Patti's husband, Bob, had not shown up. Nor had Wyatt. Nor had Hesta's husband, John, or Melanie's husband, Michael. The only man who'd come to the hospital was Rema's husband, Scott. Of course, it was unclear whether Scott was present to visit Rema or Hesta, but nevertheless, he showed up. Did this mean that she could narrow the suspects down to four?

Deep in contemplation as she walked out of the courtroom, Mac was surprised at the sight of the man occupying the last row.

"Scott? What brings you here? Shouldn't you be tending to your wife? Or your girlfriend?"

Scott stood to his full six feet seven inch height, towering over Mac, who was a strong five foot nine, and said, "Keeping an eye on you."

"What's that supposed to mean?" Mac asked.

"Whatever you think it means." With that, he turned and walked away.

Mac followed behind him, anxious to press him about Rema and Hesta, but as soon as they exited the courtroom, they were swarmed by reporters. Mac was certain that the press would focus on the Chandler Craig case, but it seemed like most of them were more excited to interview Scott. He loved the celebrity status.

As Scott was encircled in a crowd of reporters, Mac slipped down the stairs and out the side door of the courthouse. She had something that she needed to take care of.

Chapter 25

"Hesta," Mac said after returning to the hospital from the courthouse, "of all the people in your world, and all the opportunities to hook up with just about anyone, why would you choose Scott Setliff?"

"It's not like I planned it, Mac. Things like that just happen."

"No, they don't," Mac said. "You let them happen or make them happen, but they don't *just* happen. She's one of your best friends, Hesta. How could you do it to her?"

"Rema? She's not one of my best friends. She hasn't been for a very long time." Hesta used the mechanical device to adjust her hospital bed in a more upright position. Her long dark hair was dirty and matted to her scalp and her light green eyes were flat without the usual dark eyeliner, but somehow Hesta still looked beautiful. "Mac, sometimes I think that you live in the past. You think that everything is the way it was when we were in college, but it's not. People change. Circumstances cause people to do things that they might never have done."

"I don't get what you're saying to me," Mac said.

"The five of us were great friends in college, but some of us were better friends than others. Rema and Mel were best friends and you and Mel were best friends. It was the friendship triangle that was bound for destruction unless other friends were pulled in. Patti was someone everyone liked because she was so sweet and kind and would never hurt a fly. She balanced your energy. I was part of your group only because I was a roommate and I was edgy and crazy and didn't really care what anyone thought of me. I have always enjoyed our friendship, don't get me wrong, but it has never played as important of a role in my life as it probably has for you and the others."

"You always show up to our get-togethers," Mac offered.

"I do," Hesta admitted. "I enjoy our friendship. I don't think you're getting me here. Our friendship is nice. It is just not *everything* to me. I like our weekends once a year. They are entertaining. But they are simply that. A fun weekend with old friends. For me, it is a getaway from New York, but by the end of our time together, I am craving my life in the city. I don't miss John when I'm gone, but I miss my job and the power struggle of getting the story and being with the right people at the right time. My job is tantalizing."

"But you named us beneficiaries for your estate and your life insurance. Why would you do that if we are not close friends?"

"You are close. You are my best friends, but it's hard to explain. I don't need more than that. I'm emotionally distant, according to my shrink."

"So why Scott? You must run into a million powerful men in New York every week. Why hook up with him?"

"It's a long story."

"I'm here until Friday," Mac said, as she walked over to the tray at the foot of Hesta's hospital bed and poured herself and Hesta a cup of water.

Hesta took a long sip from the cup and placed it on the table beside her. "Can't believe that they won't let me smoke."

"You've gone for three days without a cigarette. Maybe you're ready to quit."

"I'll get fat. And I won't be able to write."

Mac shook her head. Hesta always had an answer.

"You were telling me about Scott."

"I was?" Hesta said, in a teasing manner. "I guess I was." She took a deep breath which caused her to cough. "Oh God that hurts," she said, pointing to her crotch.

"What did the doctor say about that? Can they do plastic surgery?"

"They do sex change operations according to the doctor and they claim that it is possible to rebuild it a little, but sensation will not likely be recovered, so what's the point?" Hesta said. "I can still have children. He did not penetrate me, so I don't have to worry about diseases."

"That's good news."

"If you consider going through life without your clitoris good news, then I guess so."

"We are alive, Hesta. We are lucky. He killed two other people up there before he got to us. We're lucky that we're not dead."

Hesta nodded.

"You started telling me about Scott," Mac reminded her. Hesta looked sheepishly at her friend, knowing that she'd been caught trying to evade the subject.

"Scott and I had a fling while we were in college. Rema had gone home from a party early one night and I stayed. I think you were there, but my memory is a bit foggy. Anyway, at the end of the night, he invited me to his place and I stupidly went. We had sport sex. It was entertaining and rough, but otherwise no big deal to me. It only happened that one time when we were in college and it pretty much slipped my mind.

"But years later after he'd been drafted by the NFL to play wide receiver for the Broncos, I was assigned to cover a pre-game story for the company I worked for prior to forming GPG. I called Rema to get Scott's number so that he could get me a locker room pass. My assignment was only to cover some stupid op-ed on the stadium and what it meant to New Yorkers. I figured that if I could get inside and add a personal touch from the locker room, that maybe my boss would give me better crap to cover. Well, it worked. My boss liked my story and Scott liked me. We hooked up that night at his hotel room after the game and had a round of drinks followed by sport sex. This time, I liked it a lot more. Probably because I was married to John by then and my sex life sucked. So I made it a point to hook up with him when he was in town. No big deal really. Just fun. But I guess our fun has lasted longer than it should."

"Are you in love with him?" Mac asked.

Hesta ran her fingers through her hair. "Oh, that hurts," she said. "How many stitches did I get in my shoulder?"

"A few. Are you in love with him?"

"I don't know. I don't think so. I think our relationship is an adrenaline rush. We are both adrenaline junkies."

"Is he in love with you?"

"Scott? He's in love with himself. And it's not like I am his only fling. By his account, he's had hundreds of lovers over the years. I can't imagine him singling me out. I'm just a number."

"That must feel good," Mac said in a mocking tone. "I wonder what number Rema is? Zero? Maybe he wanted her out of the picture."

"You don't really believe that crap do you? No one hired that Craig guy to kill us. That was his delusion. The guy is a nut. A serial killer. Rema said so herself when we rode down in the ambulance together. None of us really thinks that our husbands are involved. Hell, John could care less what I do. Bob is too much of a weenie to do something so stupid. Wyatt hasn't been married to you long enough to hate you. And Michael actually loves Mel—even if they are going through rough times. That whole story is a bunch of shit. You're the legal eagle of the group. Can't believe that you'd fall for that one."

Mac contemplated Hesta's words. Maybe she was right. Silence hung over them for a bit but instead of discomfort, it brought relief. "Am I the only one who has hung on to the *Fabulous Five* notion all these years, and the rest of you have been too polite to tell me that it really doesn't matter much any more?"

Hesta looked her friend in the eye. Her heart told her not to answer honestly, so she used her fall-back smart ass slant. "You were crucified for us."

Mac let out a tiny chuckle. "I told you that all those religious symbols at that cabin stood for something. Little did I know that they'd plant the seed for some lunatic to adopt for a torture strategy."

Hesta smiled. "Will you ever go back?"

"To the Kilkenny-Kerry?" Mac asked.

"Yes."

Mac thought about the implication of Hesta's question. Her family cabin held within it her heart and soul. It was what connected her both to the past and the future.

"Yes. I will go back. Lightning doesn't often strike the same place twice."

"If it could," Hesta said, "it would find its way to my mother-in-law in a hurry."

Chapter 26

"Gardner, this is Mary MacIntosh," she said into a pay phone. "Would you mind if I stopped by your office later today? There's something that I need to discuss with you."

"I can only spare a few minutes. I'm swamped at the moment. Fall semester just started at the university and the crime rate quadruples this time of year. I'm staring at three date rape cases from last weekend."

"I'll be brief. Are you still in the Justice Center off Canyon and Sixth?"

"Yes."

"I'm at the hospital now. I'll be there in a few minutes."

Mac walked the Boulder Creek trail at a brisk pace and arrived at the beautiful Justice Center within ten minutes. Like the court house, the Justice Center was built of stone, and was positioned along Boulder Creek and on the mountain road that led to Nederland. The building had a sense of peacefulness about it and one often spotted a deer munching on the grass outside. Mac bounded up the stairs to the fourth floor and made her appearance known to Gardner's administrative assistant.

"What can I do for you?"

"Would you mind terribly if I borrowed some office space for a few hours? I promise not to access any of your confidential information. I just need internet service and a phone so that I can call my paralegal. She's the best in the world and I need to catch up some. Looks like I'm going to miss the better part of this week at my office."

"I don't mind, but don't tell Sam Barakosh. That guy is the biggest officious intermeddler I've ever encountered."

Mac agreed. She remembered hearing rumors in law school that he hid research books so that other students wouldn't be able to get their writing assignments completed on time.

Gardner escorted Mac to an empty cubicle and logged her into the computer.

"If you need anything, ask Brenda. She'll set you up."

"Does she have a shower? I just noticed that I smell."

"I noticed it in court but I didn't have the heart to tell you," Gardner laughed. "When was your last shower?"

"Friday."

"It's Tuesday."

"I know."

"Suppose you're going to ask to come over to my house later to borrow amenities," he said, this time with a wink.

"You're not that lucky," Mac shot back. "Just got married last year."

"So I'm told," he said as he walked out of the cubicle. "Don't get me in trouble with my boss."

"You are the boss." To that, Mac received no response. She quickly booted into the internet and picked up the phone to call Pam. After five minutes of explaining everything to her beloved but nosey paralegal, Mac set about the task she'd come for. Pam had strict marching orders and no one was better than Pam at spying, prying and otherwise hacking into other people's business.

* * *

After leaving his office for the day, Gardiner Smiley got an unusual call on his cell phone. The voice asked, "Where is she?"

"She's at my office right now. I have it under control."

"You'd better."

* * *

Hours later, Mac returned to the hospital to visit Melanie. When she entered the room she found Melanie reclined in her bed and talking on the phone. Mel motioned for Mac to sit while she finished her conversation.

"I should be released tomorrow, Michael. You don't need to come. I can fly home on my own." There was silence for a moment. "I don't want the boys to see me in a hospital room. It will scare them." Pause. "Fifteen stitches isn't that many, and I only received a pint of blood. I'm feeling better each hour." Pause. "The pinky finger is the best one to lose if you're going to lose a finger." Pause. "I'm fine, honey. Really. What I want to talk about is your job. I've been thinking a lot this weekend about us and our family being happy and I've decided that if you really want to move to Oregon or Washington, or wherever it is you want to go, I will relocate my business. We can make it work." Pause. "Well, you don't need to decide right now. Just know that I am open to discussing the matter." Pause. "Michael, don't say that. It's not true. I mean what I'm telling you. The boys and I will adjust. We'll find a new great neighborhood with great schools and make new friends. We're a family." Pause. "I thought you'd be happy to hear the news." Pause. "What's that supposed to mean?" Pause.

Mac watched her friend struggle to fight back the tears. She went into the bathroom and grabbed a handful of tissues and gave them to Melanie. She readily accepted and dabbed her eyes.

"I need to go," Melanie said to her husband. "I'll call you back after you've had some time to think."

With that, she handed Mac the phone to hang up. Mel's left arm was in a sling to keep her from re-opening the gash on her shoulder and her left hand was heavily bandaged where her pinky was severed. The transfusion bag was nearing the end of its procedure and her friend's color was coming back to her face. "You are looking better," Mac offered.

"I feel worse," Mel said. Slow tears turned into a steady stream. "I thought he would be ecstatic when I told him that I was willing to move and relocate my business but he said that it was too late for that. He wouldn't say why or what he meant. He just kept saying that it was too late."

Mac walked over and sat on the edge of her friend's bed. She was still wearing the hemp hiking outfit that Melanie had given to her.

"Maybe he has re-thought his position and realizes how good life is. Maybe your brush with death has made him come to realize how important you are to him and the boys and that it is too late to discuss moving."

"That's not what it sounded like. His tone was resentful and angry. It wasn't grateful or appreciative. He's never been great at hiding his feelings."

"Wyatt's not great at showing his. At least you know where you stand."

"I'm not sure that I do. His voice sounded different this time. He's been acting very weird around me for the past few months. He's very critical of everything I do. I used to walk on water. Now I can barely tread it. I think that he is very jealous of my business and the fact that I balance it with the boys' schedules. He gets very easily overwhelmed with multi-tasking, and I run circles around him at night getting everything ready for the next day. I think he feels inferior and that has bred bitterness."

"It is hard to tell on the phone, Mel. Maybe when you see him in person tomorrow, things will appear differently."

"When I told him that I would have to come back for the trial, he wasn't too happy about it. Here I am lying in a hospital room—the victim of a serious crime—and he's annoyed that I might have to be a witness in court."

Mac didn't know what else to say at this point. There was obviously some hostility and any effort to placate her friend was being rebuffed.

"Can I ask you something?" Mac said, changing the subject. Melanie nodded. "Is our friendship important to you? What I mean by that is . . . am I the only one who cares if the five of us are friends?"

"What makes you say that? You and I have been best friends for over twenty years. You are my 'go-to' whenever I need a shoulder to cry on or an ear to listen. I cherish our friendship."

"What about the others? Do you cherish your friendships with them?"

Melanie was quiet for a moment. She pulled her knees up to her chest and adjusted the sheet. "Patti and I are good friends. We keep in touch independently. But honestly, if it weren't for you organizing our yearly reunions, I'm not sure that I would keep in touch with Hesta or Rema.

I love them. Don't take this the wrong way. It's just that neither of them make an effort toward our friendship and after so many years, it doesn't seem worth my time. I've tried to keep in touch with them. Rema never returns my phone calls and Hesta does only to the extent that she needs something."

Mac contemplated this idea. She'd never questioned the notion that these friendships were real. In fact, these friendships had served as the basis for much of her feelings of security and confidence. She often bragged to new acquaintances that she had friendships that rooted back to college days. Mac had not kept in close touch with anyone from childhood, and her family was somewhat estranged. *The Five* served as the gateway into adulthood and had been her mental refuge from the pain of the past.

"Things are never going to be the same, are they?" Mac asked.

Mel shook her head in the negative. "Not with Hesta and Rema shagging the same man."

"What about us?" Mac asked.

Melanie motioned for Mac to rest her head on her right shoulder. "You are my best friend. Nothing will ever come between us."

Chapter 27

Pam picked up the line on the first ring. Mac listened intently and took notes as Pam recited the results from her research. "I haven't got a call back from my friend in Casper about Chandler Craig, but she's pretty resourceful and I think she might be able to get in touch with her former boyfriend who was a sheriff at Juvi when Chandler was there. I confirmed that Korinne Craig is Chandler's mother and she died in a car accident shortly after he was born. No father named on the birth certificate. Korinne's sister adopted him. She was a nurse in Douglas for a long time, but her whereabouts are unknown. I'm still following leads on that one. Her first husband was Thomas Lee and it is confirmed that he is the same man that Nederland Police call Old Man Lee who was found dead in the cabin near where you were. The other lady found dead in Old Man Lee's cabin is Carolyn Patterson. Chandler killed her daughter and two grandsons when he was 12. She apparently followed him from the day he was released from the correctional facility and it could be said that the hunter became the hunted. She'd written him many letters while he was in Juvi, all promising that she would make sure that justice was served some day."

"Good work," Mac said, before Pam broke in again.

"Not done. I have my paralegal networking group working on favors for me–like I do for them when you don't give me enough work. I've asked for research regarding who Korinne was dating around the time Chandler was born. Should be easy to come by–even though it was twenty-two years ago. Douglas, Wyoming is a small community. People don't have much else to do but talk about glory days. Also have folks tapping into visitor logs from Juvi in Casper to see who visited Chandler over the nine years that he was housed there. Also, I know some people who know some people who work there, so they'll pinch hit for me. I think that covers him. I kept my research on the contacts at USAMRID, so I'm working that channel for serial killer copy cat stuff to see who Chandler's heroes are. It seems like he's most like Ed Gein, but he certainly has a little Jeffrey Dahmer twist.

"Now, I've also plugged into profiles on all five husbands. I've included Wyatt just to be thorough, but you know how I feel about Wyatt and I want you to know that I am deeply disturbed that you've asked me to include him in the search. He is the nicest man you'll ever meet and if he learns that you don't trust him and he dumps your ass, and you can pardon my disrespect right now because I love you as a boss but think you are an idiot as a wife if you even think he has anything to do with this, then I'm first in line to marry that hunk of a cowboy. I'll let you know what I find out. I'm in the middle of it right now. Scott Setliff is a perfect ass, by the way. Womanizer 101. Might be in some financial trouble with these car dealerships. Will get back to you on him.

"Anything else you want me to do? I'm jacked on Red Bull and the ex has my daughter tonight, so I'm free and geared up."

Mac was afraid to respond. Pam was never shy on words, but when she got fired up on a legal assignment, she was hydrogen minus the oxygen.

"I love Wyatt. I'm just being fair to my friends by including all of our husbands in the search, Pam. I trust him and I don't think he is involved. Are we clear about that?"

"Whatever, boss. You've always been paranoid and you've never trusted a man, and I can understand that based on Greg and that creep Jeffrey who thank God you didn't marry, but Wyatt's a good guy and you don't give him credit for simply being simple."

"Pam."

"Yes."

"I left my cell phone at the cabin. The only way to reach me is through the District Attorney's Office or the hospital. Please don't talk to anyone else about what I've asked you to do. Please make sure that your friends don't leak any of this. This case is going to be a headliner for Gardiner

Smiley and I don't want to screw it up. I just need some answers for the sake of my friends. I'll fill you in on the details when I get home."

"Sure thing, Mac. You know I don't gossip."

"I know. I just don't know your paralegal network, so I'm just putting it out there so that we are clear."

"Got it."

"Can you call Wyatt and remind him to feed Ted? He forgets and now my sweet housecat is becoming a mouser and it disgusts me that he kills and guts mice on my back doorstep."

"Got it. Anything else?"

Mac was quiet for a moment. "I don't think so."

"Okay. Signing off."

"Pam, thank you."

"For what?"

"For being loyal."

"I've got your back. You know that."

"I do know that."

* * *

Patti Poeny had married Bob Poeny the summer they graduated from college. They'd met in math lab and had accomplished their secondary education teaching credentials by student teaching together in Denver. They were both mild natured and studious in college. Bob rarely went out. Patti was more outgoing, but only went out when the *Fabulous Five* were doing something together. Otherwise, Patti and Bob were found together studying in the library or watching a movie in the student lounge. They played tennis, but Patti was much better than Bob. Both loved to play cards, but Patti was better at card counting and could beat him at just about any card game. They enjoyed solving algorithms, but it came more naturally to Patti. Both came from big families, but Patti's family was solid, Bob's was a little sketchy.

Bob did not like to discuss his childhood. He showed up with Patti and the kids for family events, but the minute the opportunity presented itself, he found an excuse to leave. "Too much chaos," was often the justification, or "too much religion."

Bob's family was Presbyterian until he turned seven. And then, for some unknown reason, all nine of them were suddenly Mormon. He had no quibbles growing up Mormon. In fact, he liked the certainty of it all. But what he did not appreciate, as time went by, was the expectation that he would live his life according to someone else's plan.

Moving to Idaho was actually Patti's idea. She felt that Bob needed some separation from the Utah band. Boise was a nice compromise–plenty of Mormon influence, but enough opportunity that if one changed one's mind about religion, one would not be ostracized from the community. They both got teaching jobs in Boise right out of college and established themselves in the community. When Jason was born, Patti stopped teaching, and as a good Mormon wife, rapidly produced more children in rapid order. Jaime and Jonathon were her "Irish twins," and after the birth of Jonathon, Patti started having female problems.

Several miscarriages in rapid sequence encouraged her to visit her doctor. Ovarian cancer did not run in her family, but genetics were not the only factor in the development of this perilous disease. Patti had a hysterectomy at age 35, which promptly brought on the signs of menopause, and it wasn't long before her sex drive completely dried up.

Bob was very supportive of his wife during this time, constantly reminding her that their faith would get them through this. But, as they say, sometimes faith is not enough. When the boys progressed through puberty and started bringing their buxom girlfriends to the house, Bob felt a stirring deep within. Going to bed at nine each night after watching the news only to find his plump wife eating a large bowl of buttered popcorn in bed while reading her latest romance novel eventually changed Bob's ideals regarding faith.

With amazing determination, he studied for and passed his real estate broker's examination, resigned from his fifteen year teaching position at the local high school, and promptly became a top seller in high end residential real estate. Hair plugs were a must. Botox was necessary around the forehead and hairline to cover the plugs. Daily tennis and early morning jogging helped reduce his waistline, and to top it all off, he purchased a new sports car with his first big sales commission.

Patti soon learned that the changes were not all professionally related. The tennis came with it a cute mixed-doubles partner who had no children and appeared to be enjoying her twenties. Late night client dinners had become customary. Early morning breakfast meetings were also frequent. Patti, her book and her bowl of popcorn had a permanent and lonely place on the right side of the queen-sized bed.

Patti was no dummy, however, and she reminded herself that algorithms were her specialty. She developed a logical step-by-step procedure for solving this mathematical problem in a finite number of steps. The first step involved a private investigator.

* * *

"Patti, it's Mac. You made it home okay?"

"Jason picked me up from the airport two hours ago. I'm fine. How are things there? How is Mel?"

"First of all, if you need me, call me from this number. I don't have my cell yet."

"Nor do I. Everything is still at the cabin."

"Nicole is bringing it down to me now and I will ship your phone to you express mail. I think I'll just keep your suitcase here because it will too expensive to ship and you are probably going to be asked to come back on Friday for a continued arraignment hearing."

"I don't know if I can make it, Mac. I have a lot of issues to take care of here."

"Bob?"

"I hired a divorce attorney before my plane took off from Denver. It's not easy to get an attorney to represent you when you are Mormon in Idaho, but luckily I've been mulling it over for some time. It will be nasty, I'm told, and expensive, but luckily Bob closed on another house in Sun Valley over the weekend so there should be plenty of cash to blow on attorney's fees."

"I don't mean to be impolite, Patti, but you've been putting up with this from him for a few years by your account. Why the hurry? Maybe it's not the best time in the world to make decisions, you know, right after enduring something terribly stressful."

"Having someone cheat on you right under your nose is terribly stressful too. This weekend reminded me that life is short and I am not going to live it feeling bad about myself. I deserve better."

"You do, Patti. Just take your time. Divorce is tricky and emotional, and I was just considering the possibility that you might need a little decompression time before making big decisions."

"Thank you for your concern, but I'm a big girl."

"I know you are. Which leads me to ask you something. Please don't take offense. It has been suggested by some that perhaps I am the only one that glues our friendship together. What I mean to say is that perhaps if I didn't badger everyone to get together every year, that maybe the five of us would no longer be close friends. How do you weigh in on this poll?" Mac sucked in her breath while awaiting Patti's response.

"Actually, you and Mel are my best friends. You always have been. Can't say that I feel the love from Hesta or Rema, but that has always been the case as well. So, maybe it is true that you are the glue that keeps us together, but when we are all together, I have always really enjoyed our mix. We all bring such different life experiences to our friendship. I can't imagine life without all five of us."

Mac smiled into the phone. "I feel the same way."

"Hesta doesn't," Patti offered. "But that's just her way. She has a way of not letting people in and sabotaging anyone that could possibly love her, so don't let her words burn through you, which is exactly what you are doing right now. I've been her roommate and I've seen her ways. She acts like she has it all together, but the truth is that she is the loneliest of us all. I've also been Melanie's roommate, and despite her pickiness about neatness, she is a genuine friend. She loves us exactly how we are. One of these days, loneliness is going to stare Rema in the face and she's going to have to figure out when not to run away, but as far as friendships go, she loves us. I think that we are the only stable thing in Rema's life."

"You are right, Patti. Thank you."

"For what?"

"Being so perceptive."

"Algorithms, my friend."

"Algorithms," Mac repeated as she hung up the phone.

Chapter 28

When Nicole arrived at the hospital, she was greeted by an entourage of reporters. They shoved microphones in her face and asked her ten questions at once regarding "The Cabin Killer," as they monikered him. She was perplexed by the notion that they knew who she was and otherwise annoyed by their angle. "Did you personally see the crime scene?" "Was it bloody?" "Can you confirm that there were severed body parts?"

Nicole did not bother answering audibly and simply shrugged her shoulders as she kept on walking. When she arrived at Melanie's room carrying three duffle bags and one rolling suitcase, Mac greeted her with open arms.

"Thank you," Mac said, as she snagged her duffle and headed for Mel's hospital room bathroom. "I'll be out in a flash."

"How have you been able to avoid the press?" Nicole asked. "They haven't shown any interviews of any of you on the news."

"The hospital won't let them in," Mac said through the closed bathroom door, "which is nice, and when I've left for court and a meeting, they've allowed me to borrow scrubs and a mask and I've left through the back door of the ER. Rema left in scrubs too, and we haven't seen her since this morning. Patti somehow slipped into a cab without being noticed. The District Attorney was good enough to get her special permission to fly without identification. To say the least, it has been an interesting day."

"I brought all the cell phones and purses, except for Rema's. I couldn't find hers."

"She doesn't carry one. She only carries a fanny pack with some cash in it."

"That girl is off her rocker," Nicole said.

"When she learns what is going on around here, she'll be even more so," Melanie said. While Mac showered and changed clothes, Mel filled Nicole in on the drama regarding Scott and Hesta.

"Whewee," Nicole said. "Fireworks are going to be blasting. Rema doesn't know yet?"

"We don't think so. She was locked in the cabin when Hesta told us in the garage, and then she rode down to Boulder in an ambulance with Hesta, but Hesta did not fess up. That would have been a good time to tell her because they were alone and could have sorted some things out, but I think that Hesta was too afraid to talk about it. Rema was discharged from the hospital this morning and she left to take care of something. Scott was here this morning and he saw both Hesta and Rema, but we don't know what they talked about. Mac said that Scott was at the court hearing, which is strange, but knowing that megalomaniac, he was probably hoping for a little spotlight time in the media."

"He used to be the sportscaster for all the Bronco's stuff, but I don't think his contract was renewed last season," Nicole said. "And the only reason I know this is because Max said something about it. He's a big football fan. I could care less. Anyway, Max said that he wasn't doing the golf promos either and that a few of his dealerships are up for sale, so maybe things aren't so good for him."

"Speaking of Max," Melanie said, "where is he?"

"Still up in Nederland dealing with the cabin. Once the crime scene investigators are done, he's offered to close it up for the winter. He's overseeing them up there to make sure that nothing gets ruined."

"He's a good guy," Mel said.

"One in a million," Nicole agreed. "He's my second husband and I'm his third wife."

"Really?"

"Really. We got it right this time around. Sometimes it takes a few bites at the apple to find the flavor that suits you. Nellie was married five times. Her first two husbands died early from natural causes. If you ask her, she'll tell you that she married her last three husbands just to have someone around the house. She just happened to keep outliving them. Life is lonely when you fly solo for too long."

Mel thought about that statement for a moment. She was about to reply when Rema walked into the room wearing sweaty scrubs. Mel smirked at her obsessed friend. "Out for a run?"

"I have to clear my head. It's the only way I can think," Rema said.

"You have stitches in your ear and you lost a lot of blood. Did the doctor say it was okay?"

Rema simply shook her head. Of course the doctor did not give her permission to exercise, let alone run twenty miles, but that was not the issue for Rema.

Mac walked out of the bathroom in clean clothes and a towel wrapped around her head. She took one look at Rema and her dirty scrubs and rolled her eyes.

Nicole motioned to Rema to come and sit with her on the windowsill bench. She put her arm around Rema and said, "I think there is something you should know."

Melanie interrupted. "I think Hesta should tell her."

"Tell me what?" Rema said, pulling away from Nicole's embrace. "That Scott and Hesta get it on a few times a year?"

Melanie's eyes flew open wide. Mac walked over and sat next to Rema. Rema immediately stood and started pacing the diminutive space between the bed and the door. "I don't care about it," Rema said. "I suppose you've all known about it for years and didn't have the courtesy to tell me. We've been getting together for these sham girls weekends for years and all along, I've been the butt of your jokes."

"Rema! That is the furthest thing from the truth," Mac said. "We just found out about it while we were tied up in the garage together. The rest of us had no idea, otherwise, we would have told you about it long ago. Believe me. We would not have kept this from you and you've never been the butt of jokes." Mac stood and coaxed Rema to sit down between herself and Nicole.

"How could you not care?" Melanie said.

"Do you have any idea how many girls that man has boned since I met him? I'm not an idiot."

"But she's your friend."

"Obviously not," Rema said. "She's never been my friend. She was your friend and somehow I've managed to believe that the rest of you were my friends."

"We are your friends," Mac said. "You just don't let us in. The minute we get close, you run away."

"Can you blame me?" Rema said, tears welling in her eyes. "The minute I get close to someone, they burn me."

"I've never burned you," Mac said.

"Neither have I," Melanie offered.

"Scott has burned you. So has Hesta," Nicole said to Rema in her mediator's tongue. "It hurts and it is not right, but you can only hold them accountable for their actions. Your other friends didn't know about it. The bigger issue is why you've been putting up with this behavior all these years."

Rema was quiet for a moment. She stood and removed her top, revealing her flat chest and sweaty jog bra. She wadded the scrub top into a ball and wiped her face with it. "I'm not sure why I've never left him. I think about it all the time when I'm running. I've pictured the moment so many times in my head. But somehow, when it comes down to it, I chicken out. Maybe it is because I don't want to be alone. Maybe it's because he is so emotionally distant that he feels safe for me. I don't have to be emotionally available for him."

Nicole stood and went over to Rema and gave her a hug. "Then we need to figure out why you don't want an emotionally supportive relationship."

Mac knew that her friend was in good hands. Nicole was a psychology professor at the university and could ferret out issues more gently than a lamb.

Nicole led Rema out of Melanie's room and arm in arm, they walked down the corridor.

* * *

"I did a little snooping," Pam said to Mac when she called her bubbly paralegal from the cell phone that Nicole had retrieved from the cabin. "My friend's ex-hubby was a guard at Wyoming's Training School's Youth Correctional Center where Chandler Craig was. Apparently Chandler was a very popular kid there and the guards liked him a lot. They gave him special privileges over the years, including internet access. The kid even made music videos when he was there. According to my friend's ex, right before Chandler was released on his twenty-first birthday, he had a visitor who came to see him several times. This was news in that Chandler had no other visitors the entire time he was housed there—and that was about nine years. She is trying to get in touch with her ex's friend who is still a guard there to see what the sign-in log says. He said that the log is probably in storage by now because it has been several months and they go through a log every few weeks, but she promised to get back to me as soon as possible."

"Do we know what he did on the computer when he had internet access?" Mac asked while pacing the corridor outside Melanie's room.

"No. I asked about that, but I guess it is pretty hard to tell because several of the kids 'on cart,' meaning the kids who'd earned credit for good behavior, had access on the same computer, so it would be hard to figure out who was using it when. The guard is going to look into the history on the computer, but he said that it's hard to tell who was using it based on the way the kids log on and off."

"What about the obituary for Chandler's biological mom?"

"As I already told you, I'm online searching for the archives, but I may have to pay for an archive search because some of the smaller newspapers such as Douglas didn't put everything online nine years ago, believe it or not. I'm working on it. I did find out from the high school administrator that her name was Korinne Craig and the administrator confirmed that she died in a car accident the summer before her senior year. When I

Google her, I don't find anything, but I'm still working on it. The police report from the murders Chandler committed in Douglas were part of an archived file and I was able to confirm that Chandler's aunt was Kristine Craig and she was formerly married to John Lee, which I think is the same guy you refer to as Old Man Lee who was killed in Nederland. Google puts Kristine Craig in Buffalo, Wyoming, so I'm hoping to get an address or phone number and pay her a visit. Kristine and John Lee divorced when Chandler was young and she remarried a guy named John Aries. I guess she liked guys named John. She divorced him too. Not sure what his status is, but checking."

"You've been busy," Mac said to Pam. Mac knew that Pam lived for these kinds of assignments.

"I've also managed to complete all of the discovery on the Wynn case and served it on opposing counsel. And Megan said that you got appointed on another juvenile case due to a conflict of interest by both the public defender and juvenile defender. The court wanted to know when you'd be back and we thought it would be tomorrow, but maybe we should call the court and let them know that you are delayed."

"I think that's a good idea. If some other attorney can make a special appearance for me, I can play catch up when I get back. It might not be until the weekend though, depending on what happens on Chandler's competency hearing and whether his criminal case goes forward, or whether he is found mentally incapable to stand trial."

"I'll see what I can arrange. It's after five, so the courts are closed for the day. I'll call back tomorrow."

"Were you able to do personal profiles on all five of our husbands?"
"You mean four of the five?"

"I need you to do one for all five, including Wyatt. If the district attorney or my girlfriends find out that I ruled him out without conducting the same investigation on him, they won't believe that I'm unbiased in my search."

"You shouldn't be unbiased. You're married to a good man who would never hurt a fly."

"Then we have nothing to worry about, do we?"

Chapter 29

"Who were you talking to?"

"Oh, Scott, I didn't see you there," Mac said, as she quickly shut off her iPhone and slid it into the front pocket of her blue jeans. "Just checking in at the office. I was supposed to be back tomorrow, but it looks like we might be here a few more days. What is it, Thursday already? Seems like I've been away for a month."

Scott walked another step closer to Mac and glared at her. He crossed his bulky arms over his burly chest and cornered her. "It sounded like you were doing something else. You got something you want to talk to me about? Because if you do, I'm all ears. If you don't, I'm going to tail you until you tell me what kind of shit you're trying to pull."

"Is that a threat, Scott? Because if it is, I'm happy to call my classmate at the district attorney's office and let him know that I'm being harassed and threatened."

"Good luck. That Smiley guy is flirty with me. He already asked for my autograph."

Mac hoped that Gardner was using the autograph ploy to try to get a DNA sample from Scott, but it did cross her mind that Gardiner Smiley was an accomplished athlete and might be smitten over a former NFL football star.

"Move, please," Mac said.

"I'll move because you asked nicely, but you'd better watch what you're doing. I don't take kindly to frame-up jobs."

"If you have nothing to hide, then you have nothing to worry about, do you, Scott?" Mac said, as she briskly stepped around his sturdy frame. "By the way, I'm on my way to see Hesta. We have a few loose ends to tie up."

Mac walked away from Scott and quickly pulled her cell phone out of her pocket, texting Melanie as she walked toward Hesta's room.

"Scott outside your room. Threatened me. Be careful what you say to him. Warn Nicole if you see her."

* * *

Dr. Grayson was a well respected psychiatrist who taught at Anschultz Medical Center at the University of Colorado at Denver while maintaining an active private practice. He had developed a forte in expert psychiatric evaluations, especially for use in the courtroom setting. It didn't hurt matters that Dr. Grayson was particularly attractive, with longish blond hair, tan skin from his healthy outdoor lifestyle, and sky-blue eyes. Juries loved him—especially the women. He was incredibly articulate and unshakeable on the witness stand. Gardiner Smiley was pleased that he was conducting the evaluation for the prosecution.

Due to his busy schedule during the day, Dr. Grayson preferred to perform his psyche evaluations during the evening hours. Each evaluation took about two hours and if they could be arranged from five to seven in the evening, he would still have an hour or more of daylight this time of year for a bike ride up the canyon trail. He made arrangements that evening to visit Chandler Craig at the jail and to conduct his evaluation in an attorney interview room. The evaluation would be recorded for the purpose of Dr. Grayson's report preparation, but the tape recording itself would remain confidential pursuant to the Welfare and Institutions Code.

"Hey, Dale," Dr. Grayson said, greeting the deputy sheriff who was in charge of guarding Chandler during the evaluation. Dale stood six foot eight and looked like the sturdiest built man on the force, juxtaposed by a teddy bear demeanor. Dale had worn many hats over the course of his career, including seventeen years on the beat as a police officer, a part time screenplay writer, and, for a few years in between the beat and joining the sheriff's department, he owned a crematorium where he specialized in using nitrous oxide to dispose of a corpse instead of the heat of a kiln. He could carry on a conversation regarding any topic, and had a great sense of humor. Dr. Grayson often told him that his life would be the perfect script for a movie if he was able to force himself to commit some heinous crime, because Dale could cover his tracks better than anyone due to his knowledge of criminal law and his experience in forensics. They would often laugh about the prospects and sometimes even create fictional scenarios while they waited for a defendant to be escorted into an interview room.

The door opened and Dale stood at attention. Two armed deputies escorted a shackled Chandler Craig into the room. Chandler was seated across from Dr. Grayson and his hands and feet were cuffed to the chair. "Are you a spitter?" Dale asked, his pliable voice converted into austere command. Chandler looked up at the giant and shook his head in the negative. "If you even think about spitting, you'll be in need of dental work, do I make myself clear?" Chandler nodded in the affirmative. "You'll answer with a 'Yes, sir' or a 'No, sir' when you address me or the good doctor over there." Chandler again nodded.

"Good evening," Dr. Grayson started, pressing his index and middle fingers on the play and record buttons of the tape recorder. He briefly explained the purpose of the interview, much a repeat of what the judge had told Chandler in court. "Let's begin with a basic understanding of your upbringing. My notes indicate that your mom died in a car accident shortly after you were born and that your aunt adopted you. Would you agree with this statement?"

Chandler just stared at the doctor, squinting at him with a formidable attitude. Dale took a step closer to Chandler as a hint to answer before he spoke. "Better be a 'Yes, sir' coming out of your mouth, son."

Chandler did not flinch. Dr. Grayson wasn't daunted by Chandler's silence—it wasn't an uncommon beginning in such an interview. His custom and practice was to continue documenting the history as noted in the file Usually if something was asserted that the defendant strongly disagreed with, the defendant would start talking. In his report, he simply noted a lack of response and associated it with acquiescence.

"You had a stepfather who didn't treat you very well, right?"

No response.

"And that was a man by the name of John Lee, correct?"

Again, silence.

Dr. Grayson knew not to pursue any line of questioning regarding the pending crimes, so he did not pursue any issues Chandler might have had with Old Man Lee. The room was situated with a two-way mirror, and the public defender was watching the interview.

"Chandler, I'm going to continue to ask you a number of questions in the form of statements. If you don't answer, I will assume that you agree with my assertions, so if you don't agree, you need to answer and explain. I've told you why I'm here and what determination the court has asked that I render. The court will heavily rely on my written report when making its ruling this Friday. I want your hearing to be fair. I'm not here to render legal advice. Your attorney is on the other side of that glass. If you'd like me to take a break so that you can speak with him about your legal strategy, I'm okay with that. I've done these evaluations many times and I don't want you to think that your silence is going to help your case."

Chandler did not move or speak. The only thing he did was breathe and blink.

Dr. Grayson looked toward the two-way glass to see whether the attorney wanted to interrupt for a short recess, but when there was no tap on the window or knock on the door, the doctor assumed that the attorney had no objection to continuing the interview.

Dr. Grayson went through a detailed history of Chandler's childhood, including reading to him the signed sworn statement that Chandler had given to Detective Brown in connection with the Patterson and Robinson murders. Chandler did not even hint at responding.

"I know that you were ordered to undergo intense psychological examination and therapy when you were housed at the maximum-security detention facility in Wyoming. Did you undergo treatment?" No response. "I understand from reviewing your medical records from that facility that you withdrew from the diagnostic and treatment program. You told doctors that you were afraid that the psychiatric examination might result in you being placed in a psychiatric facility for a commitment beyond your twenty-first birthday. Now that seems like you were using excellent logic, wouldn't you agree?"

Dale took another step forward, knowing that this was a crucial portion of the interview. He put his hefty left paw on Chandler's right shoulder and gave it a firm squeeze. Nevertheless, Chandler did not flinch and he did not speak.

"You appear to be a very clever young man. You knew that if you avoided the psychiatric treatment that the court would lose jurisdiction of you at age twenty-one and you would walk away a free man, right?"

Dr. Grayson stood up to stretch his legs. He stayed on his side of the table, as instructed by Dale many times. He took a deep breath and stretched his neck, looking to the stained gypsum wallboard that lined the ceiling. His thought process diverted momentarily to asbestos and whether the building was in compliance with state-of-the-art building codes. He'd recently built his own medical facility and used mineral fiber ceilings to enhance the "green" approach, substituting fiberglass components of expanded volcanic perlite in the research facility. He was very proud of his new office but the "green" factor had caused him to go over budget by two hundred fifty thousand dollars. He needed to double his court appearance time to make up the budget deficit. This was one of the reasons that Dr. Grayson agreed to take the Chandler Craig case.

Dr. Grayson looked down again at the defendant and then took his seat. He guessed that Chandler was not going to answer any of his questions, again relying on the Fifth Amendment to save him, so Dr. Grayson decided to get everything on the record required to ensure a complete report, and otherwise get out of the jail and enjoy his evening road race up the canyon on his new carbon monocoque-frame triathlon bike.

"So, let's talk about Wanda Sue Patterson and her two boys, Chance and Bridger. Now, I'm allowed to talk about these acts due to the fact that you've already served your time for these crimes and you can't be held accountable for them again. If your attorney objects, he'll come in and say something." Dr. Grayson paused for a moment to ensure that Sam

Barakosh had no problem with this line of questioning. "You told Detective Brown that you entered their home to steal some things, is that true?" No response. "But they came home in the middle of it, so you hit Wanda Sue in the kitchen and then used a stereo chord to strangle her. The kids were screaming and causing a fuss so you grabbed a kitchen knife, right?

"The little one, Bridger was his name and he was only about five years old, started running out of the kitchen, which is where you'd dragged his mom, so you went after him and stabbed him in the back. You left the knife in his back and then went back into the kitchen and got another knife out of the drawer. The older boy, Chance, was pulling at his mom's hand so you cut his hand off. He started screaming–"

"That's all a lie. I never told Detective Brown that."

"Which part?" Dr. Grayson said, perking up a bit.

"I was there. At the townhouse. It was on Fairway Drive. But I had a friend there with me and he did all the killing. I tried to stop him but he jabbed me in the hand with his knife. He told me that if I ever ratted him out that he would kill me."

Dale took his hand off Chandler's shoulder and took a step back.

"So you are telling me that you didn't kill the Patterson family."

"No, I didn't."

"Then why did you say that you did? Why would you serve the time in custody for a crime that you now claim you didn't do?"

"Because my friend told me to do it."

"Who is your friend?" Dr. Grayson asked, running his left hand through his thick blond hair while taking copious notes with his right.

"I can't say."

"You can't say–or you *won't* say. There is a difference."

"I can't."

"Why?"

"I can't tell you why."

"Okay. Did this friend ever visit you while you were at the detention facility?"

"I can't say."

"Did you ever communicate with this friend after you were questioned by Detective Brown?"

"I can't say."

"Have you communicated with this friend since you were released on your twenty-first birthday?"

"I can't say."

"Are you afraid that this person is going to harm you, or is this another one of your lies? I'm told that you like to make up lies so that professionals like me are confused by your stories."

"I can't say."

"Let's focus on this alleged friend. How did you meet this friend? Is he related to you? Did you know him or her well before the crime took place? Did you know him or her when the Robinson stabbing happened? Was this friend involved in the Robinson murder?"

The line of questioning continued for a good hour, and with each question, Chandler Craig answered the same way. Dale even tried a little strong arm tactic, to which Sam Barakosh gave a light tap on the window, but to which Chandler did not sway in his new line of thinking.

"Was this friend involved in the murders in Nederland?"

The door to the interview room swiftly opened and Sam Barakosh marched in. He held up his five fingers toward Chandler. Chandler looked to his right and then to his left and then put his chin down to his chest, only raising his eyes to Dr. Grayson, and in a menacing tone of voice never before heard by anyone present in the room, he said, "I invoke my Fifth Amendment rights."

"Okay," Dr. Grayson said. "I get that. I'll focus on another topic." Sam whispered into Chandler's ear for a few seconds and then left the room.

"Do you hear voices in your head?"

"I hear a voice telling me that you're part of a big fucking conspiracy to keep me locked up."

"You are using the word 'conspiracy.' Do you think that there are some people out there who are ganging up on you and trying to get you into trouble?"

Chandler's face turned crimson and he stood, taking the chair that he was cuffed to with him. "I don't have to take your bullshit, you hear me!" he screamed.

Dale grabbed him by both shoulders and shoved him to the ground. The chair made a horrendous clang upon touchdown. "Don't ever do that again," Dale shouted in a tone Dr. Grayson had never heard from what he deemed "The Gentle Giant."

"You seem angry," Dr. Grayson taunted. "Are you angry because I'm not falling for your lies? The ladies at the cabin told me what you told them and some of it is not true. Do you like to make things up to justify your behavior?"

Chandler swayed his head from side to side. His jaw was tightly clenched and his face turned nearly purple.

"Do you know the difference between right and wrong?" No response. "Do you understand that you are being charged with murder?" No response. "Do you believe that you suffer from mental illness?" No response. "Can you help Sam Barakosh prepare your defense?" No response. "Are you willing to try some medicine that might help you think more clearly?"

"I'm not taking your fucking meds."

"Have you tried psychotropic medication before?"

"I told you that I'm not taking your shit."

"In lieu of medication, do you think therapy would help you?" No answer. "Do you feel that you are a danger to yourself? What I mean by that is whether you think you might hurt yourself if you were left to your own devices?"

"I'm gonna fucking hurt you if you don't stop asking me these fucking questions."

"Is that a threat, Mr. Craig?"

Chandler shook his head from side to side.

"No, you mean it is not a threat? You are shaking your head in a negative fashion. Does that mean that you're just messing with me, or does that mean that if Dale uncuffed you and left you in here alone with me, that you would hurt me in some way?"

Sam Barakosh re-entered the room, again holding his hand up in the air. "I think you've covered all the questions the judge asked of you. Why don't we take a little break?"

Chapter 30

"I'm sitting in Kristine Craig's living room in Buffalo. Will text you when I'm done," was the text message Mac received from her paralegal Pam later Thursday evening.

Mac walked into Hesta's room and sat down in the chair next to her bed. "How are you feeling?" Mac asked.

Hesta did not respond. She stared blankly across the room, as still as a statue.

"Hesta? Are you okay?"

"No," she said. "And I don't want to talk about it."

"If it makes you feel any better, your neck is looking better. I think that Melanie is going to get released tomorrow. Her blood count is improving. They are not sure about the nerve damage in her shoulder. The doctor said that they are going to have to wait a few weeks until the wound heals and then do an MRI to see what the tissue looks like. She's worried because she loves to row–I guess she's part of a rowing team in the Bay Area–and she thinks that she might not be able to do that anymore if there is nerve damage there."

"Well guess what? Not being able to row a stupid boat is nothing compared to never having pleasurable sex again. Have you ever considered that?"

Mac inhaled heavily and quietly considered Hesta's statement. "I've thought about it since yesterday, Hesta. I really don't know what to say other than 'I'm sorry.' I can't imagine what you are feeling."

"I can imagine what Rema is thinking. She's thinking that God has a mysterious way of punishing people for their bad acts and the fact that I got my sexuality mutilated is poetic justice."

"Rema is not like that–nor has she ever been that type of person. No matter how hurt or betrayed Rema feels, she would never blight you. It is just not the way she operates. She is handling this like she handles everything–she went for a long run to think about it. When she came back, she was very calm. She's talking with Nicole right now."

"Send Nicole my way when she's done. My shrink in New York isn't going to be enough. I think I'm going to need one from every state."

It was good for Mac to hear Hesta joke.

"Will do. Not to change the subject, but has Scott been by lately?"

"Why?" Hesta asked, in a slightly different tone.

"Well, I saw him out in the hallway and I think it is fair to say that he wasn't terribly pleasant toward me. In fact, one might say that he was a bit tyrannical. You know me well enough to know that if someone bullies me, I don't respond well. My high school boyfriend bullied me, and it is my promise to myself to never be bullied by a man again."

Hesta looked bored by Mac's exposition. Mac leaned in and touched Hesta's left hand. Mac's hands were still tightly bandaged to protect her wounds. Hesta looked down and put her right hand lightly on Mac's. "This isn't your fault, you know," Hesta said.

"What isn't my fault?"

"The fact that this happened. You don't need to find someone to blame."

"I'm not trying to find *someone* to blame. I'm trying to figure out if Chandler Craig was hired to kill one of us. I know that he is probably just a mentally ill person and that we were probably just unlucky to have met up with him, but there is this tiny seed that has been planted in my mind and until I can be sure that it is not the case, then I won't be able to sleep. Maybe I'm the paranoid one, but the thought of one of our husbands doing such a thing has really jostled me."

"Think about it. The guy has killed at least six people that we've been made aware of. Maybe he has killed a bunch more. He told us that he kills for fun."

"If he killed strictly for fun, we'd all be dead now. He messed around and toyed with us for days."

"That's not unheard of in the serial killer world, is it?"

"No. It's not."

"I've read accounts of these things where the killer has kept women tied to beds for months or hidden in caves. Maybe this guy hit the mother lode with all five of us and couldn't decide who to kill first."

"Or maybe one of our husbands hired him and he was trying to figure out which of us was the right one."

"That is utterly ridiculous if you think long and hard about it. Let's just assume you are right for a moment and talk this through. If one of our husbands wanted us dead and somehow happened across Chandler Craig, he would have told him exactly who he wanted dead–describing his wife with particularity to make sure that the job was done right. Craig knew our names. He knew who each of us was and over time, figured out who our husbands were. He could have taken care of business. The real deal is that had all of this been true, he simply would have killed us all anyway to avoid having a witness identify him. So, if you follow that logic, we are all dead. If you follow the serial killer logic, it is more likely that he toys with us and plays mental games with us."

Mac considered Hesta's observation. "I suppose you're right." She paused for a moment and rested her head on the rail of Hesta's bed. "Then why is it that I have this sickening feeling in my stomach that what he said was true?"

Hesta hesitated before answering. "How are things *really* between you and Wyatt?"

* * *

"Wake up," Hesta said to Mac. She had fallen asleep sitting up in a chair with her head resting on Hesta's hospital bed.

Mac pulled her head up and felt the stiffness in her back and legs. Her hands ached terribly. "What time is it?" Mac asked.

"I'm not sure, but it's almost Friday morning. The nurse was going to make you leave, but I insisted that she let you stay. Your phone keeps beeping and it is driving me nuts. I would have thrown the damn thing out the window if I could have found it."

Mac reached down into the front pocket of her blue jeans and retrieved her cell phone. Pam had been leaving her email attachments on her iPhone all night long. Mac stood and walked into Hesta's bathroom and closed the door behind her.

From the emails, Mac gathered that Pam's conversation with Kristine Craig had gone well. She learned that Kristine divorced John Aries not long after Chandler was sentenced and that she moved to Buffalo with her two younger children that she had with Aries not long after that. According to the synopsis that Pam wrote for Mac,

> "She got a nursing job in Buffalo and had been able to live a fairly normal life. After time, people forgot about Chandler for the most part. Carolyn Patterson tried hard to rally citizen interest groups, but nothing much happened as a result. Some law professor pushed hard to have Wyoming's juvenile law changed so that there wasn't concurrent jurisdiction with the juvenile and adult court, citing Chandler Craig's case as an example of poor law, but again, the law remained unchanged in Wyoming as far as Kristine knew. Her natural children grew up with their father's name of Aries and stood apart from the past, so they were not associated with the acts of their cousin.
>
> "When asked about Korinne's boyfriend in high school and the biological father of Chandler, Kristine remained unsure. She knew that Korinne's boyfriend's name was Kevin because they both started with a "K" and that was a big deal to her little sister, but whether Kevin was the father of the child was always an issue of dispute. Kevin did not deny that he was sexually active with her, but made it very clear that he was away at football camp in

Montana most of that preceding summer when the baby was conceived and when he learned that she was pregnant, he broke up with her. The whole issue was messy in that Korinne's parents thought that Kevin was shirking his responsibilities, whereas Kevin and his family felt that Korinne was a promiscuous young girl and that someone else was the father.

"Regardless of the accusations, the fact remained that Chandler Craig was born in those days as a "bastard" child and no name was listed as the father on the birth certificate. When asked about other possible fathers, Kristine remembered her sister saying that it was some guy that she met at the Wyoming State Fair that summer. She never did know his last name, and it was a needle in a haystack to Kristine once Korinne was dead, so it was never pursued. The social service agency was thrilled when Kristine agreed to take Chandler in and raise him, although she admits that she never formally adopted him, because if she did, the agency would have stopped paying her as much money. Apparently long term foster care pays more than adoption."

Mac took a break from the information that Pam had sent and freshened up. She flushed the toilet once so that Hesta could hear her, and then continued reading the attachment to the second email that Pam had sent.

"I completed background checks on all five of your husbands. If Wyatt finds out, he will never forgive me so I'm letting it stand in writing that I protest on his behalf. Starting with him first, he has no criminal record. He was born in Sheridan and as you should know, still lives here. His prints are not in CODIS because he has never committed a crime and he has never applied for a license that requires fingerprints or a background check. He doesn't own a cell phone so I can't trace his phone records. He pays his taxes. He owns part of the ranch with his parents and the ranch house is paid off in full. He has one half-brother, Greg, who you should know well enough. I didn't check more into Greg because he is an asshole. Sorry boss. You married the right brother.

"Next in order was John Knotingham. His name sounds as snooty as his background check. Born in White Plains, New York. Raised in New York City. He has a criminal record–mostly drug related. He has never served time in jail. Arrests include possession of a controlled substance (felony) and possession with intent to sell (felony). Somehow he was able to go to rehab in lieu of prison. Money? He attended New York University and is listed on his Twitter as a writer. Not published, I might add. People who visit his Twitter, Facebook and LinkedIn page are mostly men. Gay? His mother is high society. His father is dead. He is an only child. Cannot find any contacts with the State of Wyoming or Colorado. Can't find any links to Chandler Craig, but still looking."

"Call me for the rest. I'm sleeping at the office."

Chapter 31

Mac walked out of the bathroom and into a den of wolves. Gardner Smiley sat perched on the windowsill ledge with an irksome look on his face. He was dressed in his customary dark suit and white shirt with his tie draped around his neck, untied. He was working on his double knot while Hesta wasted no time filling him in on Mac's theory of the case. Her entrance into the hospital room interrupted Hesta's discourse.

"When you told me that you needed to borrow a little office space," Gardiner Smiley said to Mac, "I naturally assumed that you needed a place to hang your hat for a few days and work on your cases in Wyoming. I never dreamed that you'd use the district attorney's office as your gateway to discovery on a rampant theory on the case wherein you are a percipient witness. Just wait until Sam Barakosh gets wind of this. He'll move for a mistrial, knowing him, and he'll try to get us both disbarred. Are you out of your mind?"

"I told you that I was going to poke around a little."

"I was under the distinct impression that you were playing catch up. Did you do anything on the DA website that would get us into trouble? What I'm asking is whether you accessed any of our databases for criminal records or things of that nature?"

"Not at all, Gardiner. I logged into my personal email through the internet explorer. That's all. I had my paralegal do her work from our computers at my office. I didn't even attempt to log into your system."

"Why are you so hell-bent on the idea that this is a murder-for-hire case? Just because some deranged serial killer tells you that he was hired to kill you doesn't mean that it's true."

"I know," Mac said, feeling embarrassed. "I just can't overlook it."

"One thing that I've learned over the years is that I have to pick a theory in a case and stick with it. Right now, I'm fighting the insanity plea. I think Chandler Craig is perfectly sane and simply a homicidal maniac. If you continue to pursue your theory, it would be very easy to confuse a jury and Sam might get an acquittal or a hung jury out of the case. Is that what you want?"

"Of course not," Mac said. "But if someone did hire him to kill one of us, I want to know that."

"More than you want him behind bars?" Gardiner said, cinching his tie closely to his neck.

"No. But how can I sleep at night if I think that one of our husbands was involved?"

"How can you sleep at night if this guy walks. If he walks, he will probably find you. He found Carolyn Patterson and she was one of the only links to his past. He found her and he killed her and he dismembered her body. Is that the kind of justice you are seeking for you and your friends, Mac? You survived a horrific ordeal and I'm sure that you are still in a state of shock. I certainly would be. But let's think this through clearly. If we can't settle on a theory and we confuse the jury with misleading ideas and this killer goes free, then who's going to protect you?"

"How could he possibly go free?" Mac asked. "You have five witnesses who can identify him and tell, in detail, what he did. That will certainly get you a conviction on kidnapping and aggravated assault with great bodily injury. Five counts each should put him away for a long time. This is not counting the notion that you can tie him to Carolyn Patterson and John Lee."

"What if the judge finds that he is not competent to stand trial?" Gardiner Smiley said.

"Then he gets the psychiatric help that he so much needs."

"Not necessarily true. He refused all psychiatric evaluation and medication as a minor. Why would he take advantage of it as an adult?"

"Because he would be placed in a lock-down psyche facility. He would have no choice in the matter," Mac said.

"Sure he would. He could refuse therapy and medication."

"The court can forcibly medicate him."

"Not without due process," Gardiner stated.

"The court can order milieu therapy in addition to medication and if he refuses, can find him in contempt of court."

"So what? If he is adjudicated incompetent, all they can do is tack on time to his sentence once he is found competent to stand trial–and even then, the same standard of proof applies, so a jury could still hang. In this state, a hung jury is tantamount to an acquittal. Taxpayers don't like us to try a case more than once."

"Not too confident of your trial abilities, are you?" Mac said flippantly.

"I'm very confident. I'm also savvy enough and seasoned enough to know not to thicken the plot beyond the average intelligence of humans. And my experience has shown me that the law of averages continues to decrease with each generation. Remember, Boulder is comprised of young people, many of whom are freedom oriented."

With that, Gardiner stood and walked toward the door. Mac was quiet for a minute, thinking of what he'd said.

"Bye, Hesta," he said to her. "I hope you are doing okay." Hesta waved to him and silently mouthed "okay."

He then turned to Mac and said, "And I'm glad to see that you showered. You'll make a better witness." He then flashed Mac an odd hand signal that she did not understand. The signal was a peace sign flashed first with the palm of his hand showing, and then he flipped his hand so that his palm and the peace sign were facing him.

* * *

Mac heard her cell phone ringing and walked over to answer it.

"It's not going to be as easy as I thought it would be," Patti said to Mac over the phone. "When I told the boys that I was divorcing their father,

176

they all got very angry with me. My middle son told me that I am selfish and am only thinking of what is best for me. He thinks that I should stick it out and go to counseling so that we can remain a family."

Mac walked out of Hesta's room and dashed down the hospital corridor towards Melanie's room. There was a 'no cell phone' policy in the hospital and so far, she'd broken it a dozen or more times already. She waved to Melanie as she entered her room and noticed that her friend had gotten out of bed and was dressed in street clothes. Mac pointed to the phone and mouthed the word "Patti" and continued talking.

"That is a normal reaction for kids. It is their own feeling of self-preservation that wants the family to stay together. He is at a very vulnerable age. Isn't he fourteen? Right in the middle of puberty and trying to figure out who he is in the world. Having his family break up in the middle of his inner turmoil is going to be very hard. He will probably act out and be fairly defiant."

"He is already the most defiant of the three boys," Patti said.

"They all might be a bit insolent at first."

"My oldest isn't. He seems to understand. He sees how much Bob has changed."

"He's one year shy of college and just that much more mature. Plus this might not affect his life as much as it does the younger two because he has more independence. This is all normal, Patti."

"I feel like I'm letting them down."

"Bob let them down."

"He will probably buy them nice things and they will still love him and resent me for screwing up their family."

"Who had the affair? You or Bob?"

"That won't matter to them."

"Well then focus on what is important to you. What do you want your boys to learn from this experience? Do you want them to treat their wives like Bob is treating you? Do you want them to think that they can walk all over the women in their lives and the women should just take it? The deal is, Patti, they might find that the women they date won't put up with that sort of nonsense and your boys will be stupefied when the girl breaks up with them because she wants to be treated with respect."

"I know. You're right. I just thought that this would be easier." "It's going to get a lot harder before it gets easier."

"I know," Patti said, her voice thickening with sobs.

"You don't have to get divorced, Patti. You can separate for a time and see if there is anything salvageable in the marriage. Have you talked with Bob about it?"

"No. He's in Sun Valley. Probably with *her*."

"Why the hurry in filing the papers then?"

"Because I'm angry and hurt and deflated and I want him to feel the same way I do. I want to see the shock on his face when he learns that I'm not going to take it anymore."

"Okay. I can understand that. You can have that. But remember, filing for divorce and going through with it aren't necessarily a matched pair. You have plenty of time to think things over. It's taken over twenty years for the two of you to build a life together and allow it to drift apart. You have time on your side to see if you can repair it."

"That means that once again, I swallow my pride and he wins."

"Not necessarily. It means that you are mature enough to at least consider what is best for you and your family. Divorce may end up being what is best. All I'm trying to say to you is that you don't have to decide today."

* * *

"Maybe you should be the counselor," Nicole said to Mac as they helped Melanie get dressed. "I didn't make it that far with Rema. She listened to my advice for about five minutes before she decided that she needed to be alone."

"Don't take it personally. No one gets in. She's kept us all at bay for years."

"No wonder Scott is on the lamb in the marriage. She's impenetrable."

"Speaking of impenetrable," Mac said to Nicole, knowing that her segue was inappropriate, "Hesta would like to speak with you."

As Nicole left and made her way down to Hesta's room, Mac helped Melanie button her shirt. "No over-the-head hemp shirts for you for awhile, huh?" Mac asked. Melanie was restricted from raising her arm up until the wound healed.

"Are you going home today?" Mac asked.

"Yes. I don't know what I'll find when I get there, but I know that Charlie and William will be happy to see me."

"I'm sure that they will. You are superwoman."

"Not to Michael."

"Yes, I think you are to Michael. That's probably why you intimidate him a little."

"Maybe. I've been thinking a lot about it. I'm going to work really hard on not being so super."

"Meaning?"

"I'm going to do what my mom told me to do. She said to make a bad meal every now and then so my good meals taste better. And I'm going to tell Michael when I screw up instead of covering it up and fixing it before he ever finds out about it. I'm not superwoman. I'm just a woman who loves her family and has a lot of energy."

Mac buttoned Mel's last button and pulled her in for a light hug, cognizant of the pain in her friend's shoulder. "Are you really willing to move so that Michael is happy?"

"Yes, I guess so. I hate the thought of it. I love my life, but if my husband hates our life, then I guess I shouldn't love it so much."

"You don't sound convinced."

"I'm not. I'm going to have to go home and try it all out for size. I need to tell him in person what I'm willing to do and see what his reaction is. I feel like there is more to the story than I know. He's never been that cold to me as he was on the phone. Something is up and I need to talk to him in person to figure it out. Having the boys around will ground me. They always have."

Mac zipped up her duffle bag and helped her off the bed. "My secretary Megan arranged for a driver to take to you to the airport."

"Thank you," Mel said.

"You will probably have to come back in a few days. It seems like the DA wants to push for a hearing on competency. He will probably need you to testify about your conversations with Chandler."

"I know. I'm prepared. Mr. Smiley stopped by early this morning."

"I'm torn," Mac said. "I really think that this man needs help, but he's been able to avoid help for eight years. If he's not going to get the help he needs in a lock-down psyche ward, then he needs to be in prison."

"That's your world, not mine."

"What do you mean?"

"I don't think that prison helps people," Melanie said with schoolgirl innocence.

"Even after a man shoved a knife into your shoulder–an injury that may preclude you from doing something you love for the rest of your life, you think that he should roam free so that he can perpetrate crimes on other innocent victims?"

"No. But I don't think he will get better no matter what. I think he is wired to hurt people."

"Why do you say that?" Mac had spent thousands of hours with her friends over the years, and it was fascinating to her that she was just getting to know them. "So you don't believe in rehabilitation of criminals?"

"No."

"What if the person had been abused and just needed intense counseling?"

"No."

"What if the person was an addict from heredity and just needed substance abuse therapy to keep them from committing drug-related offenses?"

"No."

"What is the purpose of our system, in your eyes?"

"To make people pay for the crimes they've committed."

"What if Charlie or William did something stupid, like a lot of teenagers do? Let's just say for conversation sake that William, when he is older, goes to a high school party and there are some cute girls there. One of the girls is someone that he has been crushing on for years. Of course, as his mother, he's never told you this stuff. Anyway, this girl starts mashing with him and after giving him the first blow job of his life, convinces him to pop a pill because it 'will be fun.' William is beside himself in puberty and pops a pill. This pill is Ecstasy. William is now high and has sex for the first time with this girl that he's been admiring for years. He is on a high of all highs.

She convinces him to take a swig of water, which is really vodka, and he swallows half of it before choking it up. He is now half drunk and high on "E" and it is curfew time. He knows that his mom will kick his butt if he breaks curfew so he drives home under the influence. He doesn't brake in time for the homeless Bay Area guy who is crossing the road in the dark against traffic signals and accidentally kills him. Should your son be locked up for life? Or, under you suggestion, does he walk free, getting no consequences, so the next time, he loads up on heroin and runs down a family of five in the minivan on their way to church?"

Melanie stared at her friend for some time. She felt like she was greeting a stranger. "I guess I will have to think about your hypothetical and get back to you after I've passed the bar exam."

With that, she hoisted her duffle over her right shoulder and made her way to the nurse's station.

Chapter 32

"Who says crime doesn't pay?" Mac said as she spoke to Pam on her cell phone while she watched Melanie leave the hospital. 'We all arrived five days ago with perfectly normal screwed up lives. We are all being discharged from a hospital a few days later with marriages on the brink of disaster and our bodies mutilated. I'm sure someone in Hell is having a good laugh."

Pam had a good sense of humor, which could be verified by many folks at the Mint Bar in downtown Sheridan, Wyoming, but she did not laugh at her boss's joke.

"Michael Dylan hasn't had a perfect record," Pam said with an air of authority. "Or to put it another way, I'm surprised that he was able to pass the moral turpitude portion of the California Bar Exam. I'm told that they are sticklers out there for ethics."

"They have to be. Can you imagine if they weren't?" Mac said. "So what news do you have about Michael that is so sultry?"

"Well, he has a criminal record. He was involved in a case of insurance fraud while he was in law school and he somehow managed to get his California law license anyway, which strikes me as odd. When I got my paralegal license, I was held to the same ethical standard as attorneys and they made me disclose every speeding ticket I've had, so I can't imagine how a person can defraud an insurance company and still get a license."

"Maybe it got cleared up somehow," Mac offered.

"I think someone got paid off."

"Pam, you do have a flair for drama."

"No, I'm serious. He was charged with filing a false insurance claim for a flood that happened to his apartment in law school. He claimed that all sorts of his stuff got water damaged and filed a claim for replacement value. Apparently his roommate found out and let the insurance company know that all of Michael's was in storage and that it was unharmed. That's pretty serious stuff."

"It is. But that was a long time ago and who knows what happened with the State Bar. Maybe they didn't catch it or something."

"Well," Pam said, "that is just the beginning. I'm not certain about the details, but it looks like he is currently under investigation for some ponzi scam. There is an indictment pending, according to my friend at the U.S. Attorney's Office."

Mac was shocked by the news. Michael had the aura of pristine ethics. Mac always thought of him as an extreme passive-aggressive, but not in the criminal sense. He usually had the demeanor that everything was under control.

"I wonder if Melanie knows about any of this. I would think she would mention it. She did say that he sounded very different and distant on the phone and kept saying that 'it was too late.' Maybe he was trying to convince her to move in order to get away from this problem." "It's not like the U.S. Attorney's Office wouldn't find him in a different state."

"Maybe he was just telling Mel that he wanted to move to a different state, but maybe he truly intended to leave the country. I knew an attorney a few years ago that got mixed up in a real estate tax scandal and in the middle of the night, he and his family vanished. His wife and two kids completely uprooted. Another attorney acquaintance of mine says that they moved to southern Spain because his parents were from there and he had family there that could hide them. I'm not sure if it is true, but it is a good way to dodge federal prison."

"He might want to fill in his wife before this gets much further. Maybe you should tell her so that she has time to think it over during her flight home."

Mac thought about it for a second. "How did you get the information if it isn't a matter of public record?"

"A friend of a friend. I can't mention names. But you don't have to tell her any of that. She's going to be focused on the issue, not the source."

"You don't know Melanie. She'll focus on the issue and the source and about twenty other things all at the same time. She'd want to know the source and if it turned out bogus, she would go ballistic."

"Do as you like. As a friend, I'd hedge my bets and tell, but that's just me."

"I'll think about it. What else do you have? You said that you have information on all five of the husbands."

"As for Patti, Bob Poeny has made some recent changes in his life. He's gone from a sixty thousand dollar salary a year to about a two million dollar income a year. The real estate market has boomed for him and he's not even associated with an agency. He's on his own. I don't know how he is able to get all the good listings, because usually the guys new in the business get all the low-end junk and the guys at the top of the heap get the best listings. Bob has managed to get some of the sweet properties up in the Sun Valley area and in the swankier parts of Boise. Nice houses on nice acreage. And if you look at the days on the market, his houses sell within thirty days or so of listing, so he's got something going on that is allowing him to get the good properties and get them sold fast."

"Pam, that's entrepreneurialism. In America, that's not illegal or unscrupulous. It is to be commended. He must have a good marketing system in place."

"Maybe, but I'm not so sure. Somehow all of his buyers are pre-qualified, and in today's mortgage world, that's not easy to do. I'm still looking into it, but something tells me that it is fishy."

"You are paranoid, but it makes you good at your job," Mac said.

"He is a member of three tennis clubs and a golf club and is involved in a lot of foundations and clubs."

"Part of marketing."

"And he has a mistress."

"Part of marketing."

"What?"

"Just kidding. Patti knows about the twenty-something ding-a-ling. She said that he's lost a lot of weight, got hair plugs or a transplant of some kind, and drives a two-seater sports car. Typical mid-lifer."

"He just bought a condo by one of the tennis clubs where he is a member. I'm sure it's going to be a rental. He wouldn't put his ding-a-ling in a nice condo conveniently located above the tennis club, would he?"

"Sarcasm. Paranoia. You are on fire today."

"I didn't get much sleep and I've cleaned out the office supply of Red Bulls."

"I bought a case last week."

"See what I mean?"

"So, you've covered everyone but Scott Setliff. Saving the best for last?"

"You know I've had a crush on him for a long time. Torques me off that you've never had the courtesy to get me an autograph."

"I'm working on it," Mac said as she took a long pull from her double latte that Nicole had the courtesy to deliver. She took a nibble of the lemon poppy seed muffin, realizing that for the first time in days, she was hungry.

Normally, she ran or swam every morning and stopped at a local coffee shop in Sheridan on her way to work. She missed her morning routine and missed getting exercise. She felt like she was still being kept prisoner and wanted nothing else than to strap on a pair of running shoes and go out for a run, but she hurt her Achilles tendon earlier in the year and was stuck swimming until it was completely healed. She was very tempted to give the tendon a try, just to get away from the hospital and sweat for an hour. She thought about how that might feel on her hands–which were throbbing constantly. Maybe if she held them up high when she ran, they wouldn't hurt so much.

"Are you listening to me?" Pam said.

"Oh. Yes. I'm sorry. I lost my train of thought for a minute. I was thinking about going out for some exercise. I'm a little stir crazy."

"I'm sure you are–knowing you and your inability to sit still for very long. The scoop on Scott Setliff will make you want to run–without the use of performance enhancement drugs," Pam said.

"What are you talking about? He never got charged with doping when he was in the NFL."

"I didn't say that he did, but when I tell you what he's being investigated for, you are going to be in shock. You know that 'friend of a friend' who told me about Michael's pending indictment with the U.S. Attorney's Office? Well, it is a coincidence, but federal and state agents are investigating Scott Setliff also."

"For what?"

"It all started out as a simple audit of his car dealerships. Apparently, one of his accountants was a whistle-blower and called the IRS to report suspicious activity. Scott has owned three dealerships in Colorado for nearly ten years, but about four years ago, the dealerships started losing money. He sells mostly big American-made SUVs, and with increased gas prices and the surge to promote 'green' lifestyles, sales for the SUVs dropped considerably. So, the dealerships took a huge loss a few years back. Well, the market hasn't changed much and the SUVs still aren't selling, but about two years ago, the dealerships were back in the black. The accountant told some investigators at the IRS that Scott was selling a lot of pimped out SUVs to professional athletes."

"That's not a crime, Pam. Most those guys have more money than they know what to do with, and their egos tend to be slightly inflated. They love those pimped out rides. One could argue that Scott capitalized on a market and that's good business."

"If that was all there was to it, then you are right, and at first that was how IRS agents felt about it. The athletes were paying ridiculous amounts of money for their jacked up vehicles, but it is free market enterprise and simple supply and demand. But one of the IRS agents who was assigned to the case was somewhat of a sports aficionado and studied the list of purchasers, finding a common denominator amongst Scott's clientele. The common denominator was suspected or confirmed use of performance enhancement drugs."

"Pam, most of them use the stuff in one form or another," Mac said. "It's standard operating procedure for most of the football players and body builders. They just keep finding better ways to hide it."

"Maybe. But the IRS agent is a purist of sorts and finds cheating to be appalling. Probably why he makes such a good IRS guy. So, the agent calls his buddy at the Attorney General's office and tells him what he knows and also what he suspects. The AG, who is up for reelection next year, has taken the case with gusto. The audit showed car sales to about seventy-five high profile professional athletes–mostly football players, but not exclusively. Some are professional baseball players, hockey, wrestling, track, cyclists . . . you name it. The deal is that they are all pretty well known and all performing extremely well in their last two seasons. None of them have tested positive for 'PEDs' as they call them, but some of them are highly suspicious characters."

"So they think Scott is pimping the cars with PEDs?" Mac said, with heavy sarcasm. "He's lining the dash with the drugs and they lick their car every day? Or he's designed an engine that runs on the stuff and these athletes huff on the exhaust?"

"Mac," Pam said, "this is serious."

"It's ridiculous. Sounds like an overzealous Attorney General hoping to get headlines for re-election. My advice is to be careful if your platform includes trying to take down many of America's heroes. Americans love their athletes, even if they are doping. It's strange, but true."

"It's not ridiculous if you would stop interrupting and let me finish," Pam said. "I've been working around the clock for forty-eight hours straight gathering more information than most private investigators can get in a month."

"I'm sorry," Mac said, drowning the rest of her coffee and filling her mouth with the muffin. "I'll listen," she said, with a muffled voice.

"My friend faxed me the first few pages of the indictment. It is eighty-seven pages in all. It contains multiple counts of drug trafficking charges as well as racketeering charges. I've promised not to show it to any other soul and to shred it after I saw it, which I will, sometime soon. It links Scott Setliff and the sale of these pimped up SUVs to the performance drugs. The indictment claims that on hundreds of occasions over the last several years, that he has hidden the drugs either in a secret compartment in the dash, or in hollowed out bumpers or other secret compartments under the back seat. The list of drugs is phenomenal. The indictments lists androstendione, methandriol, oxabolone, prasterone, androstane, zilpaterol, raloxifene, probenecide, and furosemide. Some of them are the more common steroids, but some of them are masking agents like diuretics and anti-estrogen therapy drugs.

"Apparently Scott has a connection in Canada and used his dealership to launder the money by importing the drugs, putting them in the car, and then jacking up the price by charging for upgrades that never happened.

Many of the athletes listed in the indictment are top performers. I only got the first few as listed. This is highly confidential. When the story breaks, it is going to be big time."

"Wow," is all Mac could manage, trying to swallow her huge bite. She walked down to the water fountain to get a drink of water to wash down the muffin. Still holding her cell phone to her ear she said, "How do you think this relates to Rema? Is she involved? Did she know about it? Did she find out and now Scott wants her dead?"

"That is what I don't know yet. It seems highly probable that Rema knew of the audit. They file a joint income tax return. Maybe she questioned him about the audit and did a little snooping on her own. Maybe the feds contacted her and gave her some type of immunity if she told them what she knew. I don't know much about spousal immunity, but I've seen it used on *Law and Order*."

"She's never mentioned it," Mac said.

"Maybe she's not supposed to. Or maybe she doesn't know. I have no idea, but what I do know is that this would definitely give a guy a reason to want to shut his wife up."

"Yes, it does," Mac agreed. "It is a reason to get her out of the picture. But think of all the thugs that Scott must know. So many of the NFL athletes are criminals otherwise engaged in a professional sport. Football is like a crime diversion program for some of them and the minute their careers are over, their crime sprees resume."

"Half of them don't wait until their careers are over to commit crimes," Pam said.

"Exactly. Scott must have many contacts with these sorts of guys. Why not have one of them, or one of the guys they know, do the job. Why Chandler Craig? How? How did they know each other?"

"That's the needle in the haystack, but I'm working on it," Pam said.

"What if Scott is Chandler's biological father?" Mac said, surprised that she hadn't thought of it before.

"What did you just say?" a voice boomed from the hospital corridor.

"Oh, God. I've got to go. Scott's here and I think he heard me. Call you back."

The line went dead.

Chapter 33

"What did you just say?" Scott's voice boomed down the hospital hallway. The nurse on duty at the nursing station rose to her feet and held her index finger to her lips suggesting that he quiet down.

Mac slid her cell phone into the front pocket of her blue jeans and started walking in the direction of Hesta's room. He followed her in.

"I asked you a question and I expect an answer." Scott's normally tanned face turned red with anger.

"What is going on?" Hesta said.

"This so-called friend of yours is trying to hang this on me."

"Hang what on you?" Hesta said.

"This stupid murder plot which doesn't even exist. Some freak goes crazy in the mountains and tells you that he's been hired to kill you and Mac somehow thinks that I'm the culprit," Scott said.

Hesta pushed the bed incline button and sat up. Mac could see her heart rate increasing on the monitor above Hesta's right shoulder. "Mac?" Hesta said.

Mac nervously grabbed a hold of her long auburn hair and twisted it into a knot at the nape of her neck.

"Mac? Do you think Scott is involved?"

"I just overheard her talking on her cell to someone. She was talking about me being the father of that creep."

"The *father*?" Hesta said. "I think you've got the wrong guy."

"How do you know?" Mac asked her friend in a defiant tone.

Hesta looked at Scott and then shrugged her shoulders. He nodded at her–as if they spoke in secret code. "Mac, Scott has been infertile for a very long time."

Mac was surprised by this assertion. "I thought that you wanted kids with Rema and the reason that you didn't have them was because of her running."

"That's what I told her," Scott said. "She wouldn't have understood the real reason."

Mac looked at Scott, who leaned against the wall near the door. He was wearing a blue button down shirt and tan pants, as if he had a business meeting to attend.

"You lied to your wife for all those years?"

"It is very complicated. You won't understand it any better than Rema would."

"Try me," Mac said.

"I don't have time right now. I have something I've got to take care of."

"Unfinished business?" Mac said, sardonically.

"None of *your* business, that's for sure," Scott said in an equally derisive tone as he walked out of the room.

Mac waited a few moments before she spoke to Hesta. "How long have you known this?"

"A long time. I know I should have said something but I was being selfish. The conversation would have naturally led to the fact that I knew something intimate about Rema's husband, and it would highlight a topic that I was not prepared to discuss. There is so much more to this story than I can ever explain. The history is as old as our friendship, and it is more complex than any novel that I could publish. If it weren't for the obvious, I would have slid the plot over to John so that he could write something worth publishing, but that would implicate me, and I've always been selfish. I'm very sorry. I know that I have let you and our friendship down."

"Hesta, I'm not here to judge you. And I'm sorry that you and Rema and Scott are involved in something that is not going to turn out well. I feel sorry for all of you to the extent that people are going to get hurt in this."

"Why do you think that Scott is Chandler Craig's father? That seems so 'left field' to me."

Mac walked over and poured a glass of water for her friend and offered it to her. She sat on the edge of her hospital bed and put her hand on Hesta's feet. "I don't have any real basis for my suspicion. It is just me being me. I hate it when I can't solve a problem and this is one of those fact patterns that has me baffled. Somehow, one of the five guys has to have some connection to this kid and that's the only thing that I can think of based on the fact that no father is named on his birth certificate."

"I think you are hunting down the wrong dog, or whatever that saying is."

"That dog won't hunt? Is that what you are saying?" Mac asked, a slight smile curving her lips.

"Yeah. Sorry. They have me doped up on something good. The pain down there," she said, pointing to her crotch, "is unbelievable."

"I can only imagine," Mac said. "I'm sorry."

Hesta nodded. "What I mean is that I don't believe that kid had any reason to torture us other than the fact that he loves to harm people. He's one of the Ted Bundy's of the world. No kid kills their neighbors without having a major screw loose. And then he tracked down the stepfather that he hated and killed him? And the mother of the woman he killed? This guy is a hunter." Hesta took another sip of water before proceeding. "And I certainly don't agree that Scott has anything to do with it."

"Then why was he in court? And why is he stalking me in this hospital, eavesdropping on my conversations? He's paranoid about something," Mac said, baiting Hesta to see if she knew anything about the car dealership indictment.

"He's paranoid because I've just told all of you that we are having an affair. He knows that there is going to be major fallout from it."

"What about his business? Is everything okay on that front?" Mac asked.

"As far as I know, his business is doing better than ever. He just renewed his contract with ESPN as a network sportscaster for this and next season and he says that car sales have improved some. He complains that he doesn't get the spokesperson contracts like he used to for sporting lines and food and that sort of thing, but he kind of expected that. The brand names tend to switch and get the younger guys to endorse products to capture a broader market, I guess. I see it in publishing all the time. So, if you are asking me whether he is financially stressed, I think that the answer is 'no.'"

"If he divorced Rema, would that change your opinion on his financial strength?"

"Absolutely. That's why he's never done it. She'd get half of everything, and I know that he doesn't like that idea very much. He just pays off her credit card and provides her with anything she wants and she seems to be happy enough. As long as she has the money to train and race, she doesn't seem to be very needy in the financial category."

"Is there any category that she is needy?" Mac asked.

"Not that I know. I don't think that she and Scott talk much at all and I don't think she puts any demands on his schedule, if that's what you mean. She doesn't insist that he come to any of her races and he is not part of her support crew on the trail. She hires the people she needs for that and Scott pays for whatever Adidas doesn't pay. She gets some stuff sponsored, but I don't think it is a lot. I think it frustrates her that she hasn't achieved Ironman status fame and fortune."

"Does Scott care if she does?"

"No. In all honesty, Mac, they are just friends as far as I can tell. And I don't think that either of them wants more than that."

"What about you, Hesta? What do you want from your relationship with Scott?"

Hesta was one of the toughest women Mac had ever known. She took the New York publishing world by storm and never let anyone push her around. Based on this, it took Mac by surprise to see her friend's eyes well up with tears.

"I love him."

Mac instinctively pulled her hand away from Hesta's feet.

"I thought you said that he was just a distraction. A good romp in the hay?"

"He was at first."

"And then?"

"It's been a lot of years. You grow accustomed to someone. He's the only consistent lover I've ever had."

"But he has other lovers."

"He used to. Not any more."

"And he's married. To your friend."

"He is filing for divorce. We've talked about it for a long time and we both finally agreed that life was too short and that we both needed to leave our spouses and move on together."

"Don't you think that it makes my theory more likely? You said he didn't divorce Rema in the past due to financial reasons. If he had her sniped, then he wouldn't have to deal with it."

"I'm trying not to be offended by this conversation, but as my therapist would say, you are obsessing about this murder-for-hire plot. It doesn't exist, Mac. How many ways can I tell you the same thing? Not to mention the fact that you keep implicating the man that I just admitted to being in love with."

Mac could think of nothing more to say. She couldn't possibly tell her friend about the federal indictment that was on a bullet train heading in the direction of the man that she just admitted to being in love with. She reached over and patted her friend on the leg.

"Have you told John?"

"Not exactly. I've tried to tell him so many times, but every time I try to talk to him about something serious, he changes the subject or walks away. Our lines of communication are on the analog dial."

"How will he take it?"

"I really don't think he cares, other than the financial part."

"I thought you said that you two have a prenup."

"Not exactly. I wish we did. When we got married, his mom made me sign this thing that said that I can't inherit any money from his trust account. I stupidly signed it. When I asked you about it, you told me that I wouldn't have the right to inherit from her estate anyway, so that the document didn't mean much."

"That's true."

"But had I been smarter, I would have insisted on a mutual prenuptial agreement, and that way, he wouldn't get any of my business."

"I wish I would have given you that advice. I never did estate planning and it wasn't my forte."

"Hindsight," Hesta said, rolling her eyes. Mac nodded.

"When do you get to go home?" Mac asked.

"It depends on what I decide about surgery. I still need to think about it."

"How long can you think about it? Is there a timeframe in which you need to act before scar tissue develops or something of that nature?"

"Yes. I need to have it done soon, but I want to get other medical opinions and I prefer to have it done in New York so that I can work when I'm recovering."

Mac nodded and gathered her duffle bag and purse. "I'm going to check into a hotel. I'll be back a little later."

"Can you please be happy for me?" Hesta asked.

Mac was a terrible liar, but managed nevertheless to give her friend a faint smile on the way out.

Chapter 34

Mac hadn't been checked into her hotel for five minutes before hastily tying the laces to her running shoes and gliding up the Boulder Creek Trail. Her hands were throbbing and her tendon felt a little tight, but the freedom of movement was worth it. It had been months since she'd allowed herself to run, hoping that the rest and acupuncture would cure her injury. Two miles up the trail she attained a steady and comfortable pace. When her cell phone rang, she was inclined to ignore the call. Noticing that it was from Gardiner Smiley, she fumbled with her bandaged hands to hit the right button after deciding that she should pick up.

"Where in the hell are you?" his voice boomed into the phone.

"Running. Why?"

"You'd better keep on running because you've created a nightmare for me at my office."

"Why?" Mac asked, slowing down to a jog.

"Someone in my office was talking with someone at the AG's and they said that you know about the indictment pending on Scott Setliff."

Mac was hesitant to respond. She sensed that it could be some kind of setup.

"You there?" he yelled. "Yes, I'm listening."

"Well?"

"Well, what?"

"What do you know?"

"I know the very basic allegations. Nothing more."

"Do you have any idea what this could do to the case or to my career? This indictment has been brewing for a year and it has required the use of dozens of special agents. The feds have gone to painstaking levels to get immunity agreements from some pretty high rolling folks for the testimony that is the basis for the indictment. When this thing hits, heads are going to roll. The fact that it could be leaked by you or someone in your office is of grave concern. I can't express to you how deep and how dangerous this whole thing is. People will go out of their way to make sure that you don't talk. It's that important. Am I clear?"

"No. Are you trying to tell me that I have a bull's eye on my back and that the feds might be willing to gun me down to ensure that their case isn't leaked? Because if that's what you are telling me, then I'm afraid that I'm on the wrong side of the law."

"I'm not saying that exactly, but I am telling you that careers are going to be made and broken from this deal. People have put their lives on the line doing undercover work on this. Keeping you quiet might be of importance to some of the guys posing as suppliers. Lives are at stake here. We were not planning to launch this thing for another week or two while agents confirm every single detail. If it leaks, then we have to launch prematurely, and that's not going to make some people very happy."

"Okay. What does *that* mean exactly?" Mac asked, slowing down to a walk, but looking over her shoulder in both directions.

"You were just talking to Scott Setliff at the hospital, were you not?"

"Yes. How did you know?"

"Because you are being tailed."

"By whom?"

"Local force at the direction of feds. What did you say to Scott?"

"I told him that I thought he was the father to Chandler Craig. He denied it."

"That's *all* you said?"

"Pretty much."

"What else?"

"That was the conversation. He overheard me talking to my paralegal–"

"Pam?" Gardiner interrupted.

"How'd you know her name?"

"She's in hot water. The person she spoke to at the AG's has already been terminated. Your paralegal has a copy of a document that is not for public consumption. They are on their way to your office in Sheridan now to retrieve it."

"Oh boy," Mac said. "Can I warn her?"

"Not officially."

"She's feisty. If she is bullied, she might fight back and get into serious trouble. Or hurt. This girl doesn't take crap from anyone."

"Then warn her, but tell her to fully cooperate, otherwise it won't go well. There could be an investigation into her ethics and she could lose her license. So could you."

"For what?" Mac said, raising her voice considerably. "I didn't do anything."

"You are her boss and you directed her to conduct an investigation regarding this ridiculous theory you have regarding the Chandler Craig matter."

"I didn't direct her to contact federal agents, but regardless of what I did or didn't tell her to do, I'm not throwing her under the bus."

"Mac, I'm on your side. I'm trying to help you. I need you to understand how crucial it is for you and Pam to cooperate and to not speak to anyone about this indictment."

"I got that much. I haven't told anyone. Are you sure that you're on my side, because your tone doesn't suggest it at the moment."

"Do you have a copy of the indictment?"

"No."

"Have you seen a copy of it?"

"No."

"How many pages does Pam have?"

"I don't know. I think she said seven or eight."

"Do you know what pages? Are there any names listed?"

"A few, but she didn't say whose."

"Are you sure?"

"Yes, Gardiner, I am sure. What difference does that make?"

"You have no idea. Have you told anyone about this?"

"I already answered that. No. I have not spoken to anyone about it."

"Not Hesta?"

"No."

"Are you sure?"

"Yes."

"Agents are there right now with her, so let me ask you this one more time. Are you sure you haven't told Hesta or anyone else about this?"

"Yes. I'm sure."

"Good. Then go back to your hotel as fast as your legs will take you. I'm sending someone over in about twenty minutes to get you. Be ready."

* * *

Melanie Dylan made the drive from the Oakland airport to Berkeley with a renewed sense of self. No longer did she cling to the idea that her life was perfect and that she had to keep the status quo for happiness and stability. Instead, she felt the purpose to live in a manner that allowed all four of them to be a happy family–together, no matter what. She could move her business. She did not like the idea of laying off her hard workers that had been with her for a decade, but if it meant keeping her family unit intact, then it was worth it.

She turned from Main Street to Arlington to Thousand Oaks Boulevard and came to a stop in her driveway on San Juan Road. She loved her

Thousand Oaks neighborhood just north of Berkeley–so close to San Francisco, yet so close to the educated elite of the UC. All walks of life lived among her and she enjoyed the fact that her children were educated in public schools along with some of the most diversely populated youth around.

Melanie parked her Volvo station wagon in the driveway of her two-story Tudor-style home and walked up the brick pathway to the front door. She could hear her golden retriever barking in the backyard as she approached and made a mental note to take him and the boys to Tilden Park over the weekend.

When she put her key in the lock, she was happily surprised to see both boys waiting at the front window for her. She opened the door and was greeted enthusiastically by Charlie and William. "Be careful boys," she quickly warned them. "Didn't Daddy tell you that my shoulder and my hand both got hurt on my trip?"

"Dad's not home," Charlie said with the authoritative voice of the oldest man in the house. It was Wednesday evening at nearly eight o'clock. Michael was always home from work by seven.

"Is Myra still here?" Melanie asked.

"No. She went home when Dad got home from work, but he had to go somewhere tonight and so Sammy is here."

"Oh. Okay. Well, you love Sammy. Is she playing checkers with you?"

"No. She's in the kitchen studying. She has a test tomorrow."

Melanie walked into the kitchen to find Samantha, their high school senior-date-night babysitter sitting at the granite counter studying Trigonometry. "Hi, Sammy. Big test tomorrow?"

Sammy looked up and nodded before looking back at her book. When it registered in her mind that Melanie had a sling on her arm and her hand in a large bandage, her head shot back up. "What happened?"

"A little accident up in the mountains. I'll be fine. Where is Michael?"

"I'm not sure. He called last minute and said that he had an emergency at work and asked for me to watch the boys. I told him that I couldn't because I have this huge test tomorrow, but he begged. I felt bad so I came, but I told him that I would have to study and the boys would have to watch a movie. He said it was okay. I hope that's okay with you."

"They are in good hands. Let's go upstairs, boys. Charlie, can you get my bag for me?"

The boys followed Melanie upstairs and into her bedroom. She looked at her queen-sized bed and grimaced at the fact that it had not been made that morning. Before she could make a snide remark under her breath, she reminded herself that she was home to make peace and that she was going to have to let go of some of her silly demands in order to have a happy family.

"William, honey, can you push down on the drain stopper and turn on the hot water in the tub, please?"

"Okay, mommy. Do you need a bath?"

"You two need a bath first."

"You mean in your tub?" they both said in unison. Melanie had redesigned her master suite a few months prior and had added a large Jacuzzi tub. The boys had begged to use it many times, but Melanie did not want the imported Italian travertine to get soap stains, so she'd cordoned the boys to their own bathroom.

"Sure. Why not."

"Yeah! Can we use bubble bath?" Charlie said with a sparkle in his eye.

"Sure."

"Mom, you should go on vacation more. You come home happy," Charlie said.

Melanie smiled at her adorable children who were scurrying to undress as quickly as they could. She loved seeing their slightly tanned little backs against the white of their bums. Soon their summer swimming tans would fade.

"You are going to have to be very careful climbing into the tub. I can't really help you much tonight. My arm has a boo-boo."

"Did you fall down?"

"No. Not really. I sort of bumped into something really sharp."

The beauty of children was that they were so easily distracted by the whim of something new. Impulse control was certainly not either of her boys' strong suits, and the thought of romping in mom's tub was much more exciting than talking about her injury.

"How much can I use?" William said as he dumped a cup full of suds into the bath.

"Oh, wow, that should do it," Melanie said, knowing that the jets would likely boil the bubbles to the ceiling. She'd be lucky if she could find the boys in the white froth. "Where did Daddy go?" she asked them once she got them both in the tub and they began rubbing shampoo into each other's hair.

"Work. He said that he would be gone for a long time."

"Like past your bedtime?"

"I don't know," Charlie said. "He took his suitcase that has wheels."

"Suitcase?" Melanie said out loud. She quickly stood and went to her husband's walk-in closet. Sure enough, his suitcase was gone and so were some of his clothes. Melanie had insisted on color-coding the entire his- and- hers walk-in, and it was quite easy to know if anything was out of place. She noted that a number of his business suits were missing, as well as shirts. She opened his underwear drawer to find that most of his boxers were gone. She quickly opened the hamper to see if the laundry had been piling up for days, which would account for the low volume of underwear, but the hamper was empty, except for a shirt and a pair of dark socks.

Melanie peeked around the closet door to check on the boys, who were happily playing in their giant bubble storm. She then darted to her nightstand to see if Michael had left her a note. He had not. She ran to the top of the staircase landing and leaned over to shout at Sammy to come upstairs for a moment.

"Where did Michael say he was going?" Mel asked.

"He didn't. He left you a note in the office downstairs."

"Can you watch the boys for a minute? I need to read the note."

Sammy took a deep breath and headed into Mel's bathroom. The stress from her examination was showing in her expression.

Melanie ran down the stairs, clutching her left elbow with her right hand. Her shoulder and her hand were both throbbing and she needed to take her pain medicine in the worst way. She was overdue in taking it but didn't dare before the drive home.

She saw the envelope sitting on the hemp-covered chair. She picked it up and read Michael's neatly printed note.

> "Dear Mel: Things have become rather complicated at work. I can't go into the details right now. Suffice it to say, I may find myself in a little bit of trouble. My intentions were good, but I may have done something that is going to get me into hot water with a few of my clients. After you read this, please burn it, because it could be used against me in a hearing. I love you and the boys very much. Please understand that I need to stay away for a few weeks until the dust clears. I am working on getting some things in place for our future, but can't discuss them yet. I am so sorry. I should have listened to you. Love, M"

Melanie read the note again and then took it with her to the kitchen. She turned on the gas burner from her Viking range and lit the note on fire. She quickly walked it over to her dual sink and turned on the faucet. She dropped the flaming note in and watched it disintegrate into ashes.

Chapter 35

Chandler Craig paced his cell, angry at himself for speaking to Dr. Grayson. Somehow, that pompous man had set him off. His plan was not to speak at all during the evaluation. When Chandler was undergoing the battery of psychiatric evaluations at the juvenile detention center, it was easy to set his chin to his chest and look upward toward the white coats. He never said one word during the twenty-some times they tried to elicit information from him. How could he have let Dr. Grayson get under his skin? The guy had a knack about him to incite Chandler. It was like Dr. Grayson was mocking him the entire time.

And why hadn't he been taken to the doctor's office for the interview? Isn't that what he'd been promised? He swore that Judge Brooks, "Mr. State-The-Law-One-Hundred-Times," had agreed to him being transported to the shrink's office for the interview.

Chandler was used to the way things worked in juvenile land, where kids were given some slack and were treated with respect. He was maddened to find himself in a world where he was treated like a common thief. He was better than the rest of these thugs that were housed around him. He was clever and resourceful and able to charm his way into the graces of the wardens at Juvi. What was wrong with the guards? They all seemed to hate their jobs.

Chandler looked forward to Wednesday's evaluation with Dr. Witt. He reminded himself to say nothing at all. The Fifth Amendment had been his friend for nine years. Remaining silent had worked well. Chandler was learning that the lies he was starting to tell "for the fun of it" were coming back to bite him. So, he decided to return to Plan A which was utilizing the Fifth Amendment and remaining silent. And, if he was transported to Dr. Witt's office, wherever that may be, he would employ Plan B.

* * *

"What a bunch of assholes," Pam said to Mac over the phone.

"Did you do as I asked?" Mac asked, while pacing the floor of her hotel room.

"Yes, I gave them the eight-page fax and showed them confirmation on the fax machine that it was all that I'd received. But that wasn't good enough for them. They rummaged through this entire office. I told them that they had no search warrant and no right, but I didn't call the police because you said not to."

"Thank you. We want to stay friends with the Attorney General."

"After you called, I called Chops to come over. He was having a beer at the Mint Bar. He kept them from tearing up the place too much. I think they might have if he wasn't here."

Chops was one of the guys who hung out at the Mint Bar and drove a rapped out Harley. He was huge and tattooed and willing to engage in a fight without much provocation.

"Probably a good call," Mac admitted.

"He said he would stick around for a while to make sure that they don't come back."

"I think we might be in some trouble, Pam, so I need you to do exactly as I ask. If the feds show up again, let them in and be courteous, but also let them know that they need to follow the law. I think that they are threatening to take away our licenses so we are going to need to watch what we do."

"Take away our licenses? On what basis?"

"Pam, you got your hands on a federal indictment before it was filed and served." Pam was quiet for a second. "Even in Wyoming, the law is the law."

"I'm sorry, Mac. I hope I didn't get you into trouble. I should have thought about it longer. I'm so used to getting my hands on what I need because I know practically everyone in the state."

"Your Polish connection is great. It makes for really fun Elks Club weddings, but when we are dealing with the law, we need to remember boundaries."

"What was that noise?" Pam asked.

"Oh. That must be Gardiner Smiley knocking on my hotel room door.

He's the District Attorney who tipped me off and allowed me to call you. He's completely freaked that this is going to go sideways and told me that he was going to come over and pick me up. I'll text you in a few minutes to let you know what I need you to do next. I have some new leads on the Chandler Craig case."

Mac pulled aside the curtain covering the window to her hotel room to make sure that it was the DA.

"Shit," she said, pushing the curtain closed as quickly as she could. She dove to the ground and crawled to the bathroom as a wave of gunshots fired into her hotel room.

"Mac," Pam shouted into the phone. "What's going on?"

Mac did not answer.

* * *

Michael drove to the airport and boarded a plane to Denver, as he had been instructed to do. He carried with him a briefcase full of documents per the instructions he'd been given. He was to exit the plane once it landed and proceed directly to the Southwest baggage claim west exit. There, he would meet his contact.

* * *

Mac scrambled to her feet once inside the hotel room bathroom and shut and locked the door behind her. She ended the call with Pam and dialed 9-1-1. She looked around to see if there was a way to escape, but it seemed as if the walls were closing in on her.

"9-1-1. State the nature of your emergency."

"I'm at the Quality Inn. A man is shooting at me in my hotel room."

"Where are you in the room?"

"Bathroom."

"Get into the bathtub with the door locked and stay down. Officers have been dispatched."

"I'm in the tub," Mac said.

"Good. Stay calm. Police will be there. What room are you in?"

"Two Fourteen."

"Can you describe the assailant?"

"Yes, but you might not believe me when I tell you who it is."

"Ma'am, we don't play games. Is this a prank call, because if it is, you will be charged."

"This is no prank," Mac whispered into the phone.

Another round of gunshot reverberated through the room.

"Ma'am, lay down in the tub. The porcelain will protect you. Stay calm and try to describe for me what your assailant looks like."

"Scott Setliff."

"He looks like the football player?"

"He is the football player," Mac said.

"Ma'am, it is a very serious violation to crank call emergency services."

"This is no joke!" Mac yelled. "He is shooting at me."

Chapter 36

John Knotingham was deeply detached from his wife's emotional side. This was due to the fact that he had rarely seen Hesta shed a tear, in addition to the fact that he did not care. He blamed Hesta for every curse in his life, as it was obviously her fault that he was unpublished and virtually unnoticed by New York's media circuit. Therefore, in fairness to John and his ability to safely place blame, he was completely taken off guard by Hesta's telephone call.

"Hello, John," she said, in a rather formal tone. "This is Hesta. I'm calling from the hospital in Boulder."

"Oh. Hello," John said. There was a brief pause in the conversation wherein John was unsure what to say. "Is–are–is everything okay?"

"Yes and no. Mostly no, actually," Hesta said. "I'm still in shock, I guess. We were at Mac's cabin in Colorado and this crazy guy attacked us and held us hostage. It was horrible. He tortured–"

"I saw it on the news," John said with a tone so flat that rocks could skip on it.

"Then why didn't you call me?"

"Uh, I, well, I wasn't sure that it was you."

"Why didn't you call anyway just to make sure that I was okay?"

"I tried, but I couldn't get through."

"I checked my logged calls, John, and your number wasn't among them."

There was a slight pause before John responded. "Well, obviously you are alive."

"Yeah, Husband of Twenty Years, I'm alive. You sound disappointed."

"I'm not disappointed, Hesta. I'm just wondering why you are calling *me*. Normally I'm the last person you would call."

"Oh, God. You've been talking to your mom today, haven't you? How many have you taken?"

"How many what?"

"Pills, John. Oxycontin. Paxil. Zyprexa."

"Fuck you."

"No, John. Fuck you. Are you loaded?"

"Since when do you care?"

"I care that you don't overdose. You mix the drugs and the booze and I'm afraid your heart is going to shut down."

"Like yours?"

Hesta felt the sting of the comment.

"John, there was a man at the cabin who tried to kill us. He told each of us that one of our husbands had hired him to kill one of us and it was up to us to persuade him that we were not it. Now I know that you and I aren't the quintessential married couple, but is it to the point where you are hiring a guy Bronx-style to kill me?"

"If I wanted that, it would have been done years ago."

"Exactly," Hesta said, before reflecting on the comment. "Do you know a guy by the name of Chandler Craig?"

"Never met him."

"Did you hire someone to kill me?"

"No. If I did that, then I'd have no way to get Setliff's cash."

"What?"

"If you were dead, Setliff wouldn't send me any more money."

"Scott sends you money?"

"Yes, princess. It is called blackmail. My trust fund ran dry a few months ago. Luckily, Setliff was willing to help me out. I do a few errands for him and he pays me on time with cash."

* * *

Pam heard the gunshots through Mac's phone before the line disconnected, so she quickly called the Boulder Police Department. They promised that dispatch had a unit responding. Pam insisted on backup. She then called the hotel manager and reported the incident. He promised that he would check into it, but claimed that he had not heard a thing.

"Typical," Pam said to herself. Chops, who was still sitting in the office looked up at Pam. "Sounded like about eight rounds were emptied into Mac's hotel room and the manager didn't hear a thing."

"Maybe he was paid not to hear," Chops said.

Pam considered that possibility. Her thoughts were interrupted by the phone ringing. She answered.

"This is Kristine Craig, the woman you came to see in Buffalo–" "Hi Kristine. How can I help you?"

"Remember when you told me that if I thought of anything else about the baby's father, to call you? Well, I hadn't done so in years, but I decided to go up into the attic and get down Korinne's box of keepsakes. I looked through them and I found a few letters that I had never seen before. They are from this lady in New York named Maria."

"What did the letters say?"

"Let me back up," Kristine said. "There were other letters too. One was from a kid named John. Now mind you, these letters are old and they are not dated and I'm not sure if they are in response to something Korinne did or said. She was a disturbed teenager if you ask me. I know that I'm her sister and I should defend her after all these years, but something about her was not right. She was a very angry child and she did mean things sometimes without much of a prompting. So it is entirely possible that she threatened this Maria person in some way. Korinne had a way of dredging up a fight."

"What did the letter from John say?"

"He said that he didn't remember her and had no idea what she was talking about and to leave him alone. His letter was short. There is only one letter from John."

"What about from Maria?"

"They were a bit more terse. I can copy them and send them to you if you want. They are handwritten and old–at least twenty years now–and hard to read in spots. I think the mice got into them a little. There was a hole chewed in the bottom of the box."

"Sure. Copies would be good. Can you give me an idea of what the letters were about?" Pam's patience were starting to stiffen.

"Korinne must have accused this John kid of being the father of the baby. Maria indicates in her letter than no son of hers would bother with some lowlife girl from nowhere. She said that her son was at some high class dude ranch in Wyoming and his whereabouts had been accounted for by the owners of the ranch. She threatened that if Korinne kept bothering them, that she would have the police investigate the matter."

"I take it that you never heard from Maria or John?" Pam asked.

"Not a word, but remember, Korinne lived with our parents at the time. They were both chronic alcoholics. I don't know whether Maria contacted my parents, but I can only imagine how my dad would have handled threats. He had a terrible temper. So did my mom, for that matter."

"Do the letters identify the dude ranch? There must be one hundred or more in this state."

"Back then dude ranches were few and far between. Deer Fork was the only one I remember, but the letters don't identify the name of the ranch."

"What else do the letters say?"

"Well, this Maria lady told Korinne to get an abortion and that she would pay for it. Of course, I don't know how Korinne responded, but she must have written back, and a subsequent letter must have enclosed a check because the letter references it and what the money is to be used for. I gather that Korinne cashed the check, based on the next letter in the chain. Maria stated that the money was supposed to be for an abortion and that since Korinne didn't use it for that purpose, that it was up to her to be responsible for the raising of a child. Maria continued to deny that her son had any involvement and told Korinne to never contact them again."

"Was that the end of it?"

"No. Korinne must have written back because there was one last letter, and it also must have had a check in it. The tone of the last letter sounds like she was agreeing to something. Maybe Korinne said that if she sent one last check, then Korinne would never contact them again. Like I said, I'm not sure because I don't have the benefit of both sides of the communication. But the last letter does reference another check, stating that it is the last one that would be sent and if Korinne ever contacted them again, she would contact authorities in Douglas, Wyoming and have Korinne charged with extortion."

"So that was the end of it, as far as you know?"

"I guess. Korinne had the baby and was killed shortly thereafter. That's all I know."

"Did Maria use her last name?"

"Yes. Knotingham."

Chapter 37

"Ted Bundy was the last serial killer to escape from a Colorado jail. Since then, we don't take any chances," Deputy Sheriff Dale said to Sam Barakosh.

"I'm not asking that my client go without police supervision. It is simply and patently unfair that my client has to be interviewed in a jail setting by a psychiatrist who is preparing a report for the most important hearing my client will ever face. How can the court rely on a report that is so biased toward the prosecution?"

"I don't make the rules, Sam. I just follow them. And ever since Ted Bundy broke loose and went on a killing spree, our state had a bad name for a long time, so the legislature in Colorado passed a law that all inmate psychiatric evaluations were conducted at the facility, and not at the professional's office."

"My client's due process rights are being violated."

"Take it up with the legislature."

"I don't have time. My client is going to go crazy when I tell him that he can't be transported. I told him that I'd make sure that it happened."

"You shouldn't promise your clients things you can't do. The law has been in place for a very long time. As long as I can remember, and I've been here almost seventeen years."

"I know," Sam said in despair. "I've done a fair number of these competency hearings, but none of my clients have ever requested that the interview be elsewhere, so I didn't think it was a big deal. I guess I should have figured it out before I made any promises to Chandler."

"Guess so," Dale said. His waistband radio barked a command. Dale unhooked the clip and pulled the two-way to his ear. "Shots fired at a downtown hotel," Dale said to Sam. "You're probably going to have a new client soon if they catch the guy. This town is not as safe as it used to be."

"No, it's not," Sam said, thinking about his own safety when he must deliver the bad news to Chandler Craig.

* * *

Laying flat in the bathtub as instructed by the 9-1-1 officer, Mac slipped her cell phone into the back pocket of her running shorts and zipped it closed. She had often joked with her running pals that a back pocket in running gear was a stupid idea. Her opinion now changed.

She heard the door to the bathroom turn and when the intruder discovered that it was locked, she felt the whiz of the bullet over her head. In rapid succession, she heard a second round of shots and then heard the door to the bathroom smash open.

"Get up," a voice commanded. Mac looked up to see the crazed eyes of Scott Setliff standing over her holding a pistol. "Stand," he ordered. She obeyed, pushing herself up gingerly with her bandaged and throbbing hands. "Come with me. We're going for a ride."

"Scott, please don't do this," Mac begged. "This is only going to get you into more trouble."

"Shut up. I have a big problem with you and your stupid office worker digging into my past. Once the two of you are gone, it's going to be business as usual."

"This has nothing to do with me or Pam, Scott. They were on to you before we ever did anything."

"Yeah, right. You expect me to believe that? All fingers point to you."

Scott grabbed Mac by the elbow and rubbed the nose of the gun into the small of her back while leading her out of the hotel room and through the hallway of the second story of the hotel.

"Scott, please."

"I told you to shut up. Now we are going to walk to the back stairs. You will be perfectly quiet. You will get in the car without a sound. If you don't, you will die. It is very simple."

Mac could not believe her luck. She'd survived a serial killer and now she was about to be kidnapped by a football star gone mad. She thought of running, but was fairly certain that he'd shoot her. If she complied and got into the car, it was likely that she'd never be seen again.

She chose to take a ride, hoping that help was on its way.

* * *

"Well, I'll be damned if it ain't the tallest guy on the force," Nederland Marshall Pat Redley said to Dale, who was manning the intake desk Friday afternoon at the jail. Dale picked up overtime shifts whenever he was able so that he could fund his daughter's college tuition.

"Red," Dale responded. "What brings you down the mountain?"

"Cabin Killer," Red said. "I had to file my report before the case is heard on Friday. Hey, did you hear the gunshot call over the two-way?" Dale nodded, patting his radio. "Heard it is that Mary MacIntosh lady. Same one that was at the Kilkenny-Kerry. Something fishy is going on with her."

"How'd you hear that?"

"There was a back up call for extra officer support. Two collaborating 9-1-1 calls. One was from her secretary, I guess, or something to that effect. Suspect was described as Scott Setliff."

"Football player?"

"Yep."

"That's weird," Dale said.

"What's really weird is that Setliff's wife was at the cabin with the MacIntosh lady," Red said. "Glad that it is out of my jurisdiction. It's going to be enough trouble if I get called to testify at the Cabin Killer case. I hate being in a courtroom."

"You hate being inside," Dale said to Red.

"That's right. The way I see it, I can either be fly fishin' on a nice peaceful stream, or I can be sitting for hours or days waiting to be called as a witness. I think the former is a better use of my natural resources."

Dale smiled at his old friend, noting that Red had not changed much since the days they served together on the force.

* * *

"The District Attorney knows your involvement with the performance enhancement drugs," Mac said to Scott Setliff on the way to his car. "He warned me that you were out to get me, so they will be looking for you right away."

"I told you to clam it."

"If you stop this right now, maybe you can work out a deal for yourself. I won't press charges, I promise. You can work out a plea with the DA and your life won't be forever ruined."

"I never wanted it to get to this point, Mac, and I'm truly sorry that you are involved for Rema's sake, but now you are and I have to protect myself."

"By harming me, Scott? Do you really think that's going to help? I heard about the indictment that the Attorney General is filing. Do you want them to add kidnapping to the RICO and drug trafficking allegations?"

"The indictment is a scam."

"A scam? Scott, the AG's office doesn't scam people. It's for real."

"It was a scam for you."

"Now I think you are suffering from delusions. Do you really believe this? Why would the AG's office prepare an eighty-something page indictment to scam me? I'm an officer of the court. What difference does it make to me how you run your car dealership and whether you run a steroid business on the side?"

"It was Gardiner Smiley's idea to throw you off."

"Throw me off from what, Scott? I am completely confused. The DA is trying to throw me off by creating an AG indictment which, the minute it gets into my paralegal's hands, the DA goes nuts? That makes no sense."

"Then he was right. He is smarter than you."

"Maybe he is, Scott. But that doesn't explain a lot of stuff."

"He can do the explaining. I'm just supposed to deliver you alive."

"I guess that's supposed to be some kind of relief. Where are you taking me?"

"To meet some of our friends. I will allow you to sit in the front seat with your hands tied behind your back so long as you behave. If you make a single gesture to anyone that we pass along the way, you will be transferred to the trunk. Ever ridden in the trunk of a Corvette?"

"Can't say I have."

"Then keep it that way."

Chapter 38

Rema had charged twenty-three miles up the canyon before deciding to turn around and head back to Boulder. A forty-six mile run would be a good day, she decided. She had missed two full days of running while being held by the weirdo at the cabin and there was no way that she'd get the new Adidas sponsorship unless she won the Pike's Peak race. Good, hard training was in order. And, she thought that if the media outside the hospital saw her running, that perhaps Adidas or Nike might see a clip and recognize her dedication to the sport.

As she rounded back down the mountain following the roadside trail, she thought of her girlfriends and what they had endured together. Maybe she needed more time with humans and less time alone. Obviously, running away from her marriage full time hadn't brought her much happiness. The most joy she'd felt in the last year was the few moments the women had together at the Kilkenny-Kerry before the maniac arrived. She wished that she had enjoyed that time more–taken it all in and absorbed it. At the time, she was feeling guilty for having a margarita and for eating food that wouldn't agree with her digestive tract for training. Did life have to be all about taking care of business? Isn't some business in life to take care of oneself? One's friendships? One's loved ones?

Rema had been extremely remiss in her efforts to serve others. She wasn't there for her sister when she was sick with breast cancer. She barely showed up for her mom when she was dying of uterine cancer. At her mother's funeral, Rema could easily have volunteered to help her sister with the kids while she underwent chemotherapy, but the kids were seven and nine, and how would she get her long runs in? They didn't fit in a baby jogger anymore and they were too whiny to ride a bike alongside her.

Rema recounted her selfish ways while merging from the trail back to the road that led into Boulder. As she crossed over, she saw Red's official car en route. She waved to him and he pulled to the side of the narrow canyon road.

"Hey you! Aren't you one of the ladies from the cabin? Scott Setliff's wife?" Red asked.

Rema could only grimace at the thought of being associated with her asshole of a husband.

"Yes. In name only," Rema added, more to make herself feel better than anything else.

"There's been a report that your husband has fired shots at your friend Mary MacIntosh at the Quality Inn Hotel. Heard it on the two-way. Hop in and I'll drive you there."

Rema agreed and scurried her sweaty and tired body into his car. "Scott is such a fucking prick. If he hurts my friend, I'm going to personally kill the son-of-a-bitch." Rema was surprised by her own language. She'd never talked this way before.

"Don't blame you," Red said.

After talking about Mac's situation and her marriage for a bit, she turned and asked, "Got anything to eat? You guys always have food in here."

Red motioned toward the glove box where she found beef jerky, granola bars and a cup-o-soup container. All contents shifted to the right as Red flipped a U-turn and headed back into Boulder.

* * *

Pam called the Boulder police for the seventh time in ten minutes. They assured her that officers had been dispatched, but there was no word from the force. Pam's anxiety grew exponentially, as Mac had not called her back and the police could not give her any more details about the situation.

Next, she called her friend who had sent her the few pages of the proposed indictment. When she learned that her friend had not lost her job, and that she was not in any trouble, Pam's blood pressure rose.

Pam made a few more calls to her connections throughout the state. It was possible that she knew half of the people who lived in Wyoming. She'd grown up in Sheridan, as had her parents and her parents' parents. They were both from large families and their respective brothers and sisters had filtered out into other small towns. Eventually, Pam had uncles, aunts, cousins, nieces and nephews in just about every part of Wyoming. And each of these people knew of a friend of a friend. It is what made Pam so good at her job.

So when she called her friend whose boyfriend had been a guard at Juvi when Chandler was there, it was not impossible to ascertain that Chandler had only one visitor during the entire time that he lived at the detention facility. What was interesting was that the visitor was a woman.

Kristine Craig said that she had never visited Chandler. As much as she had wanted to, she couldn't bring herself to do it. The boy had destroyed two of her marriages and she was afraid to expose him further to her natural born children. She felt that she needed to sever the ties with this kid. He was a bad apple.

There were no other family members connected to Chandler. Chandler's mother was dead. Chandler's grandmother on his mother's side was a blackout drunk who died of sclerosis when Chandler was thirteen. He was a ward of the State. He was alone in this world.

Pam pressed on for information. In order to visit anyone at a lockdown facility, an application had to be made. The applicant had to pass certain security pre-screening in order to get permission to visit. Only one woman had made such an application, and it had been very recent. The application revealed that she was related by blood to Chandler. In fact, she was his paternal grandmother.

* * *

Red turned the volume on his radio higher so that he could better hear the communications of the Boulder Police Department. An APB had been issued for a red Chevrolet Corvette with Colorado plates belonging to Scott Setliff. It had last been seen heading southwest on Highway 36.

"He's heading to Denver," Rema said.

"How do you know?" asked Red.

"I just know. His dealerships are there. Our house is there. His asshole business guys are there. He knows the city well. My bet is that he'll go to the Arvada dealership. That's where he spends most of his time."

"I know a shortcut. I can take the 93 to the 72. Are you sure that's where he'll go?"

"I'm not sure of anything right now, Red, but it is my best guess."

"Let's try to cut him off at the pass."

Rema shoved another granola bar into her mouth and then pulled the lip off the Cup-O-Noodles and started eating the dry noodles raw out of the container.

"You have weird eating habits," Red said. "Most people add hot water to those things."

"Do you have any hot water?"

"No."

"Then what's your point?" Rema joked.

Red knew full well that there wasn't a woman on the planet that he truly understood and had long ago resigned himself to simply focus on the task at hand. Presently, his task was to find a red Corvette and pray that Mac was inside it and alive.

* * *

Michael's flight landed in Denver on time and the stiff in the unmarked white car was waiting for him where they had agreed. Michael carried a briefcase full of the information that had been requested. He left a copy of the documents at home in the room over the garage. Michael left a note to Melanie under her pillow that read, "If something happens to me, you'll find the answers where the sun don't shine."

Anyone else reading the note would think it a rude way to address one's wife. Melanie would know exactly what he meant. When they bought the house, Melanie wanted the downstairs room as a music and art room for the children. She intended to have a grand piano as the focal point of the room and ensure that her boys were well versed in the arts. She wanted to convert the room over the garage into Michael's home office so that he would have a quiet place to work on evenings and weekends if need be, and his work wouldn't disrupt the home, and the children wouldn't disrupt his work.

When Michael and Mel entered the room above the garage, they turned on the overhead bulb and each looked at one another and at the exact same time said, "This is where the sun don't shine." At the moment, they both laughed hysterically, as they often said the same thing at the same time or had the same thought simultaneously. Being that the comment was so off kilter, they both remarked at their silliness and how much they thought alike. The room was dark and the only window faced west, so by the time that the sun got to that side of the house, it was blocked by the large ficus trees. They both knew that Michael could not work in a dingy room and, instead, made the garage room a playroom, allowing Michael's office to be in the east wing of the house.

Michael thought of that moment in time as he greeted the man wearing the black suit and dark red tie. "This way sir," the man said. "The name is James and we will be driving downtown today."

Michael had never been to what he believed was the federal building in downtown Denver and upon arrival, was surprised by its grandeur. He walked through the high arch doors and through security before climbing the marble staircase to the second floor. "This place is very nice," Michael said to James in an effort at polite conversation. "Feds pour a ton of dough into their buildings. The state buildings are all falling apart. Guess it pays to be at the top."

James nodded.

Michael did not feel like he was at the top at the moment—the only thing that he could feel was his nervous stomach acting up. Had he done the right thing by contacting authorities? He had never thought of himself as the whistle-blower type, but under the circumstances, he could not get his client to listen to the voice of reason, and if Michael didn't make the call, and the client's business was audited, Michael's neck would be on the line. It wasn't worth losing his law practice and his license to practice over one client–albeit, a well-paying, long-time client.

When he entered the large conference room, he was surprised to see how many people were there, all very busy speaking on their cell phones. Michael overheard more than one conversation and the theme seemed to be the same. "Can you guarantee confirmation of the source?" It appeared to Michael that something was about to launch and that the agents were covering their bases.

James escorted Michael past the men in suits and introduced him to a man who, coincidentally, had the name of Michael. The men exchanged pleasantries before the federal agent got down to business.

"Tell me exactly how you came to be a tax advisor to Scott Setliff?"

Michael explained the details of their wives being friends in college and that at one of their weddings–he thought it was Hesta's–Scott told him that his NFL career was nearly over and that he was looking into buying a car dealership to supplement his income. Michael, being a young associate attorney at a big firm, scampered at the idea of having a big name client in his book of business. He hastily agreed and helped structure a number of partnerships and limited liability agreements between Scott and some other capital sources. As time went on, the equity partners changed from time to time, and new agreements were drafted. Different tax laws changed allowing for new structuring, and every step of the way, Michael worked with a number of other attorneys to ensure that Scott's businesses had the best tax status possible.

"So, did something change?" the federal agent asked. "What prompted you to call us?"

"I'm not an accountant and I never analyzed the books as if I was his accountant, but in the sense that I was responsible for tax structuring, I had to be able to make sense of the numbers. As I delved a little deeper into the figures last year, I noticed that car sales were way down and that for a period of time, the books reflected this. But suddenly, things changed. The volume of cars did not significantly increase, but what did increase was the sales price for some of these cars. Now, in a time of economic downturn, most folks are looking for a bargain and certainly don't pay above market for cars. I poked around, called his corporate office asking for supplemental documents—and of course, as his long-standing attorney—they were provided to me without question. It didn't take long to digest the fact that the same folks—professional athletes almost exclusively—were buying cars at inflated prices. Now, I know that most of these guys have too much money on their hands and love to brag about punking their rides and all that garbage, so it didn't jump out at me at first. But I have always had that sixth sense about things and I knew that something was wrong, and I didn't want to be associated with it.

"I had been asked over the years by Scott and some of his financial advisors to structure deals that would be highly beneficial for Scott, but were, in my opinion, not congruent with tax law and corporate holdings. I'm very conservative by nature, and I won't touch anything out of my ethical comfort zone, but it appeared to me that this was the goal of his financial team. I decided to pay a surprise visit to his Arvada shop about six months ago, since this was the location where all of the high priced cars were inventoried. What I saw blew me away. On the back wall to the body shop, there was a shelving unit. It looked like any other parts shelf, but when I came in unannounced, the shelving unit was pulled open away from the wall. It was like a hidden room in there. In the room were vials upon vials of stuff. It took me a minute to figure out what the names on the boxes stood for. I'd never heard of drugs such as oxymetholone or mesterotone. I typed as many as I could into my Blackberry to research later. I figured that they were barbiturates or stimulants or some other street drug, which freaked me out of course. I saw them stuffing vials of stuff into compartments of the cars. I slowly backed out of there unnoticed and caught the first flight back home.

"I told my law partner about what I'd seen. We'd started out as associates together and he'd always been jealous about this great NFL client that I had. When the two of us researched the names of the drugs and figured out that they were prohibited performance enhancement drugs, we were shocked and disappointed at first. And then we were scared. I was particularly worried that someone had seen me there. My partner was worried that our firm would be associated somehow with the trafficking of these drugs. My partner and I were both worried about being disbarred by the State of California for involvement in such a ring. We both agreed that it needed to be reported. So, I called the ethics hotline for the California State Bar and explained the situation to them without mentioning names. I was told that I could expect a return telephone call the next day. I did get that call the next day and the man on the other end of the phone was very insistent that I be forthcoming with the alleged perpetrators of the fraud and my precise knowledge. I complied, at the behest of my partner. We turned over some evidence and agreed to have a meeting in Sacramento. My partner and I both met with state and federal people about what was going on. I turned over the list of names of other professional athletes that had been identified as purchasers of these cars and then I agreed to do something that I was terribly uncomfortable with."

"What was that?" the federal agent pressed.

"I agreed to carry on representing Scott Setliff and act as if I knew nothing. I agreed to gather as much evidence as I could against my client and turn it over to the feds. I've done everything that has been asked of me. But all the while, I've been terrified for the safety of my family."

Chapter 39

"Why didn't you tell me, Pam? Oh my God!" Wyatt said, shouting into the phone that had been recently installed in the barn.

"She said that you knew."

"When she called, it was from her cell phone and I could hardly make it out. She said something about her car being impounded and that she wouldn't be home for a few more days. She said her hands hurt and that was about all I could figure out from our broken line."

"Wyatt, your wife and her friends were held hostage in the cabin. They were tortured and maimed. Mac's hands were nailed to a bedpost. The man who did it hid her car at another cabin where he'd killed two other people. They were searching her car for evidence."

"Is she still in the hospital? She doesn't answer her cell."

"No. She was released and she got a hotel room so that she could be in Boulder for the killer's continued arraignment hearing and to be with her friends who were badly hurt. Her hotel room was gunned down and she was kidnapped and no one knows where she is."

"Shit. You should have called me Pam. You've known about this for days and you didn't call."

"I thought you knew and that you were too busy. She said that she asked you to come to Boulder to be with her and that you said that you were too busy with the ranch."

"I'm never to busy for her. I would never have allowed this to happen. If I had gone there Monday, she would be safe. Oh my God. What do I do?"

"Either you get your ass in a truck and drive like a bat out of hell to Boulder, which will take you seven hours, or call your dad's nutty friend and ask him to fly you there."

"I'll call Stu. If he's reasonably sober, I'll let him fly me."

"You hate airplanes, Wyatt. Mac says that you won't take any trips with her because you hate to fly."

"I do hate to fly. But she's my wife."

And she suspected you of being involved in this, Pam thought to herself. *My boss is an idiot.*

* * *

Mac's legal secretary, Megan, walked into Mac's law office on time and perky, as usual. When Pam filled her in on what had taken place over the past fifteen hours, Megan's demeanor plummeted like a rock sinking in a lake.

"How can I help?" Megan asked.

"I need to figure out who visited Chandler Craig while he was at the detention center in Casper. I have a pretty good idea of who it is and I've narrowed it down to two people." Pam said. "Here are their names," she said, handing Megan a yellow sticky note. "Here is the number of a guard there. Mention my name and hopefully he will help you."

Megan dashed to her desk and got busy dialing. If there was one thing Megan was great at—it was sweet talking on the phone. The minute Megan picked up her line, the back line started ringing. Pam picked it up to find a frantic Melanie on the line.

"Where is Mac?" Melanie asked. "She doesn't answer her phone and she doesn't pick up my pages at the hospital?"

Pam filled her in.

"Oh God. Scott? So it was him. Have they found them? Is Mac okay?"

"Doubtful. I heard at least six gunshots. I called 9-1-1 and they swear that officers have been dispatched. Wyatt is on the way. She was supposed to be meeting Gardiner Smiley."

"That's weird, because Gardiner Smiley called my house this afternoon and left a message on my answering machine looking for Michael. Now Michael has disappeared."

Pam shook her head. "I'm confused. How does the District Attorney know Michael?"

"I don't know." Melanie said. She thought about it for a moment and then said, "Michael did legal work for Scott."

"You're kidding, right?" Pam said.

"No. He's been a client for years, but I have no idea what that has to do with the DA."

"Me either. I'll call you if I hear anything. Call me if you hear from Michael."

She promised that she would.

Pam hung up and started making a flowchart like Mac had taught her to do when trying to figure something out. She charted all the people that could possibly be involved based on what she knew, drawing arrows to connect certain persons with motive. As she contemplated all the issues, Megan interrupted her thoughts.

"Maria Knotingham."

Pam looked up at Megan, whose five foot petite frame stood over Pam's desk. Megan's spiked blond hair stood on end and her large blue eyes flew wide with excitement. Pam took the sticky note from her and gave her a thumbs up sign. "If John's mom visited Chandler Craig, that confirms that John is probably Chandler's father." Pam drew a line from John to Chandler on her flow chart. "Why would John want his wife dead?"

"Money," Megan said without hesitation. "Or love. But my bet is money."

Pam nodded. "I have another number I need you to call. It's Mac's private investigator. He can find out financials on anyone. Have him pull recent financials on both Maria and John Knotingham. Also, have him find out if Hesta had a life insurance policy and who the named beneficiary is."

Megan saluted and marched back to the phone. She had adrenaline flowing through her veins. And a lot of strong coffee.

* * *

Michael had spent hours discussing over and over again the situation at Scott Setliff's Arvada car dealership. The agents grilled him about each person who was there in such detail that he felt like he was the criminal in an interrogation room. Next came the document review, where they sat and painstakingly went through each entry regarding profit and loss centers for the dealership and franchise. After the fifth hour, he asked to use the restroom.

"Sure," James said. "Leave your cell phone here with the team. I will escort you."

"You think I'm going to take off?" Michael said in an accusatory manner.

"Relax," James said. "We just want to make sure that you are safe."

"Am I safe?" Michael asked. He knew that it was a rhetorical question, as they weren't going to answer in the negative, but the thought had crossed his mind that he really didn't know who these people were, and for all he knew, he was part of the sting–or worse, part of the reverse-sting.

* * *

Melanie got the boys out of the bath and they quietly watched a movie. Her bones ached from exhaustion. She was too wired and nervous to sleep, but she needed to lie down just for a minute. She gingerly slid onto her bed, pulling her second pillow out to rest her elbow. Her shoulder wound was aching terribly. She pushed her top pillow up so that her neck was comfortable and in doing so, she saw a piece of paper. She sat up and quickly pulled it open. It was a note from Michael. All it said was: "If something happens to me, you'll find the answers where the sun don't shine."

Melanie rose in an instant and dashed to the room above the garage, stopping momentarily in the kitchen to grab a flashlight and keys.

Chapter 40

The pain shooting up Mac's arms was something she could not endure much longer. She could feel the wetness around her wounds, meaning that they had begun to bleed again. Scott had bound her hands behind her back and strapped her into the front seat of his car. Not long after traveling south on Highway 36, he pulled off on the Bloomfield exit and continued into a remote area, and after a few minutes of driving, he pulled over and stopped the car. He walked around the back, lifted the trunk, and then walked to the passenger side. It was in this precise moment, Mac knew that she was soon to be dead.

Mac was confident that Scott was going to walk her into the cow pasture and pull the trigger. She assumed that he had a shovel in his trunk to bury her body, and a plastic bag to dispose of any evidence.

She felt the sting of the tears rolling down her cheeks and incredibly, for that split second in time, the pain in her body left her. She chose to see the beauty of the mountains one last time and to appreciate the love of the sun shining brightly on the Flatirons. The rolling hills were very green and there were black cows grazing in the pasture. She thought of the smell of freshly cut grass—one of her favorite things—and imagined that she could inhale it. She saw imagery of her majestic and loveable cat, Ted, who was so much more of a dog than a cat. She imagined her four friends, happy and laughing at the Kilkenny-Kerry, before the maniac arrived. And then she thought of Wyatt—her sweet, cowboy husband who had never harmed a creature in his life. How could she have even considered that he would have harmed her? A pang of guilt overwhelmed her and then she instantaneously quashed it, knowing that her last thoughts must be of positive things.

When Scott opened the passenger door, she expected to see his gun in his hand. He reached in, unbuckled her seatbelt, and pulled her loose from the seat. She had a vision of biting him in the shoulder, kicking him in the groin, and then running for help, but she knew that he would run her down and kill her if she did. *What difference did it make at this point?*

To her great astonishment, he did not walk her into the field, but instead shoved her into the trunk of the car and hastily sped off. Her shoulder hurt from the impact and her legs were skewed at odd angles, but, for the grace of a higher being, she was still alive.

With her hands bound behind her back, she was still able to reach the back zipper pocket of her running short. Mac pulled out the phone and tried to figure out which was the top end and which was the bottom. The charger end was at the top of her iPhone, so when she found it, she could picture in her mind what the screen looked like. The wonderful thing about touch screen technology was that if you were looking at the screen, you could touch it. Blind, as she was at the moment vis-à-vis the phone, she had no idea what she was touching. She racked her brain trying to remember what the initial screen looked like and what area to hit to get to the phone, but it was no use.

Her body rattled around with each bump the Corvette endured, and it was hard enough just to keep the phone in her hands.

"*That's it,*" Mac said to herself out loud. She decided that she needed to slide the phone under her waist up her chest and to her chin. If she could see the screen, she could touch it with her nose or her tongue, and she could dial for help.

If only it was that easy. Mac found out that it was not.

* * *

Wyatt truly hated to fly, and the worst possible scenario for him was the single engine prop. Nevertheless, he was sitting as the co-pilot, next to his hopefully sober friend Stu, and together they had a flight plan to Boulder's executive airport.

"Goin' to be a bit bumpy. Winds are from the north," Stu said.

"Great," Wyatt replied. "I have motion sickness."

"How can a guy like you get sick from a few bumps? You ride bucking broncos all day long. That's a whole lot rougher than this."

"It's different," Wyatt said. "I can control the horse."

Stu laughed. "Maybe if you do the flyin' you'll feel better. He let go of the wheel and motioned to Wyatt to grab the controls.

"Not funny, Stu. Take the controls," Wyatt said angrily.

"Okay, big boy. Settle down. I'm used to flyin' your old man around and he likes to fly the plane."

"I'm not my dad."

"Obviously."

"Can we talk about something else?" Wyatt asked.

"Sure. What'dya have in mind?"

"Why did you divorce your wife," Wyatt asked.

* * *

"We're coming up on the 72," Rema said to Red.

"I see that. Lived here all my life. I know these parts like the back of my hand. And, with the modern era of signs, I can read." Out of the corner of his eye, he saw Rema roll her eyes at him. He immediately corrected himself. "I meant to say, 'thanks.'"

Rema was hungry and tired and her usual cranky self after she'd run too long on not enough fuel. The Cup-O-Noodles without water was a bad idea, as the sodium content in that small cup had nearly sent her into cardiac arrest. She drank the bottle of water that Red offered, and then reached for his half empty bottle. Somehow, he sensed that he should not admonish her, and with his good sense, he kept quiet. She would have guzzled it anyway, and it likely would have started an argument.

Despite the fact that they were chasing a bad guy that was probably the most famous man in Colorado, and despite the fact that his fly fishing had been interrupted three days in a row, and despite the fact that his sleepy and quaint town of Nederland was now consistently on the national nightly news, Red was feeling more alive than ever.

"What's that?" Rema yelled out.

"Red Corvette"

"Step on it."

"Then he'll see us. I'm driving a squad car, in case you haven't noticed."

"Radio it in."

"I will when I have confirmation of the plates."

"Radio it in anyway. Get a jump on it."

"That's not how we do things."

"Do you have a cell phone?" Rema asked. Red released his right hand from the steering wheel and shoved his old Samsung in her direction. "I don't have one of these," she said.

"Yeah, it's a dinosaur."

"No. I mean I don't own a cell phone. How do you turn it on?"

"It's on. Just touch the picture of the phone and dial the number you want." Rema dialed Melanie's number. Other than Mac's, it was the only one that she knew by heart.

* * *

"We're following her," Rema yelled into the cell phone.

Melanie had no idea who was calling her, as she didn't recognize the number or the extremely loud voice. "Who is this?"

"Rema. I'm with Red and we're following Scott's Corvette. He has Mac as a hostage and he's driving toward Denver."

"Michael's in Denver," Melanie said with a sudden air of animation. "And it involves Scott. He's meeting with federal agents about these cars that Scott was selling to his pro athlete buddies at an inflated price. Something about drugs in the cars."

"I think Mac must have figured it out," Rema said.

"How? I just found out five minutes ago. Michael left a copy of the documents in a secret place. This must be bad stuff."

"How's Michael involved?"

"He still does corporate tax stuff for Scott."

"Still? I had no idea."

Rema felt a tap on her leg. Red mouthed the word, "What?" She told Mel to hang on for a minute while she filled Red in on the details.

"Can you see Mac? Is she okay?" Melanie asked.

"I can't see her because Red won't pull up close enough," Rema said.

"Did you see that?" Red said to Rema. "His back tail light just went out."

"She's in the trunk," Rema said. "She once sent us a chain email about carjacking and that a woman survived one once by kicking out the tail light while locked in the trunk."

"I remember that one."

"Close the gap, Red. This is a good sign."

* * *

"Now, are you sure, Michael, that these are all the documents that you have?" the federal agent standing next to James asked.

Michael, feeling a tingling sensation at the back of his neck, responded, "Yes. This is everything. I packed up all of my files and brought them."

"These are the originals. Where are the copies?" James said.

Michael felt the glass walls of the conference room closing in on him. "I didn't have time to make copies. I'm sorry. I was home with the boys and I knew it was risky to only have one set of documents, but they are young boys and I can't take my eyes off of them for a minute or they get into trouble, and then I got the call from you, James, to take the next flight–no questions asked–so I called the babysitter and–"

"So this is it?" James said again.

"Yes."

"No other copies?"

"No." Michael looked James in the eye. The man was looking more familiar. He recognized him from somewhere, but he couldn't place him.

"Okay. You better not be fucking with me," James said. "I know where your family lives."

The hair on the back on Michael's neck stood on end. *What kind of federal agent speaks to an informant like that?* His thought was interrupted by the vibrating noise on the marble table. His cell phone was ringing and the call identifier noted that it was Melanie.

James grabbed the phone and put it into his inside jacket pocket. "We're going for a ride."

"Where?"

"To the car dealership. We need you to show us exactly what you saw and where. If you can do that, our case will be locked down tight."

Michael relaxed a little bit. For a moment there, he was feeling extremely uncomfortable with the manner in which James spoke to him. He tried to reassure himself that federal agents, especially the guys who deal in the drug trade, were probably pretty tough characters. They risked their lives during some of the sting operations and had to be very careful when gathering information prior to an indictment. Grand juries were not generous when agents put on a case that had loose ends and allowed room for doubt. Michael knew that these guys' jobs required meticulous inquiry.

He walked with James to the car that remained parked out in front of the building and together they drove north for a short bit until they jumped on Interstate 25 connecting to Interstate 70 West.

Michael and Melanie had been on this freeway so many times on their way up to Vail, Breckenridge, Copper Mountain, and Keystone. So many great memories came flooding back to him. He thought of his wife and how lucky he was to have someone as capable as her. He inventoried his heart, silently acknowledging that he had been treating her with some level of disdain recently, mostly out of jealousy for the ease of her success. He realized, on reflection, that her success was not easy. She worked tirelessly to ensure that the boys had what they needed every day and that their schedules were booked with fun and motivating events. She also worked hard to guarantee that her staff was happy and that her company met the goals that had been set. *Why have I been so hard on her?* The pressure that he'd put on her to move must have caused her so much stress. He promised himself that the minute he saw his wife, he was going to tell her how much he appreciated her and that he was willing to discuss the future and staying put in their lives with a respectful conversation, offering the give-and-take that he recently had been unwilling to bestow.

Michael relaxed, feeling a sense of inner peace. He was going to clear up this tax situation so that his name was cleared and he could focus on his family first, and his law practice second. He had a new lease on life and it felt good.

"Hey, you missed the exit to Scott's Arvada dealership," Michael said to the driver. James, who sat next to him in the back seat of the Lincoln Towncar remained silent. The driver did not respond. Michael reminded himself for a brief second about the road construction projects in the summer and late fall in this part of the country. All of the major work had to be crammed into a few good weather months before the snow storms hit. "Construction?" Michael asked.

"Change of plans," James said smoothly.

"What do you mean? I thought you wanted me to show you what I saw at the dealership?"

"We know what you saw. That's the problem."

The euphoric feeling that had just filled Michael disappeared.

"You're not federal agents, are you?"

"Not exactly," James said.

"What do you want with me?"

"Nothing. Not a thing. We want you to be as silent as a mouse."

"Where are you taking me?"

"To a place where we can be sure that you won't sing."

Chapter 41

"She is flat broke," said Bob Avery, the private investigator that Mac used for many of her cases, including the Preston Parker murder case on the ski slopes of Jackson Hole. "Maria Knotingham's high-priced lifestyle has outdone her. The baron that she married some years back, and who coincidentally died shortly thereafter, left her all of his money, which was quite a bit, but she has managed to blow through it."

"And John?"

"His only source of income was mommy dearest and Hesta. He hasn't earned a dime in years. He practically spent the interest on the trust account money before it was earned. He has a male lover who doesn't earn much either. They live a glamorous party lifestyle for men without means. Recently, there have been some deposits to John's account from a car dealership in the Denver area. I have a guy checking on those as we speak."

"Were you able to track down her flight history in the past year?"

"Yes. Two flights to Denver. Rental car from Denver where she put about 580 miles on the car each time. It's about 280 miles from Denver to Casper, so it adds up. You have to apply to visit any jail, prison or detention facility. She applied using her maiden name of Maria Sweeney. But fingerprints are a must, and hers match. She visited Chandler Craig two times in the past year; the last time was about five days before he was released. She left a package to be delivered to him upon release. Probably money."

"I thought she was broke."

"She is, but I figure that she had to source the money somehow. Craig's been able to live for months without getting a job, and it is certain that his aunt didn't give him cash. I called her. She said that she's never given the kid money. So either he's been on the take from someone, or he's stolen everything he's needed to survive these past few months in Colorado. I'm not done checking on him, just thought you might need to know some particulars right up front."

Pam thanked him and then explained with a sense of panic what Melanie told her about Mac.

"You had me researching this stuff when Mac's life is in danger? Are you nuts? Tell me everything! Damn! Does Harry know?"

Harry was Mac's legal partner and he managed the office in Jackson Hole. He was like a father to Mac, but they hadn't seen much of each other in years, outside Mac's wedding. Bob Avery had been working for Harry as a private eye for nearly twenty years. Pam was so caught up in the investigation that it hadn't dawned on her that she should have called Harry.

"I forgot," was the lame excuse she used.

"I'm calling him now. He will be furious with you and completely freaked out! He loves Mac like she is his own daughter."

"I know," Pam said with a hushed tone. She knew she'd make a mistake.

"Harry knows everyone. I know that he is friends with the Governor of Colorado. They had dinner together a few weeks ago. Harry will ruffle some feathers while I get the rest of the information you need. Who is the DA on the case? Who's the judge?"

* * *

Andrew Harrison had practiced law in Jackson Hole, Wyoming for nearly forty years. His practice ranged from criminal defense to toxic tort to family law to business litigation. He rarely turned down a case, and had made it very clear to Mac when he first hired her that she would be cross-trained in every area of the law when working for him. He liked variety and notoriety, and from this objective was known throughout the entire state of Wyoming and most of Northern Colorado simply as Harry. He handled many famous cases over the years and walked away victorious in nearly every case. His motto was preparation. He taught Mac that if she was prepared on every possible aspect of her case, that most likely she'd be able to "field the ground balls that took the awkward bounce" in the courtroom, and in life.

"Prepare for everything and you won't be surprised in Court." Harry had trained Mac well.

Because preparation was something Harry was keen on, when he made his company cell phone purchases the previous holiday season, he chose a network that provided the "Mapquest Find Me" feature.

When Harry received the call from Bob, he nearly went into cardiac arrest. Bob talked fast and Harry thought even faster, and together they were able to call the cell network, engage the "Mapquest Find Me" application, and locate through a global positioning system the whereabouts of Mac.

Bob talked Harry through the process of syncing his phone up with his laptop, and then networking the Mapquest Find Me application to Mac's computer at work. Pam logged in and could see the same screen that Harry viewed, watching as the little red dot moved from the highway interchanges onto Wadsworth to Ralston to Balsam to Reno Street.

"The dot stopped moving," Harry said to both Pam and Bob on the conference speaker phone line.

"I'm calling Gardiner Smiley and linking him," Harry said, and before he disconnected his line with Pam and Bob, he gave them both specific instructions on what to do next.

Harry was in Jackson, which was in the northwestern part of Wyoming. Even if he chartered a flight, there was no way that he could get to Denver within two hours. He knew in his heart that Mac didn't have that long to live. He'd have to take care of business the old fashioned way.

* * *

Wyatt's flight made a bumpy descent into the small executive airport outside Boulder. He borrowed Stu's phone to call Pam. She quickly talked Wyatt through the directions while Stu made arrangements for Wyatt to borrow a car from an airport employee. Money changed hands quickly and Wyatt was behind the wheel of a Prius.

"I'm too damn tall to drive this rollerskate," Wyatt said to Stu. Wyatt, wearing his standard Wrangler jeans, cowboy boots, blue button-down shirt and cowboy hat, looked out of place in the tiny white car.

"Are you trying to thank me, son?"

"Got your pistol in the plane?"

"You know I do. Never have flown without flares, food and my gun."

"I need to borrow it."

Stu held up one finger and limped toward the plane to retrieve his weapon. After nearly 70 years of the ranching life, Stu's legs and back were in chronic and constant pain. Flying, while uncomfortable to his sciatic nerve, was the only way Stu could envision retirement from ranch life. He could fly over every ranch in the state, appreciating from the air the hard work and dedication required to work the land.

Stu had been a friend of Wyatt's father for thirty-some odd years, and their relationship was solid. Passing a pistol to Butch Anderson's son was of no consequence to Stu.

"Be careful," Stu warned, as he handed his gun to Wyatt. "Sounds like these folks don't mess around."

"I'll be careful. I'm more likely to get killed driving in Denver traffic," Wyatt said, as he started the car. "What's wrong with this thing? It doesn't make noise."

"It's a hybrid. Fuel efficient. Just assume that the car is on and drive it like any other car."

Wyatt put the car in gear and took off like a rocket, heading south on the 36. He had Stu's phone on speaker mode as it lay on the passenger seat, allowing Pam to guide him to his wife.

* * *

Scott Setliff took a hard left and gunned the Corvette into a warehouse off Reno Drive in Arvada. Mac's body levitated to the top of the trunk and then crashed back down with a thud. Her cell phone ascended and flipped before sliding down toward her knees. She felt the car come to a screeching stop, sending her phone back up toward her torso. She had no luck trying to dial with her tongue and was cursing Harry for insisting on the upgraded technology. Just as she was hexing her boss, she saw a light go on her phone. She grabbed the phone with her mouth and flipped it over so that she could see the panel. "*Mapquest?*" she thought to herself. She figured that the jolt had somehow initiated an internet connection to the search engine. As she was about to try to back out of the search engine by hitting the backward arrow with her nose, she heard the door of the car open and footsteps coming toward the trunk. She nudged the phone like a hockey puck with her nose causing it to slide under the spare tire to the car.

Scott Setliff's massive frame towered over Mac. The bright light from the sun blinded her for a second as her eyes adjusted from blackness to dusk.

"Time to meet some of my friends," he said in a maniacal tone. Scott reached into the trunk and pulled Mac out by her arms. Blood had soaked through the wounds on her hands and was dripping past her fingertips. "You are a mess, Mary MacIntosh. You used to be a looker."

Mac took a deep breath, coaching herself not to take the bait. He closed the trunk and pushed her in the direction of the gray warehouse. As they walked closer to the dull green door, it opened without prompt.

"Hey, boss," a voice said. Scott did not respond. He pushed Mac inside the large and seemingly empty, unfinished interior. "We got ourselves a full house."

Mac carefully looked around as she walked on the cement floor, taking inventory of everything she saw. There were windows in the building, but none of them were below seven feet high. The metal rafters showed, as did the electrical fixtures and air vents. The main room had two rooms at the far end, with the dull green doors pulled closed. Escape routes didn't seem plentiful.

"In here," another voice called out. Scott led Mac to the far right door and opened it with his right hand. Mac's eyes flew wide open upon the sight of Michael seated in a metal folding chair with his mouth duct taped and his hands tied behind his back.

"No need for introductions, right?" Scott said with a hint of a laugh. "This is what I get for doing my wife's friend's husband a favor. He rats me out to the feds. Now I am forced to do the unthinkable."

Mac had a series of retorts she would have loved to spew, but knew better. Scott Setliff did not have a reputation in the sports industry as being cool under pressure. Mac remembered a Monday night game a few years back when the other sports announcer disagreed on the air with Scott regarding some projections for the game. Scott got visibly upset on the air and called the colleague a pompous ass on national television. The other announcer didn't appreciate the gesture, and with minimal provocation, explained to the watching public that during Scott's playing career, he had a reputation for misunderstanding the quarterback's calls. Scott was trigger happy with his fists and proceeded to punch his fellow announcer square in the jaw. All of this entertainment concluded prior to the game starting. Needless to say, both announcers were fined and suspended for several games. In the world of pro football, this made them more popular than ever.

"Are you okay?" Mac asked Michael. She noted the large gash above his left eyebrow. He shook his head back and forth. He did not look well. "It's going to be okay." Her voice cracked as she spoke. She knew that she wasn't convincing to Michael or to herself.

"We have one more guest who is going to join us for our party and then we are going to hear the choir sing," Scott said.

James left Scott in charge of Mac and Michael and momentarily left the bare room. Scott unfolded another chair and shoved Mac down on it. He grabbed a piece of rope from the high windowsill and tied Mac's thighs to the seat of the chair. She could see the roll of silver duct tape with another piece of rope on the windowsill. She wondered who it was that would be joining them in her last moments of life.

When the door swung open once again, Mac was astonished to see a very familiar face.

"Gardiner!" she said. This would be the last word Mac spoke before feeling the stifling slap of silver across her lips.

Chapter 42

Rema called Pam using Red's cell phone. "We lost them," she said. "We were on Wadsworth off the I-25 and they turned left on Ralston. By the time we got to Ralston, they were nowhere to be found. It is a maze of industrial buildings back here and they all look the same."

"Turn left on Balsam and left on Reno Street. Mac's cell is sending a signal at the corner of Balsam and Reno."

Rema wasn't savvy enough with cell phones or GPS to question Mac's employee. She repeated the information to Red, who radioed it to Arvada dispatch.

"There it is," Rema said, pointing to the red Corvette. They slowly turned around and parked around the corner.

"Wait here," Red said. He unbuttoned his shirt and strapped his gun around his waist. Rema could see that he was physically fit. She watched him fasten his shirt again and open the car door.

"You expect me to just sit here and wait?" Rema said. "No way in hell am I going to do that. My best friend is in there with my asshole husband."

"I didn't picture you as the jealous type."

"I'm not jealous, you idiot. I'm–"

"I know. Bad timing," Red said. "I don't know what is going on here, but if what you tell me is true, then these guys aren't going to monkey around."

"Then I'm going too."

Red shook his head. He knew that there was no sense in arguing with this woman. She had a mind of her own. Anyone who was willing, day after day, to run thirty miles up and down a mountain was a force to reckon with. "Fine," he said. "Stay behind me and be quiet."

* * *

Wyatt's life experience of driving consisted of back country roads, ranch land and mountain terrain. City traffic was treacherous in comparison. He navigated the tiny car in and out of the Friday rush hour of cars and trucks careening down the highway on their exodus from work. He wondered how people could live this way. He wondered what they found appealing in wasting the better part of the evening fighting traffic to get home.

Wyatt had lived his entire life on his parents' ranch, and his life was remarkably pleasing to him. He lived his days wholesomely and drew great pleasure from working the land and communing with horses. In contrast to his peaceful nature, Wyatt enjoyed hunting and fishing, like many men in the West. He was an excellent rifleman and usually only took one shot during elk season. He had never been skunked while hunting. His family enjoyed venison every year since he learned to hunt.

Fishing was a different story all together. He admittedly stunk at it. It was as if every trout in Wyoming could sense his smell. Yet, he still loved to stand on the edge of a river, casting and waiting and walking and listening.

Fishing required patience and Wyatt had plenty.

As patient as Wyatt was, he was about to lose his mind as he listened to the car tell him when to turn, following the quadrants that Stu had plugged in for him from Pam's instructions. *Who in the hell drives cars that talk to them? Are people so lonely that they like this sort of thing?*

He desperately wanted to turn the GPS system off, but he was so afraid of driving in traffic in a city that he left it on in hopes that he would not have to watch the road and try to find street signs at the same time. Pam had been very specific with directions, but it was very hard to drive and follow a map. As the GPS system reminded him to exit the freeway and take the second right hand turn, Wyatt started to appreciate the advances of modern technology.

Wadsworth. Ralston. Balsam. Reno. Bingo. There was the red Corvette. If those guys had so much as laid a hand on his wife, they were dead men. Stu provided six rounds in the chamber—that would be more than Wyatt needed for six years of elk hunting. And elk were smart.

** * **

It was no secret that Gardiner Smiley had his eye on the gubernatorial race in Colorado. It was a goal that Gardiner and Harry shared and since Harry's market was the great state of Wyoming, it was a goal that they could work together toward. Gardiner certainly had the good looks and charm to pull off a campaign, and the fact that he had a brilliant record as a crime- fighting district attorney didn't hurt matters whatsoever. Harry was also handsome and charming, yet he was twenty years senior to Gardiner—which carried with it the credential of experience. Harry's criminal defense record was notorious, but most folks—especially people in Wyoming—preferred candidates who were tough on crime and weighed on the side of the prosecution. That was the thorn in Harry's side. Gardiner lacked the wealth of experience in years of service, but he made up for the deficit by getting support from high-powered athletes, entrepreneurs, and politicians.

Gardiner met Scott Setliff while attending college in Boulder and had managed to wiggle his way into Scott's inner circle. They had become friends and before Gardiner became a district attorney, he practiced in the private sector and had negotiated many contracts for Scott before his career necessitated a sports agent.

As Gardiner climbed the corporate ladder, eventually leading to the campaign for district attorney, Scott helped him both politically and financially. They had a mutually symbiotic relationship.

What differentiated Harry and Gardiner Smiley was the fine line of ethics. Harry never even approached the line. He taught Mac early on in her career that if she could smell an ethical issue, then she'd already made a poor choice. Ethics were to be adhered to always. It was never worth it to get her toe even close to the line.

Gardiner had not been coached in the same capacity regarding ethics. He had been raised by a father whose motto was "win at all costs." His father was the guy who got kicked out of little league games for cursing at umpires and arguing calls. Gardiner was raised under the theme that if you didn't win, you either didn't train hard enough or you didn't take enough shortcuts to outwit the opponent. Fear was a weakness and it showed a lack of preparation. Fear was something that Gardiner Smiley did not embrace well. Nevertheless, Mac witnessed fear in Gardiner's eyes as he walked into the warehouse room where she and Michael remained bound to folding chairs, staring down the barrel of a gun.

"Gardiner," Mac tried to shout, encumbered by the harsh nature of duct tape.

Gardiner looked at Mac and then shook his head with a disdainful scorn. "Mac, I tried to tell you to keep your nose out of this, but you wouldn't listen. I didn't want it to turn out this way, but I'm afraid that this is out of my control. There are too many top-notch careers at stake for this to go public."

"What do you mean that you warned her?" Scott said, his voice a sharp as a razor's edge.

"She was convinced that the lunatic in the cabin had been hired by one of you to kill one of the wives. Even if it was true, I tried to dissuade her from pursuing it because I didn't want her delving into your life, Scott. I know Mac and I know her boss and neither of them leave a stone unturned. I didn't want her on your tail because, knowing her, she'd figure it out and come after you. But the more I tried to keep her away, the more she pushed and somehow, she got her hands on a federal indictment that has your name on it. I didn't even know about it, and I'm on the grand jury committee. This was top secret." Gardiner then did something very curious. He flashed Mac the same peace sign that he had flashed her at the hospital when they were in Hesta's room. Mac was unsure what to make of the hand signal, but it gave her a slight hint of hope.

"Tell me whose names are on the indictment," Scott said to Mac. She tried to make a noise, but with duct tape, it was impossible. Scott ripped the tape from her mouth, giving her a wax job that no salon could match.

Mac gasped for a breath.

"I want every name," Scott demanded.

Mac looked at Michael, searching for some clue as to what he knew. Michael looked down at the floor. *Oh God,* she thought to herself, *he knows.*

"I don't know the names. I never saw the indictment. The only name I know is yours."

"I don't believe you," Scott said. "You need to tell me right now what other names you know and who else knows about them. If this leaks and I don't warn my buddies, we'll all be dead."

The cogs in Mac's mind started spinning full speed. In that instance, she knew why Michael had been pressuring Melanie to move. She knew why Rema ran away from her husband every day. She knew why Harry had always warned her not to mesh too closely with any powerhouse with ambition. Once again, Harry was right. He was always right.

Chapter 43

Rema had only met Wyatt one time, and that was on his wedding day. She could have met him days prior to the wedding, but Rema was too busy training for an ultramarathon. Regardless of the very limited amount of time spent with the cowboy, Rema could have spotted him in any crowd. He was undeniably good-looking.

He had once been the Marlboro man, right? Rema hated the fact that she was not a great listener. Her ADHD kept her from the details of conversation. She was fairly sure that Mac told her once that he'd been the cowboy for the cigarette ads, and that he only agreed to take the job because the ranch was hurting at the time. But she was not certain of these things.

She was certain, however, that at this moment, in a remote area of Arvada, that she was staring at the man who had married her best friend.

"Wyatt?"

He looked at her like a child assessing a stranger.

"Wyatt? It's Rema. Rema Setliff. Mac's friend. Do you remember?"

All the while, Red was trying desperately to keep Rema quiet. They stood one block away from the warehouse and he had called for backup. If they were spotted and blew the plan, lives could be at stake. Red motioned for Wyatt to stay low and to join them across the street from the warehouse.

Wyatt was not accustomed to dealing with the criminal element and thought nothing of walking across an industrial park with a pistol sticking out of the waistband of his jeans. Red made several gestures in his direction, but Wyatt did not seem to understand.

"What in the hell is going on?" Wyatt asked Rema. She quickly introduced Red and explained what was going on inside the warehouse.

"Help is on its way," Red said.

"Don't think so," Rema said.

Red looked at her with a sideways glance. "I called them in."

"You don't understand. Scott has paid most of these guys off for years. He drives like a maniac, yet he's never had a ticket. He has freakish partner swap parties at our house when I'm gone and the cops don't arrest the prostitutes. He drives drunk, but no one seems to care. Believe me, the force is on the take. If you radioed in that he was your suspect, there will be no dispatch on the way."

"Then we will have to take them without backup," Wyatt said.

"You and what army?" Red said.

"Are you in or are you out? 'Cuz when it comes to my wife, I don't mess around."

Red was in. While they discussed a plan and put it into action, Rema called Pam to tell her what was happening.

* * *

"Harry, good to hear from you. How are you and Jane doing? We missed you at the Hamptons this summer," said Hal Jaffe, *the* District Attorney for New York City. Hal and Harry went to Stanford Law together many years back and had remained close friends.

"I need a favor, old friend." Harry explained the legal issues involving Maria and John Knotingham. "My investigator is faxing the documents to your office as we speak. We are under the wire."

"I'll have my number one gal look into it immediately. She's going to be pissed off that I'm dropping it on her on a Friday afternoon, but if it sticks, count on extradition. But it better be super glue!"

* * *

"Melanie?" Pam said. "Mac's law partner, Harry, just called and he told me to tell you to pack up the kids and get out of there. He said to remain available by cell and to let me know where you are."

"Should I bring the box of documents that Michael left?"

"Yes. Do you have somewhere safe to go?"

"The City. One of my rowing friends has a flat in San Francisco. She has kids that are close in age to my kids. The only problem is that it's Friday afternoon and the traffic will be terrible."

"Don't worry about the traffic. Worry about your safety. Text me her name and address and get out of there. Harry is worried that these guys might be after the records that you told me about. He thinks that they are trying to clean up the evidence trail so that the grand jury can't green light the indictment."

Melanie wasn't sure what the last statement meant, but she clearly understood that her children's safety might be at stake.

"William, Charlie. Grab your Nintendos and jump in the car. We're going for a sleepover at Zelda's in the City."

* * *

"Patti," Pam said. "Things have gotten ugly with Mac. I'll explain the details later but Harry wants you and Bob and the boys to get out of your house and to go somewhere safe for a few days."

"Bob is at his girlfriend's," Patti said with a quivering voice.

"Okay. I know that you are not in a good place right now and that you are feeling very hurt and betrayed. But I need you to focus on you and your boys for a minute."

"That's the problem, Pam. I've always been focused on the boys and now my husband is leaving me."

"Patti. Listen carefully. Scott Setliff has kidnapped Mac and we believe that his intention is to kill her because she knows about some misdealings with his car dealerships. I don't know what, if anything, you know about this, but Scott is mixed up with some shady characters–bad guys–people who are not afraid to commit acts of violence. If you want your boys to be safe, then follow Harry's advice. Quickly pack a few things and get out of your house for a few days. Don't leave Bob a note at the house. If they come looking for you, don't leave bread crumbs for the bad guys."

"Okay," Patti said, gaining some composure.

"Now, Patti. Pull yourself together right now and make it happen. We'll take care of Bob later."

* * *

Hesta sat uncomfortably in her hospital bed awaiting yet another medical opinion from a plastic surgeon. Her castration was the talk of the ward, and doctors flocked to her room for each viewing. Hesta felt like her vagina was a train wreck and passersby couldn't help but look. They were polite enough to ask her permission, but after a while, she felt like charging admission. Being a publisher, she thought of writing a memoir of her experience in Colorado, and was keeping her mind occupied by outlining the chapters and desperately trying to think up a catchy title that included the word "vagina." She thought "Vagina Viewing" was too obstetric. "Vagina Restored–a Renovation of Virginity?" Perhaps.

The consensus among the surgeons was that it would take several surgeries to recreate the overall appearances of her femininity, but that she would likely never have the sensation back as it was nearly impossible to undo the nerve damage done to the clitoris. The doctors assured her that other sexual functions would remain intact and that she could otherwise carry on a normal life–which could still include childbirth if she desired, but the clock was ticking in that regard.

Hesta had never wanted children, so the discussion with the doctors on this subject was merely polite interaction from her standpoint. But with the time on her hands, and the lack of contact with her friends over the past twenty-four hours, she started thinking about the notion. She felt quite lonely at the hospital despite the constant interruption from medical personnel. She thought about the people in her life. She had people who worked for her, and a handful of friends that she saw once or twice a year. Her husband didn't love her. Her mother-in-law loathed her. Her parents had died years ago—both heavy smokers throughout life. Who was going to care for her when she advanced in years? Thinking of her parents made her think of cigarettes. She had not had one in five days. It was the longest she'd gone without smoking since college. Perhaps it was time to take inventory of her life and to make some changes. The first essential change was dumping her deadbeat husband. That would also take care of the second change—his mother.

Next, she needed to decide what to do about Scott. She loved him, but she knew deep down that he was not the right man for her. First, he could not have children due to his overuse of steroids. In fact, Scott told her that he had a vasectomy as a result of the damage done from the performance enhancement drugs. Second, Scott did not treat her with the dignity and respect that she deserved and needed. Hesta wanted to be loved in the traditional sense, and no man had ever loved her that way. She knew that she'd always sold herself short when it came to relationships, and it was time to make some changes.

Chapter 44

"Mother!" John Knotingham yelled into the phone. "The cops are here with a search warrant. What should I do?" John was still wearing his pajama bottoms late in the afternoon. He'd been out half of the night doing the bar scene and his mind was unfocused for writing.

"I'll call my attorney right away. Don't let them in until I've called you back," Maria said. "That's odd."

"What?"

"There's a knock on my door. The doorman never called to inquire as to deliveries."

"Mom! They are knocking again at the door, insisting that I open it or they are going to forcibly enter. What should I do?"

"Oh God. They are at my door too. I need to hang up and call my lawyer."

* * *

Scott was not satisfied that Mac was telling him the truth. He nodded to the thug in the red shirt to apply a little pressure to her. Scott watched with glee as the thug kicked the back of Mac's chair, effecting a hard blow to her hands which were tied firmly behind her back. Mac screamed out in pain. She could feel her wounds open up, which sent a nauseating wave through her body.

"You'd better start talking. My patience is wearing thin."

Mac wanted to say something, but the pain was too intense. Bile rose from her stomach and she couldn't keep herself from vomiting all over the floor beneath her feet.

Scott was disgusted by the sight and switched his attention to Michael.

"Who else knows about the drugs?" Scott asked Michael. "Did you tell your wife?"

Michael shook his head in the negative. Scott walked over to where Michael was sitting and ripped the tape off his mouth. Michael winced in pain.

"I have one of my West Coast guys on his way to your house right now, Michael. They've already paid a visit to your office. I don't think your partner is very happy with you right now–that is, if they let him live. He swore that you took the documents home with you. He had better not be lying or he is better off dead. See, this deal involves a lot of people and if it goes to the grand jury and becomes public, hundreds of people are going to be fucked. Football players. Baseball players. Basketball players. Big names. Some coaches are on the take. Some trainers. I promised each and every one of them that they were untraceable, but you apparently have made a trail that leads back to me. So, you see, if this blows up, I'm dead and if I'm dead, you are dead. So, let's go over this one more time. Is this the only copy of the documents?"

Michael could feel the blood drain out of his head. The room reeked of vomit and he began to feel sick to his stomach. No matter how he answered the question, he knew that Melanie and the boys were in peril. If he was honest and she cooperated, would they leave her and the boys unharmed? He assumed that these guys were willing to do whatever it took to make sure that no documents or witnesses existed that connected them to the performance enhancement drug ring.

It was possible that Melanie had not found his note yet and knew nothing about the documents. What would she do if a few large men showed up at her doorstep demanding to search the house? Knowing her, she would go ballistic and call the police–which would piss these thugs off and they would probably hurt her.

Michael knew that he'd made a big mistake. He should have done what he initially planned to do–write his wife and children a note making up a story about how unhappy he was and that he was leaving for South

America to try to find himself. At least his family would be okay. His altruistic ideals of blowing the whistle and having the government protect him and his family had backfired. He and his family would likely end up dead and Scott Setliff and his cronies would walk—remaining American heroes for their natural athletic talent. What a crock. What a nightmare. Michael made up his mind.

"These are the originals. I did not make a copy."

The thug in the black shirt standing behind Michael hit him hard across the face.

"You are lying," Scott said.

"I'm telling the truth."

The thug kicked him in the shin.

"I don't believe you."

Michael did not respond. The thug hit him again with a closed fist to the jaw. Blood spattered across the room.

Gardiner Smiley stepped forward. "You need to be straight with us, Michael. There are a lot of people named in the indictment based on your documents. How can you expect us to believe that no one else knows about this besides you and your law partner?"

"Because I didn't tell anyone else other than Agent Rankling."

"You can't expect us to believe that you can tell one federal agent about this and an eighty-page indictment is generated a few weeks later?" Gardiner Smiley said. "That's not how the system works, Michael. It takes many agents and a lot of investigation and collaboration. Evidence is corroborated before a grand jury is involved."

"That's all I did," Michael said. "I swear to you that I didn't do more than make the call and fax the documents that I brought today."

"Agent Rankling never called you back to discuss your entries?"

"Yes. We spoke many times, but he was the only person that I dealt with. No other agents called me and I didn't tell anyone else about it." Michael paused for a moment and then continued. "I did tell the ethics people at the State Bar, but I didn't mention any names. I swear that I didn't tell anyone else."

"Not even your wife?" Gardiner Smiley asked. "You are your wife are very close, aren't you?" Michael nodded. "Of course you would tell her. You tell her everything."

Michael looked at Mac with shameful eyes. "I used to tell Mel everything, but things have changed between us in the last few years. I don't mean as much to her as I used to, and we've drifted apart. I was worried that if I told her, she would accuse me of being stupid or careless. She never liked the fact that I did business with Scott and she made her point very clear to me many times. She worried that doing business with friends could cause a problem in the friendship."

"Did it?"

Michael hesitated before answering. The thug stepped forward to entice an answer, but Gardiner held up his hand.

"Yeah, it did sometimes. I did complain to Melanie years ago when Scott would ask me to fudge on things. Sometimes he'd ask me to send a big bill for services rendered so that he could expense it against earnings. He wouldn't pay the bill. Sometimes he asked for tax structuring that wasn't legal–at least not in this country. He did business with a lot of rich people who lived on the edge financially and legally, and he wanted to do it too, but not get caught. I felt trapped. I tried to quit working for him, but he didn't take it well."

"You are full of shit, Michael," Scott said. "You had no problem accepting my checks. And you happily took on lots of my buddies' accounts."

"A long time ago. But not in recent years. When I was first going out on my own, I accepted pretty much any business that walked in the door. I had to. But when things got ugly, I wanted out."

"So you went to the feds?" Gardiner asked.

"No. I went to Scott first but he told me that the only way out was six feet under."

"Fuck you."

The thug punched Michael in the stomach so hard that the metal chair collapsed out from under him.

"Stop it!" Mac yelled.

Scott turned in her direction. "You want some attention, do you?" he asked. "Feeling left out?"

The big man left Michael rolling side to side with a chair attached to him and walked over to where Mac was seated. Scott motioned for Gardiner Smiley to join them in the interrogation. Gardiner slowly walked toward her, making the strange hand motions again.

"Who else knows the names on the indictment?" Gardiner asked her.

Mac did not answer. She knew that it was futile, based on what happened with Michael. She braced herself for the next blow that the thug was gearing up to deliver and promptly threw up again.

"I'm going to make you lick that shit off the floor," Scott said. He then nodded in the direction of the thug with the red shirt to take care of business.

Just then, the door to the room burst open.

"Don't move," Red yelled.

Chapter 45

Wyatt charged in the room behind Red, both with their guns drawn, but each with a different attitude toward resolution. Wyatt fired one round into Gardiner Smiley and one round into the thug with the black shirt before either had time to turn in his direction. He then aimed at Scott.

"Hang on," Red said to Wyatt. "Drop your weapons!" Red yelled at the three men. "Drop them now or I'll shoot.

Wyatt had patience when it came to fishing, but when it came to his wife's safety, he found that he had few. He fired purposefully into Scott Setliff's right thigh, sending him to the ground in a thud.

Wyatt's marksmanship was without question. He could mark an elk's heart from three hundred yards away, so when Gardiner Smiley and the black-shirted thug next to him were each holding their left shoulders, it was likely that each shot was placed exactly there. Neither man seemed to hear Red's command to drop their weapon. Wyatt could see a gun tucked into each of their waistbands.

Out of the corner of his eye, Red saw Wyatt aiming again at Gardiner.

"Drop your weapons or my friend will shoot you and this time it will not be in the arm."

Both Gardiner and the thug reached into their waistbands. Gardiner tossed his weapon to the cement floor near Mac's feet. She instinctively kicked it toward Wyatt. The thug in the red shirt quickly pulled his gun and aimed it at Mac's head. The sound of the gunshot ricocheted throughout the empty walls of the warehouse.

* * *

Melanie made it a practice to drive conservatively when the boys were in the car, but it was not her nature to do anything slowly. She had loaded the car with an overnight bag, threw the box of documents in the back, paid the babysitter and locked up and left within fifteen minutes of Pam's call. She would call Zelda on the way but was certain that at this time of night, her friend would be home with her two boys quietly watching a movie. Zelda was a single mom who had done well in the dot com industry in the nineties. She married a fellow dot comer, had two boys with him, and then divorced after the second baby was born. The father of her boys had no real interest in raising them and seemed perfectly content with working twenty hours a day, seven days a week at a start up company. She happily accepted full custody and enjoyed life in San Francisco. She and Melanie met out in the bay one day while taking a rowing class and became fast friends, mostly due to the fact that their boys were the exact same ages.

As Melanie turned right on Shattuck and then right again on University, she noticed that a car was following behind her. Not many other cars were on the street at this late hour. She had intended to drive directly to the 80 south, but out of caution and paranoia, turned left on San Pablo and then right on Ashby. The car behind her did the same. Melanie entered the onramp at a higher rate of speed that she normally would with William and Charlie on board. She told them that they needed to lay their heads down on the seat and try to get some rest so that they could play with their friends when they got to their house. The boys agreed. Mel called her friend, telling her everything that had happened as quickly as she could, and asking if it was okay to come over. Zelda welcomed her friend, but not without concern for herself and her own boys' safety.

"You need to call the police right after we hang up," Zelda said.

Melanie agreed.

"I think there is a car following me. I'm about to get on the Bay Bridge and I'm going to try to lose him."

"What does the car look like? I'm going to call the police too."

Melanie said that she couldn't tell. All she noted was that the car was a dark color. She hung up from Zelda and dialed 9-1-1, but before she was connected with dispatch, she felt the impact from behind and her phone flew out of her right hand.

The Volvo spun a full three hundred sixty degrees before careening into a sign that said, "San Francisco County."

* * *

Rema called for paramedic assistance and the response was extraordinarily quick. Apparently, the sound of the gunshots had been extreme due to the cavernous nature of the warehouse and adjoining businesses had also called the emergency hotline. Due to Harry's call to the Governor of Colorado, the Arvada police finally arrived simultaneously with the paramedics, demanding details on what had gone down. Red handled the inquiries while Wyatt attended to his wife.

"That was a stupid thing that you did," an officer said to Wyatt. "You're lucky that his gun didn't go off first." Wyatt agreed with the officer and apologized for taking the law into his own hands. The officer's perturbed attitude didn't change much with Wyatt's explanation of events. "Just a stupid thing to do. People like you get hostages killed."

Wyatt knew better than to argue or justify his defense, but no one was going to point a gun at his wife's head and get away with it. He was old school in many regards, and the West was still the West in some parts of the country. Wyatt brought Wyoming with him wherever he went.

Red told the police exactly what had happened, blow by blow. When he got to the end, he explained how Wyatt's shot nabbed the thug right between the eyes flipping him backwards to the ground next to Michael. Michael crawled away as quickly as he could scoot with a folding chair tied to his thighs. Wyatt held his gun steady on Gardiner Smiley while Red took aim at Scott Setliff and when the Arvada Police Department arrived, federal agents descended as well, including Agent Rankling, who immediately went to the aid of Gardiner Smiley, ensuring that his inside guy was okay.

As she watched the paramedics load him on a gurney, Mac hesitated before she approached Gardiner. "You were never on Scott's side, were you?"

"Never. I kept trying to flash you a hand signal so that you'd know that I was on your side, but I don't think you caught it."

"I noticed, but I didn't know what it meant. Your call to me was real, right? You weren't setting me up?"

"No. He got to you first. When I found out that Scott beat me to your hotel room, I immediately called Agent Rankling and reported it. He called the under cover team to back me up, and told me where to go and what to do. I'd been playing Scott for almost a year with this investigation. Michael's call was not their first tip, but his documents were the proof the feds needed in order to satisfy the grand jury inquiry."

"Why you? You're not with the FBI."

"Because I played baseball for two seasons with the Rockies. I'm friends with a lot of the guys that Scott did business with which allowed me to gather information from the inside. This ring is bigger than you know. It's the way of the world in professional sports, I'm afraid. A lot of money at stake."

"I knew you played ball in college, but I didn't know you went on to the big leagues."

"That's because I got hurt early on in my career. In the mid-nineties, I took some of the enhancements that the World Anti-Doping Agency made illegal with the 2006 Code. I did it to try to overcome injury and get back into the game, but it didn't work out for me, so I fell back on my law degree," Gardiner said. "That's how I came to know what was going on with Scott. My trainer got his stuff from one of Scott's guys. I came clean with the MLB, but I had never made a big name for myself, so it wasn't a big deal. When Scott's scheme started to unravel, the feds found my name on the PED list and contacted me to see if I would help them set up a sting. To be honest with you, Mac, I didn't really feel like I was given a choice. It's no secret that I have political aspirations, and it was made clear to me that if I helped, I would get better treatment."

"Sounds a little like blackmail."

"That's how it works. Not much different than offering immunity to a co-conspirator in exchange for testimony at trial," Gardiner said.

Mac contemplated his assertion and nodded. "Is your shoulder going to be okay? I'm really sorry that Wyatt shot you. He didn't know you were one of the good guys."

"It's the same shoulder that got injured in baseball. I needed surgery anyway," he said as the paramedics unlocked the wheels to the gurney and rolled him away.

Mac waved to him before a swarm of emergency workers surrounded her to attend to her hands which were bleeding and swollen beyond recognition. While being attended to, she turned her attention to Wyatt, who had finally escaped the scrutiny of the police officer.

"You came," she said to him.

"Of course I came," Wyatt said, holding her tightly in his arms. "I had no idea what was going on. You downplayed it like the situation was no big deal, and when you called, I was in the barn tending to a yearling that had been caught in barbed wire around the neck. We had a terrible connection and I missed half of the stuff that you said. I'm sorry that I didn't listen better and I'm sorry that I didn't come right away. Had I come Monday, none of this would have happened."

Mac felt a flurry of tears welling in her eyes. "You love me?"

"Hell, yes, I love you. I married you."

"You really love me."

Wyatt pushed the hair back from her forehead and gave her a kiss. "Enough to fly in a plane with Stu and drive a car with a half-wit engine in traffic."

"I have to tell you something," Mac said, with tears flowing rapidly down her cheeks, feeling compelled to give her act of contrition. "I made Pam investigate–"

"Ssshhhhh. I know. Pam explained everything to me. We can talk about that later. Let's get your hands fixed up. I don't reckon that you can talk without them."

Chapter 46

"All rise," the bailiff announced one week after the warehouse standoff. "Judge Brooks, presiding."

Gardiner Smiley stood at the prosecution table with his left arm in a sling. He wore his standard navy suit pants, white shirt and red tie, but not suit jacket this time. "Your Honor," he said. "I apologize for my dress. I am unable to get my jacket–"

"Not a problem, Mr. Smiley. How's the arm feeling?"

"Better, thanks." He turned to see if the cameras had caught this exchange. Harry, who was sitting in the back row of the courtroom, chuckled to himself.

Mac sat with Harry to her right and Wyatt to her left in the competency hearing for Chandler Craig. Nellie had made the trip down from Nederland, thanks to Red and Rema, who'd volunteered to drive her. Also present were Nicole and Max, but Max reminded them a few times over that he didn't plan to stay long, because Nedfest was in full swing and he didn't care to miss the best bands of late summer play in a setting that reminded him of his days at Woodstock.

"Nedfest is better than Frozen Dead Guy Days," he told Harry, "and that is saying a lot." Harry laughed out loud, capturing the watchful eye of the bailiff.

Mac looked fondly at her four friends seated in the row in front of her. Rema sat next to Melanie, who had suffered minor bruises and scrapes in the car accident, but due to the safety features of her Volvo, she and the boys had survived virtually unharmed. Police had responded immediately to the accident due to Zelda's call, and Scott's thugs were caught shortly thereafter driving the wrong way on the Bay Bridge.

Hesta sat to Melanie's right, and Patti to Hesta's right. They sat close, arm in arm, each relying on each other. They had met early in the morning for a brisk walk and a good talk before the hearing. They all agreed that their friendship was very important to each of them and that even though the experience at the Kilkenny-Kerry was horrific, it reminded them how important they were to one another. They were able to get things off their chest while being held hostage and able to have candid discussions with each other that otherwise might never have happened. They agreed, while walking, that they would always honor and respect each other and forgave each other for any indiscretions, harsh words or acts over the years. Even Rema voluntarily forgave Hesta and they both agreed that having him out of their respective lives was a good thing.

Scott was in custody with the indictment pending release any day. He would likely post bail, but would serve many years for his involvement with the crime ring.

Bob declined to join Patti on her trip back to Colorado. She took this as the sign from God to move on in her life.

Michael was present, but remained out in the hallway watching over William and Charlie.

John and Maria Knotingham were in the first row behind the prosecution table. Gardiner Smiley had them extradited in custody from the State of New York, thanks to Harry's deft legal maneuvering and his close association with *the* District Attorney. Gardiner had arranged for them to testify at the competency hearing if necessary and they were of course key witnesses in Chandler's case if the judge ruled him competent to stand trial.

Sam Barakosh remained standing while his client was ushered into the courtroom fully shackled.

Hesta watched as Chandler shuffled in, noting that technically, he was her stepson. John had never mentioned to her that he fathered a child when he was a teenage boy, as Maria had forbade him from ever discussing it with anyone other than her therapist. When Hesta learned that she was the person that Chandler was hired to kill, she was shocked.

She had never truly believed Chandler when he told them that story. Harry visited her at the hospital and explained how Maria's inheritance had run out, drying up John's trust fund, and the best that the two of them could come up with was Hesta's interest in the publishing company and her life insurance policy. She had been required to have a sizeable policy by the financiers for Gold Publishing Group, and five million dollars sounded livable to Maria. She could manage on that sum, while John could survive on the rest of Hesta's assets. The only sticking point was who to hire to get the job done.

Under pressure from New York's District Attorney's Office, Maria confessed her plot and admitted hiring Chandler Craig to kill Hesta. She provided Chandler with the names of the five and their respective husbands and offered some detail so that Chandler could "toy" with them a little, but would know which one was the right one to kill. When Maria learned that John was not the beneficiary of Hesta's life insurance policy, she was despondent. Hesta had changed the beneficiary earlier in the year from John to Mac, Rema, Melanie, and Patti. Maria's ploy had been undermined. Reluctantly, she admitted visiting Chandler at the detention facility several months prior to his projected release under the pretense of offering family support at the time of his liberation. She did offer support—in the form of cash—half down for agreeing to the job and the other half upon completion. The New York District Attorney offered a reduced sentence for the confession. Maria knew that she could never withstand the public embarrassment of a trial.

John was charged as an accomplice to the crime and was offered a similar deal. Both, however, had to agree to testify at Chandler's competency hearing. Since they had no relationship whatsoever with this young man, they both willingly agreed to a deal that would reduce their sentence by several years.

"The defendant is presumed competent at the commencement of this hearing today," the judge started. "The burden is on the defendant to prove his incompetence to stand trial by a preponderance of the evidence. The Court is in receipt of the reports from both Dr. Grayson and Dr. Witt. I have read and reviewed both reports in preparation for today's hearing.

Does either side wish to be heard with respect to either finding by the court-appointed psychiatrists?"

Sam Barakosh rose to his feet. "Yes, Your Honor. The defense disagrees with both findings of competency."

"I figured that you would, Mr. Barakosh, but don't you find it remarkable that both experts agreed that your client appears competent?" Judge Brooks thumbed through some papers he was holding and then readjusted his reading glasses which had slid part way down his nose. "Both doctors found that Chandler Craig is presently able to understand the nature and purpose of the proceedings taken against him. They both found that he is presently able to cooperate in a rational manner with counsel in presenting a defense. They both also agreed that the defendant is able to rationally determine whether he wished to be treated with antipsychotic medication and the defendant's wishes were granted. He was not ordered to take medication. Usually in these cases, the experts disagree. This is not so with Chandler Craig. Dr. Grayson cites the fact that the defendant was able to track down his former stepfather. Dr. Witt cites the fact that the defendant was able to recognize Carolyn Patterson, the mother and grandmother of his victims from his teenage killing rampage, and that he admitted to killing Carloyn Patterson prior to meeting the five ladies at the cabin near Nederland. Both doctors agree that he is able to formulate a plan and carry it out in a purposeful, deliberate manner. Both doctors also agree that your client has a strong opinion regarding antipsychotic medications and that he is able to articulate his desire not to be medicated."

"Your Honor, I object to the reading of the finding of the reports into the record," Sam Barakosh stated. "I don't see either doctor here in the courtroom at this time. If you are going to read them into the record, then they should be subject to cross-examination. I was present at both interviews conducted by Dr. Grayson and Dr. Witt, and my client refused to answer any questions, for the most part. It is impossible for me to believe that these doctors can reach a professional conclusion regarding competency when a client refuses to speak with them."

"Very well, Mr. Barakosh. Turn around. In the back row to your left you will see both court-appointed doctors. They are present and able to take the stand for cross-examination. However, in an abundance of caution, I will ask my court reporter here to strike every notation in the record where I read from their reports. Since this is a civil hearing and there is no constitutional right to a jury, you understand that it is the judge who is the fact finder, and, as such I am entitled to read, review and rely on professional reports when making my findings."

"I understand," Sam Barakosh said in a subtler tone.

"So, you may call your first witness, Mr. Barakosh."

"I call my client, Chandler Craig."

Chandler was escorted to the witness box and sworn in. He refused to agree to tell the truth, but Judge Brooks didn't seem too shaken by the defiance.

Chandler had the appearance of a very young boy on the stand. Melanie was the first to comment on the fact that he was clean shaven and his hair had been nicely trimmed. Chandler smiled at *The Five* seated in the back of the courtroom.

Mr. Barakosh asked Chandler simple questions first, about childhood and the fact that his mother was killed shortly after his birth. He acknowledged being raised by his aunt and the fact that he'd been charged with murder as a twelve-year-old. "Did you commit murder when you were twelve?"

"No. Someone else did it and I took the blame."

"Who did it?"

"I plead the Fifth," Chandler said, holding up five fingers.

"You can't be charged with that crime again. Do you understand that?"

"Yes."

"Then there is no harm in telling the judge here who did it."

"I can't. He will kill me."

"Okay. Let's move on," Sam Barakosh said, loosening his light blue tie with his left hand while holding a yellow tablet in his right. "Do you recognize some of the people in the courtroom today?"

"Yes. I know the five ladies in the back," Chandler said, granting a half smile on his face while looking at them.

"Okay. We'll get to them in a minute. Do you know these two people who are sitting in the front row?" Sam asked, pointing to Maria and John Knotingham.

"No."

"You've never seen these two before?"

"No."

"Let me make some introductions. This lady," he said, pointing to

Maria Knotingham, "is Maria. Do you remember Maria visiting you while you were at the juvenile detention facility?"

"No. She did not visit me. No one visited me when I was there. I was there nine years and I had no visitors."

"Right before you got out? Don't you remember talking with her two times?"

"That never happened."

"Okay. Let's move on. Tell me about the five ladies in the back of the courtroom that you said that you recognize. Tell me about them."

"They are the ladies who invited me for dinner in the mountains. They gave me food. They were nice to me."

"Okay. Good. Anything else?"

"The old lady in the back was mean to me," Chandler said, moving his eyes in the direction of Nellie. "She shot me with a gun for no reason."

"Okay. Well, wouldn't you agree that people usually don't go around shooting people without a reason?"

"No. People do it sometimes. And she did it to me, so I won't agree with you."

Sam looked bulge-eyed at his notebook, trying to find a different angle. "Do you know where we are today?"

Chandler scoffed at him before answering. "Of course. We are in court."

"Do you know why we are here?"

"Because the old lady shot me."

"Thank you," Sam said. "I have no further questions."

Judge Brooks looked up from the bench and watched Sam Barakosh sit down at the defense table. "Your witness," the judge said to Gardiner Smiley. Gardiner rose from his chair, leaving his notepad on the table, and walked in front of the prosecution table and then leaned back against it. He raised his leg slightly on the table and appeared relaxed and conversational.

"It must be terrible to meet your father for the first time here today. How do you feel about that?"

"Objection. Argumentative," Sam Barakosh shouted.

"Overruled. Witness may answer," Judge Brooks said.

"Mr. Craig, how does it feel to see your father for the very first time?" Gardiner asked again, this time pointing at John Knotingham, who sat smugly in the front row holding his mother's hand.

"I don't feel a thing. I don't know the man."

"Precisely. It must hurt a lot to know that this man never made the time for you and now he is here to testify against you."

Chandler's face grew a noticeably darker shade.

"When you met your grandmother for the first time, were you surprised that she offered you money to kill your stepmother," he said, pointing to Hesta in the back.

"Objection."

"I will withdraw the question," Gardiner said, pleased that he'd accomplished his goal of offending Chandler, who had turned his head slightly sideways to the left, bowed his head and glared at the district attorney.

"Now you mentioned that no one visited you when you were at the juvenile facility. How did that make you feel?"

"Mad."

"Why mad?"

"Because when other people got their visits, they got stuff to barter with. I never had anything to barter with."

"So other people had privileges that you didn't have because their families cared about them."

"Yes."

"And that made you mad."

"Yes!"

"What else makes you mad?'

Chandler pursed his lips tight. "When people like you ask me questions."

"You don't like authority figures asking you questions?"

"No."

"What about doctors?"

"No."

"Did you refuse to speak to the doctors when you were at the juvenile detention facility?"

"Yes."

"What about at the jail? When the doctor at the jail was getting those shotgun pellets out of your leg, did you speak to her?"

"Yes."

"Why would you speak to her, but not the other doctors?"

"Because she was helping me."

"Do you remember telling her how you knew that Carolyn Patterson was following you and that you turned the tables on her and hunted her like she was hunting you?"

"No. I didn't say that."

"The doctor is sitting in the third row. See her," Gardiner said, pointing to a woman wearing blue-ish gray scrubs. "You don't remember talking with her about that?"

"No!"

"Do you remember telling Patti, the blond haired lady in the second to last row, that you were going to starve her to death for a few days so that she was skinnier and then peel off her skin and make furniture out of it?"

"Objection."

"Withdrawn."

"Your Honor, he's deliberately questioning my client about the facts that support criminal charges. He knows that anything said can be used against my client at the sentencing phase on cross-examination, and he is setting my client up. I request that the court admonish Mr. Smiley."

"My apologies, Your Honor. That is not my intention with this line of questioning. I will move on." Gardiner turned toward Chandler. "Would it be fair to say that you are angry at your mother for abandoning you when you were little?"

"She did not abandon me. She died in a car accident."

"Is that what you were told? Did you know that she told your aunt that she couldn't take care of you and took off with her friends and went out partying the night she was killed?"

"That's not true. My real mom died driving home from work. My real dad was in the car with her. My aunt was babysitting and she adopted me."

"Did your aunt tell you that story?"

"Yes."

"What did your uncle say? His last name was Lee, right? You called your aunt your mom and Mr. Lee your step dad, right? What did Old Man Lee tell you about your real mom?"

"He was a LIAR!" Chandler shouted, pounding his shackled wrists on the witness stand.

"What did he tell you?"

"He was a liar and a bully. He hit her. She made him leave for telling me lies."

"Nothing further," Gardiner said, walking back around the prosecution table and sitting down.

"Any other witnesses, Mr. Barakosh?"

"No."

"You may step down, Mr. Craig."

"Does the defense rest?"

"Yes, subject to closing argument."

"Mr. Smiley, the Court is prepared to rule on the defendant's motion at this time, unless you would like to put on evidence."

"Your Honor, the prosecution has Maria and John Knotingham present. They are prepared to testify under a qualified immunity agreement, but if the defense has not met its burden of proof and the court is willing to rule, and then the state will not call witnesses."

"Defense waives argument," Sam said in defeat. The burden of proof for competency was very low, and by the statements that the judge made, the public defender knew that he had lost. His efforts were better served in the defense of the charges pending, and he knew it was better to save face until that time.

"The court finds the defendant, Chandler Craig, competent to stand trial for the charges of murder in the first degree, kidnapping, mayhem, assault and battery with grave bodily injury, and trespassing. Trial will commence three weeks from today. Court is adjourned."

Chapter 47

Gardiner Smiley made his name golden for the gubernatorial race by getting a conviction on all counts in the Chandler Craig case. The trial took nearly three weeks and each of *The Five* had to testify. None of them stuck around prior to or after they gave their testimony, as life went on and each of them had some rebuilding to do in their personal and professional lives.

Gardiner's role in the Scott Setliff sting was tantamount to exoneration of the fact that he, too, had taken performance enhancement drugs early in his professional career. He made known to the public what he did was wrong and why he did it, and that given another opportunity, he would never repeat his mistake. Athletes, both adolescents and professionals, were dying as a result of these drugs and something had to be done to stop it. The public embraced his honesty and diligence in taking down a group of fellow athletes who were cheating to enhance their performance in professional sports. Scott Setliff was sentenced to fifteen years for his role in the ring. Others who refused to cooperate weren't so lucky at sentencing.

After Gardiner announced his decision to run for Governor of Colorado, he received a prompt telephone call from Harry. "I think those performance enhancement drugs are still working on you," Harry joked. "You beat me to the punch once again."

Gardiner laughed at his friend who was a shoe-in for the Governor of Wyoming. Harry was quintessentially good looking, smart, well-known for his legal and charitable achievements, and, most recently, the author of a piece of legislation to change Wyoming's Juvenile Justice Act. Harry's proposed law explored the failures, illegalities, and inconsistencies of Wyoming's former juvenile law based on the Chandler Craig case, and enacted changes necessary so that Wyoming's youth could be adjudicated for crimes in a manner that both served the youth and the public. The law easily gained support and was passed. Harry was a hero for advocating for the rights of kids while advocating for the rights of the public safety.

At the conclusion of the sentencing hearing where Chandler Craig was given a term of twenty-five to life, *The Five* agreed to meet for another reunion. It was early December and where better to meet than in New York City? Rockefeller Center. Central Park. Tiffany's. The Nike Store (for Rema and Mac). Broadway. Nice restaurants. Shopping. Spa treatments.

The women stayed at Hesta's new private residence condominium, which was conveniently located at the newly converted Plaza on the corner of Fifth Avenue and Central Park South. Hesta had completed and published her memoir entitled "Vagina Chronicles" and it was on the Best Seller's list. She was having no troubles in the dating department, and her divorce from John was proceeding at a rapid pace.

Patti and Bob agreed to proceed with their divorce as respectfully as possible so as not to further mess up their boys. Patti had been willing to work things out, but three is a crowd in a marriage, and Bob was not willing to give up his new sex toy. Patti was working diligently on renewing her teaching credential, and looked forward to once again making money of her own. She was assured by her attorney that she would never have to worry about money again due to Bob's recent sales in the Sun Valley area, but it was important to Patti to make a new life for herself. She needed an excuse to get up early each day and get to the gym before going to class. She was losing weight and getting back into the perky shape that she enjoyed in college. With the advances of Botox, Latisse and a little Juvederm, her face looked as young as Bob's girlfriend's. Her body had a ways to go, but she was convinced that she'd get there.

Rema had some mopping up to do in order to settle the expense of the criminal matters Scott left her with. She sold all three dealerships, paid off the fines associated with his misdeeds, and promptly filed for divorce. She and Red had been dating steadily since the Chandler Craig nightmare, and although she lived in Boulder, she ran up the mountain nearly every day to see him.

Melanie and Michael agreed that they loved their life in Berkeley.

Charlie and William loved the fact that their daddy moved his law practice to the room above the garage. He was there to take them to school when mommy had a meeting and he was there to pick them up and take them to soccer or baseball or karate or art class when mommy couldn't make it. Mel's children's line continued to prosper at a rate where supply could not meet demand without outsourcing. She and Michael agreed that she would work more hours so that he could work fewer, and he would do a greater share of the parenting. Once he knocked out a few walls and added huge picture- framed windows to his new office, he took to the idea of working from home like wildfire. The tempo of their married lives changed, but their love remained constant.

Mac and Wyatt had a few issues to work out in their marriage. It was patently obvious that Mac could not live in a ranch house next to her in-laws, despite how much she enjoyed their company. She needed her own space and she needed her husband to be married to her, not his parents. The compromise was interesting. Mac had purchased a Victorian home in Sheridan before they married. She had been renting it out to a couple with two small children, but the couple had found a home to purchase, and Mac was faced with the prospect of new renters. She loved the home and was unwilling to rent it to just anyone. So, she and Wyatt agreed that she would live there during the week, and he would come for sleepovers on Tuesdays and Thursdays. She would come out to the ranch on Fridays after work, and they would stay on the ranch for the weekend. They were each happy with the changes. The only one that was unhappy was Ted, the cat. Ted used to love being at Mac's office during the day, perched on a windowsill above Main Street, watching the goings-ons of a small town all day. But once he moved to the ranch, being a barn cat was about the best thing in the entire world for a yellow tabby male with attitude. After some compromising, it was agreed that Ted would stay on the ranch. Mac got a second kitty, a grey and white Persian named Pywacket, who lived in town with her.

On a day very near Christmas, after *The Five* had enjoyed a spectacular reunion together in New York with the agreement that they would never again speak of Chandler Craig, Mac received a small gift basket and a card delivered to her law office. Megan opened it first, as she never had the patience to wait to see which client sent a gift. Her blue eyes flew open wide and she showed the card to Pam before walking it into Mac's office. Mac read the note from Kristine Craig. "Thank you for everything you and your friends did in Boulder. It took a lot of courage to face him. I never could. Happy Holidays. Kristine Craig."

Mac opened the box of chocolates and was about to sample her favorite one when she was hit with an overwhelming feeling of nausea. When Pam saw the shade of green on her boss's face, she grabbed her purse and darted across Main Street to the local pharmacy. She returned in minutes with a small package.

"Here," Pam said, shoving the brown paper bag toward Mac. "You need to pee on the stick."

Mac looked at her office staff in complete bewilderment. She'd never taken a pregnancy test before. At age forty-three, she figured that her time had passed and had become less careful during Wyatt's sleepovers.

Mac followed the directions on the package and returned to the office ten minutes later. She showed Pam and Megan the stick with the bright pink line.

"I can't believe it," Mac said. "I need to call Wyatt! He's going to be a daddy."

Wyatt was thrilled with the news, but before she could finish the conversation, she tossed the phone to Pam and darted back to the bathroom. Morning sickness was going to be a sneaky business.

* * *

Mac called her friends on a conference line and told them the news. They were all excited to learn that their friend was having a baby. Patti went on and on about educational toys. Melanie spoke about the importance of natural foods and fibers. Hesta promised her to buy her a prescription to *Working Mother* and even volunteered to fly to Wyoming to babysit.

Most surprising of all was that Rema stopped running to answer her new cell phone. She listened to Mac's news with delight and promised to buy her the best baby jogger on the market.

Six months later, *The Five* shared another reunion–a baby shower on Wyatt's ranch! He was a terrific host and even taught Hesta how to ride a horse. Their friendships had ebbed and flowed over the years, but they all agreed this time that they had never been closer. They once again agreed that they didn't wish the Kilkenny-Kerry experience on anyone, but they were all stronger and better for it. No longer did they tolerate unhappy marriages or unsatisfactory positions in life. They'd all shed their skin, so to speak, in lieu of a mid-life crisis, though that might have been a preferred route, and were now in excellent and rejuvenated places in life.

"To friendship, love, and smelly diapers," Melanie toasted with freshly squeezed Mimosas.

"To friendship," they agreed.

Books by Maureen Anne Meehan

Dying to Ski, a Mary MacIntosh novel
Snake River Secret, a Mary MacIntosh novel
Powder River Poison, a Mary MacIntosh novel
Pandemic Predator, a Mary MacIntosh novel
Poisoned by Proxy, a Mary MacIntosh novel
The Five, a Mary MacIntosh novel
Rodeo, a Mary MacIntosh novel
60 Dates in Six Months (with a Broken Neck)
Push You Away
Let Me Be

ABOUT THE AUTHOR

Maureen Anne Meehan received her bachelor's and master's degrees in education before becoming a lawyer. She lives with her family in Southern California, where she is a mental health judge and crafts legal thrillers, as well as nonfiction dating satire.